SLOE MOON

Sloe Moon Series

Volume 1: Tall Trees

Available soon:
Volume 2: Stoneharp (July 2024)
Volume 3: Crooked Hill (November 2024)
Volume 4: Eastbay
Volume 5: Halfway
Volume 6: Goldenlake

Content Warnings

Strong language, sex, violence, injury detail, one instance of attempted rape, mentions of miscarriage

SLOE MOON
TALL TREES

C. M. KUHTZ

WOLLSCHWEBER
PUBLISHING

2024 © C. M. Kuhtz

Wollschweber Publishing
www.wollschweberpublishing.com

All rights reserved.

Except for the quotation of short passages for the purposes of criticism and review, no part of this book may be reproduced in any form or by any means, electronic or mechanical, including photocopying, recording, or any information storage and retrieval system now known or to be invented, without written permission of the publisher, author, or artist.

CREDITS

Copyediting: B. N. Laux
Production: C. M. Kuhtz
Cover illustration: Casey Gerber
Cover design: C. M. Kuhtz
Logo design: Dorit Osang
Map design: C. M. Kuhtz

A catalogue record for this book is available from the British Library

ISBN 987-1-7394032-0-1 paperback
ISBN 987-1-7394032-1-8 ebook

for all of us who feel unseen

THE LANDS OF THE FAMILIES

TALL TREES

HOLLYBROOK

DARKWATER

THE FORESTS

THE
GRASSLANDS

FOALSTONES

THE STONEHARP

CLAWDIG

BEAKDIG

FEATHERDIG

THE GARRISON

WESTLIGHT

GREYCLIFFS

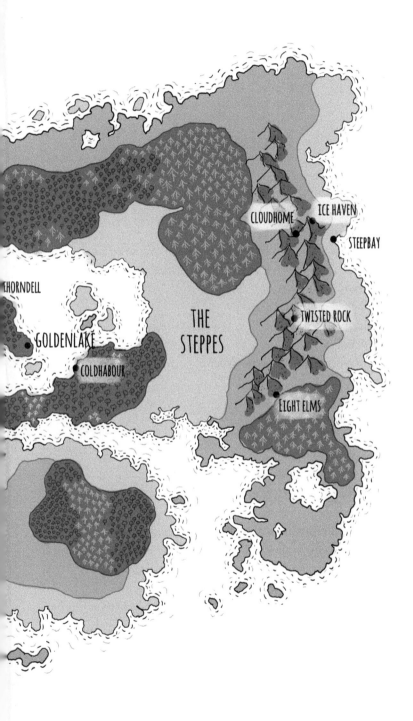

DRAMATIS PERSONAE

Pronunciation Guide

Vowels
A—as in 'marvel' (ā)
E—long, as in 'elusive' (ē) or short and flat (ə), as in 'energy'
I—like ee, as in 'feel' (ee), though sometimes more like a flat e (ə)
O—round, as in 'over' (ō)
U—like oo, as in 'moon' (oo)

Consonants
C and Q—like k, as in 'crown' (k)
J and Y—like y, as in 'yay' (y)
S—soft, as in 'zebra' (z)
W—like v, as in 'village' (v)

Humans

In Tall Trees and on the road
Ileon (Ee-lē-ōn)—a man of the Eastern Cities.
Julas (Yoolās) Raven—a distant cousin of Sloe's.
Qarim (Kāreem) Badger—Sloe's father, long presumed dead.
Qes (Kəz) Badger—Sloe's cousin and best friend.
Saon (Zā-ōn) Moon—Sloe's ex-boyfriend.
Silid (Zee-ləd) Moon—Sloe's oldest sister and heir to their mother.
Siw (Zəv) Moon—Sloe's sister, closest to them in age. A wizard's apprentice.
Sjunil (Zyoo-neel) Moon—Sloe's aunt and wizard of Tall Trees.

Sloe (Slō) Moon—youngest child of the leader of the Moons.

Sloe's mother—the leader of the Moons.

Sor (Zōr) Moon—Silid's child, living with Sloe in the Other House.

In Goldenlake

Cathil (Kāthəl) Cloud—favourite son of the leader of the Clouds and famed warrior.

Cirvi (Keer-vee) Cloud—a wizard.

Olas da Ozanil (Ōlāz dā Ōzā-neel)—a man of the Eastern Cities and negotiator.

Qati (Kātee) Badger—one of Qes' cousins.

Qerla (Kēr-lā) Badger—the first wizard of Goldenlake.

Qor (Kōr) Badger—one of Qerla Badger's apprentices. Also Qes' cousin.

Tjal na Tialin (Tyāl nā Tee-ā-leen)—a man of the Eastern Cities.

Werid (Vērət) Wolf/Werid of the Far Side—a wizard from the Eastern steppes.

In the west

Cjanis (Kyā-nəs) Cloud—one of Cathil Cloud's sisters. Also a wizard.

Rawil (Rāvəl) Owl—the commander of a garrison of warriors in the west.

Raz (Rāz) Owl—Rawil's niece.

Rion (Ree-ōn) Owl—Raz's brother.

Rovan (Rōvānn) Owl—the commander of the Beakdig garrison. Rawil's ex-husband.

Animals

Cirvi (Keer-vee)—horse.

Yoli (Yōlee)—horse.

BOOK ONE

GETTING AWAY FROM ME

"Oh fuck," my cousin Qes whispered. "Don't look."

I turned around.

"Sloe," he groaned. "I said, don't look. Didn't Saon want to give it another go just yesterday?"

I stared at the man I had left. Saon was with one of my other cousins, who sucked at Saon's tongue with loud slobbering noises. "Well, he always was a fast mover."

"He didn't deserve you."

I tried to shrug it off but the taste in my mouth was bitter, drawing the muscles in my cheeks into a desperate grimace. It wasn't the first time Saon had disappointed me.

We were attending one of the monthly assemblies and though the Roundhouse of Tall Trees was packed to the rafters, I could still hear them kissing behind me. My neck prickled. I'd been with Saon for nearly two years before coming to the conclusion that there was no reason why I couldn't try finding someone else. Apart from the fact that no one in Tall Trees was interested in me. Apart from the small, persistent voice that Saon had woken in me that constantly told me that while he didn't deserve me, I really deserved him: the excuses, the snide remarks, the off-hand cruelty that I'd become so used to before Qes joined us in the cousin exchange and had pointed them out.

From the very beginning of his stay in Tall Trees, Qes had attached himself to me and it still amused me that he became so easily offended on my behalf. While Saon was sleek and willowy, Qes and I resembled each other in build; we were both tall, fat, and broad-shouldered, though I secretly wished for his spectacular hair. It was of a blueish black, a tangled curly cloud around his head, and matched his dark eyes. His mother was my father's niece, one of the Badgers, and sometimes I wondered if my father had looked like Qes when he'd been young.

I heard the door close behind us. The strong smell of burning herbs in the braziers illuminating the house suddenly made me sneeze. I noticed the rustle of food parcels and shuffling feet—no one expected the meeting to be a short one. I could see my sisters making their way to the central platform, my mother behind them in her midnight-black cloak that was embroidered with the symbol of our family, the half-moon crest. I'd stitched some of these moons myself, the ones nearest the hem, as was expected of the youngest child of a leader.

A hush fell over the house; everyone had realized that Mother was even more displeased than usual. Most news had been bad of late, but at least it had nothing to do with me. Or so I thought. My heart skipped a painful beat. Maybe I'd made another mistake and she'd take the opportunity to tell me off in front of the whole family? In front of Saon, who obviously congratulated himself on getting away from me?

I quickly looked over my shoulder. He'd stopped kissing, though that meant he'd registered my checking up on him. I could hear his intake of breath, the noise he made when he sneered at someone. A bead of sweat trickled down between my shoulder blades and I had to suppress a shudder so violently that I didn't realize my eldest sister had started to address the assembly.

For a future leader of the Moon family, her voice was disconcertingly high and grating, the only jarring aspect in her presentation of the rightful heir. Her cloak was dark blue, dyed over and over again to achieve its rich deep colour, and her hair swept up into an impressive heap studded with bone needles and amber beads.

I forced myself to concentrate on her words: "… seen a worrying amount of hostility from the west, with our latest offering rejected." An unhappy sigh ran through the house and my sister paused, her long slender hands outstretched until we'd settled down. "We will try again, but we will have to take this kind of disrespect into consideration …"

Her dark eyes found me in the crowd and my stomach lurched. The relations between the Moons and the families of the west had been strained of late and only a few months ago, one of our most important alliances had been broken over a rejected proposal of marriage. I knew that my mother had hoped to patch up the relationship with a new set of conditions, but it felt as if a final word had been spoken. We'd lost a few dozen goats since the falling-out, with raiding parties getting deeper and deeper into our territory. No wonder my sisters felt disrespected. No one expected that the smaller settlements around Tall Trees would be able to pay their full rents this year, and it seemed the situation might be even worse.

"… decided to address the wizard council at Goldenlake …"

The sounds of distress around me grew ever louder. Attending the council meant that my mother was forced to rely on old favours—the favours of the eastern families, the Badgers and Ravens, powerful families linked to us by marriages and treaties as old as the Golden Lake itself.

"… we will decide on the attendants in the coming days." Again her eyes roamed in my direction and I felt decidedly queasy. "We will call to prayers this evening to ensure the grace of …" But I wasn't able to keep focused on her. Mother couldn't possibly plan to send me to Goldenlake?

Qes gripped my arm. "Do you think they would let me come with you?"

I forced myself to breathe in. So he'd noticed it as well …
"I don't know. I need to talk to them. There must be … there must
be a way around it."

He frowned. "But you're always talking about getting out of
Tall Trees and what about …"

"That was before."

"Before what?"

"Before the offer."

His eyes went wide, but for once he shut up. He was right. I'd
always longed to get out of the forest, to travel like my father had.
My life in Tall Trees was an endless chain of chores and when the
last of my brothers had left the village to marry a Raven, I'd felt
left behind, desperate for any sort of adventure, which more or
less had led to Saon's involvement in my life.

Of course, everything had changed. The rest of the meeting lay
under the cloud of expected measures, though there were plenty
of less disturbing things to be discussed, and I was barely able
to listen anymore. The quality of the bearnut harvest held little
fascination for me, facing another humiliation.

When we were finally released from the Roundhouse, I rubbed
my cramping thighs. "Wish me luck."

Qes' brow furrowed. "You want to do it *now*?"

"No time like the present."

"Can't you speak to them after prayers?"

I touched his elbow. "By then I might've changed my mind."
I jumped down to the trampled clay floor. My sisters had almost
reached the House of Women by the time I'd caught up with
them. "Silid!"

My eldest sister stopped so abruptly that I almost fell into her
cloak. Her eyes glinted with impatience. "Is this necessary?"

"I thought it might be."

"We're about to eat—make it quick." She glared towards my two younger sisters, who left us alone. A sharp wind blew dead leaves through the centre square of Tall Trees. It whistled between the House of the Women and the Other House, and though she was the one wearing the thick cloak, I saw Silid shudder, her complicated coiffure being blown to bits and the amber beads clicking softly against each other.

"Even if there's no other way than calling the council, you're not seriously thinking about …" I swallowed painfully.

She grimaced. "It was your honour that was called into question, Sloe. This is an opportunity to air your grievances in person, to represent your family at the council and speak for all of us—and you won't be the only representative. You could bring your sidekick."

"Qes isn't—"

Her left eyebrow arched pointedly. "Mother is giving you another chance, Sloe. You can't afford to fuck this up as well." Her voice dropped to a ragged whisper. "I know it wasn't your fault as such, but Mother is still angry about it, and you need to be seen to actually do something for us. You haven't taken on any real responsibilities so far, but there are expectations now that you are the only one left of us who Mother can use to keep the peace."

"You mean who she can sell to keep the peace."

Silid shrugged. "You must have known that this day would come. Be assured that I will endeavour to find an experienced guide for you." She gave me a last nod, then turned around to join our sisters and mother in the House of Women.

I stared after her for several moments, too terrified to move.

"I can't wait to see the lake again," Qes said over our meal of nutbread, goat cheese, and stewed apples. "It's an experience you'll never forget."

"At least one of us is looking forward to it," I grumbled into my spoon.

"It's going to be an adventure."

"No, it's going to be another opportunity for me to fail."

"Your mother wouldn't send you if she'd thought you'd fail."

"Oh, she would. She absolutely would. She would love to have another arrow in her quiver of regrets."

Qes snorted. "Silid was right, Sloe. Now that you're the only one left unmarried, you're useful again. Even she must realize that it would make much more sense to support you. She knows that you might look like him, but …" He faltered under my stare, put his bowl down, and started poking at the fire.

We had a favourite place between the birches near the river, not too far away from the village and sheltered in a little dip, with mossy rocks and soft grass; a place where we could talk and eat and be away from the others. In the summer, we'd slept there sometimes but autumn had arrived at last and even so close to the fire it was just a little bit too damp and uncomfortable. I licked my fingers and turned the slice of bread I'd placed on the flat baking stone to toast, a pleasant smell wafting up from the roasted nuts and herbs. Assembly days were set aside for reflections and prayers, but I had little motivation to join the rest of the family. I'd pray later, on my own.

I cleared my throat. "Do you think your mother would attend the council in person?"

Qes shrugged. "She might send our own wizards. I don't think she'd make the trip herself anymore. Not this late in the year, now that she prepares to stand down." He grinned. "Officially, at least. We all know that it'll take another decade for her to trust my sisters enough to do it all on their own. I bet Silid is having a similar experience."

"My mother will step away only when she dies," I said glumly. "She still has way too much fun."

"I can't imagine that today was fun." Qes scratched at his temple. "It's not an enviable position to be in, having to announce to all the family that one of the oldest treaties of our history has fallen apart under her watch."

I slid the warm bread into my bowl and started breaking it into chunks. Sometimes I desperately wished for Qes to be a little bit less reasonable. "I suppose so."

He sniffed. "Would you rather talk about—"

"Gods, no!" I spread cheese on the bread and started wolfing it down. Anything was better than thinking about the spectacle Saon had made of himself today. "Tell me about the lake."

Qes sighed happily. "It is so wide that it doesn't look like a lake—it's more like the sea. Well, what I guess what the sea would be like. Do you think we'll see the sea one day?"

"Oh, definitely. One day we'll go on that adventure, when both our spouses have died, and our hair is grey, and they finally give us a fucking break."

"You will like the lake," Qes said quietly. "I don't really understand why you're so frightened, Sloe. Shouldn't you be happy that they're giving you something more meaningful to do than herding the goats and digging over the herb gardens? This is what you were born for."

"I wish I could be so sure. I might make a passable gardener one day or the best goat herd of Tall Trees. At least no one would be chomping at the bit to get me married to one of the Clouds."

Qes seemed decidedly uncomfortable. We hadn't spoken in much detail about the offer that the Clouds rejected. The worst thing was that the whole situation only strengthened the suspicions that Saon had given me. Why would I be the chosen one to rescue the treaty? The Clouds had married the Moons since time immemorial and then the whole thing fell apart over my involvement … it made sense to me. So much sense.

I sniffed angrily. "They will laugh at me. Again. The whole council of Goldenlake will understand why the offer was refused." I rubbed at my right eye, the blue one, and Qes didn't miss the gesture.

"My uncle Qon has the same eyes. And my auntie Qay, though with her it's the other way around—the left one is blue and the right one is brown. It just means that you are half a Badger, and it will make them know that the Clouds refused both of our families. Do you need a hug?"

"No," I lied, desperately. I was half a Badger. Half a disgraced Badger, to be precise. Maybe it would've been easier if my father had still been with us, but more likely not. He hadn't exactly been an uncontroversial character.

As I turned my gaze to the skies, I could still hear him talk of places far across the sea and people who had other words for the world around us.

QUITE GOOD WITH THE GOATS

Once upon a time, my father had been a famous wizard. Then he'd lost his powers in a duel, when he'd pissed off an even more famous wizard and spent the last five years of his life as the village drunk. At least, we assumed they had been his last years; he simply didn't come back to Tall Trees. Maybe he'd been eaten by the wolves, or become a werebear, or fallen into the river and been too drunk to get out again.

He'd been my mother's fourth and last husband. Since she was past her child-bearing years, no one saw a reason to pressure her into choosing someone new. Silid's suspicion was that she'd never forgiven herself for making such a big blunder with my father, someone who'd already had a bad reputation when his name was first mentioned to her. Young and desperate for another chance to prove himself to the Badgers, he'd agreed to be married off to Tall Trees like so many others of his cousins before him; the position my mother's status had offered him an appropriate compensation for the slight chance of actually fathering his own offspring. Everyone must've been surprised by my speedy arrival, Mother's last triumph, though in the end I hadn't been enough to keep him at her side.

The Badgers were known for their stubborn nature and had always been one of our staunchest allies against the families of the west. There was no reason why it shouldn't have worked. Maybe he had other promises to keep. There'd been times when I'd hoped that he actually was dead, though the wish made me deeply ashamed—but at least it would've been a good reason for him to stay away.

Qes had known exactly who Qarim Badger was when he arrived in Tall Trees and had probably felt sorry enough for me to attach himself to my side. I couldn't recall any other Badgers coming to Tall Trees before him; there'd been lots and lots of Ravens and some Clouds, of course, before they decided to risk Mother's wrath. I should've realized that wasn't a particularly good sign.

I'd felt nervous when Silid announced the new list of cousins who would join us in Tall Trees and Qes' name came up. A Badger who'd probably been to Goldenlake, someone who'd travelled a fair bit of the forests and knew about my father's bad name. I saw him arrive on a stocky gelding, his curly hair matted and full of twigs. His round face was drawn with exhaustion, and I'd felt a jolt of disappointment. I'd hoped to meet someone who looked like me and Qes wasn't that, definitely not that. He slid from the saddle and did something strange: he threw his arms around his horse's neck and hugged it. It took me a few heartbeats to understand that his knees were shaking so hard that he was about to collapse. He used his horse to keep himself upright. He'd allowed himself to be vulnerable in front of the whole of Tall Trees because he wasn't well-travelled at all and nervous to have been chosen to come so far to the west, where the forest was deeper and tangled and could be dangerous at times, where werebears ambushed our hunting parties and the rivers swelled so much in spring that they washed away whole valleys, reordering the landscape around us. When he released his grip on the horse and turned around, I made myself smile.

"Welcome to Tall Trees," were my first words to him, a formal greeting that he took with a little shrug.

"Thank you." I saw his gaze flicker up to my eyes and then he smiled back at me. "They told me to watch out for you," he said. "Sloe Moon of Tall Trees."

Like everyone else, I'd officially received my name on my first birthday from our wizard, who was one of my aunts and mad like a ferret. She usually lived in her own hovel, half a day's march away. Silid recalled that our wizard had gone pale beneath her felted hood and uttered my name before the ceremony had even started. "Sloe—not like 'slow,' but the horribly bitter fruit."

It wasn't the name Mother had chosen for me, but the wizard refused to change her mind. "The gods are entitled to their opinion. A woman as powerful as yourself, dear sister, must still bow her head from time to time." Mother hadn't sent for her for half a year, until she'd been able to forgive her. My aunt probably had her eye on me from the start, but Mother decided that my sister Siw was going to be our next wizard and after a good bit of grumbling, they had eventually agreed.

I had four sisters and three brothers and like every woman, my mother had a few in between who'd died. Even for the plentiful Moons, that was unusual but her first marriage had been a happy one and my siblings followed each other every year; it was during my grandmother's reign, when my mother was waiting for her to die and maybe there wasn't much else to do. Silid would take over one day, with our next two sisters as advisors. My fourth sister was busy sweeping our auntie's hovel, and my brothers were living with the Ravens, the eldest particularly well-married and close to their own leader.

Family reunions could get complicated in the forests; even within the families we had countless feuds to keep track of and I couldn't remember all the cousins I was supposed to hate (apart from the one throwing himself at Saon at the assembly).

Life in Tall Trees was exceptionally well organized to keep all of us from being bored and useless. Everyone not immediately involved in government was part of the work rota, though we were allowed to specialize. Qes liked working with the horses, I was really quite good with the goats, and Saon was on his way to become the master dyer of Tall Trees.

We'd first started to talk when he came to inspect the fleeces before the annual shearing and complimented me on the condition of the animals in my small division. I'd taken the trouble to remove all the burrs, brushed out the felty bits, and had made sure that he saw the ones with the most lustrous coats last. I'd known that Silid had her mind set on a new cloak, and that Saon had been asked to select the wool for it and be involved in the dyeing. While our wizard and her apprentice were preoccupied with the gods, Saon's work was as close to magic as I could get.

I could tell that he liked to have someone to listen to, someone who appreciated his expertise and took care with the materials he needed for his craft. I would've loved to supply his herbs as well, grown by my own hands in the garden, but for the blue he had in mind he needed the good stuff, all the way from the west coast, where families traded for the rarer dyes with people from other continents. I wasn't too bad at spinning and weaving but for Silid's cloak we could only use the best; Saon wasn't a man who compromised on his vision.

Though I was disappointed, I knew that he needed to produce the best for the heir of the Moons. I'd always found him slightly intimidating, not quite as tall as me but so incredibly graceful, with a narrow face and strong black brows, a few years older than me and with the swagger of an expert. He knew how to get the very best results from the plants we processed and while others dressed in practical clothes, he liked to wear a shawl made from his dyeing samples, embroidered with a mass of spiralling patterns, pinned together on his left shoulder—something that made him stand out in the Roundhouse or at prayers.

He must've noticed early on that I began to keep an eye on him, but from his behaviour it was impossible to gauge whether he was actually interested. He talked to me, but then he talked to everyone—or at least *at* them. He had friends who liked to keep close to him and I could often hear them laugh, huddled together next to the drying racks.

Maybe one of them started teasing him about me skulking around, because I remember the moment so clearly.

"When did you choose the Other House?" he asked, a question so personal that I recoiled from him. He hadn't grown up in Tall Trees; he'd joined us from one of the other settlements to bolster our numbers. It was more than possible that his village was too small to have an Other House and that it made him anxious.

"I can't really remember," I lied. "There always were a few of us here in Tall Trees and more would come from time to time."

"There can't be that many of you now."

"We are four. Two of us married each other and one of my sister's children has also moved in, but they are still very young."

He fussed with the oiled wooden brooch that fastened his shawl. "Does it feel lonely sometimes?" he asked.

"No," I said, but of course he was right. It was lonely, so different from the bigger houses that had been built around the Other House. The House of Women had been extended the year before and the House of Men would be in the next, to fit everybody. Compared to them, the Other House felt spacious and it wasn't always easy to share with a married couple if there were no other grownups around. Like all children in Tall Trees, I'd been kept with one of my parents at the beginning, switching between the houses until I was able to decide where I wanted to live, but then my father had died and I'd been with my sisters from then on.

I could remember the old House of Women—the wide sleeping platforms, heaped with furs and mattresses stuffed with compacted bracken, the smell of the burned crystallized tree sap with which the building was cleansed every week, the warmth that hovered around the bodies sleeping in small groups. In the Other

House, I had my own platform and had become used to it, but I feared he would think me stupid if I admitted that. He had a weird glint in his eye, as if he could see right through my skull and knew everything I tried to keep from him.

"You're interesting," he said, and I felt a shudder of happiness wash over me. "We could meet in the woods."

There was no question about what he suggested to me, and I grasped at the chance. "Fine," I said, trying not to sound too eager, though he must've seen that I still shivered before him. He probably hadn't thought about me as a prospect, but then I was as close to the heart of the Moons as possible and that might've swayed him. It was as if a cloud had suddenly lifted, and the sun streamed down on my face.

A self-satisfied grin spread over his lips, because he had me and he would continue to possess my full attention for the best of two years. He was the first I lay with. He was good about it, though a bit impatient. He let me stay with the dyers when it was time for the finest of the yarn to be processed and each time the batch was lowered into the vat, I felt his anticipation.

It went so far as Silid having a word with me because I missed a lot of my own work; people were starting to talk, and though Saon had tried to keep our involvement a secret at first, no one in Tall Trees had any illusion where my heart was at. Saon and I weren't related, so there was no problem with us getting married one day, at least in theory. Saon was preoccupied with his work and the next ambitious projects that he sketched out in red ochre and coal on grass paper he'd traded for when he bought the blue dye from the west. Though I found myself deeply bored with his artistic vision, I smiled and listened and waited for him to touch me again.

For the first weeks, we met up almost every day, before he got stingier with his affection. He said things that I couldn't recall without wanting to strangle him once I understood why he'd said them. He made it clear that he preferred our relationship to be about our talks, not so much about sleeping with each other and that there were things about me that repulsed him he'd previously put up with because he valued my mind, my opinions. It probably gave him a thrill to watch me starve right in front of him and I wish Qes had joined us sooner, because he took one hard look at me and pulled a disappointed face.

"You know that he is never going to marry you?"

I gasped in shock though I knew as much. "Why not?"

"Because your mother will find someone more important for you."

"She already tried a few times," I replied, still breathless. "She won't find anyone to take me off her hands now."

"Of course she will. Someone will be clever enough to make the perfect match with you."

"Or stupid enough."

Qes' frowned. "I wish you wouldn't do this."

"What?"

"Be so mean to yourself."

"Saon says …"

"I don't really care what he says, Sloe. I'm hungry. Let's go eat."

Qes was always hungry and so I watched him eat while I worried. Growing up in a gaggle of sisters hadn't been the best way to instil a sense of self-esteem in me. All my sisters were graceful in the way Saon was, with long swishy hair and doe eyes. My hair was dark brown and I had the eyes that didn't bother Qes in the slightest but that everyone else found weird. They made my face lopsided, or at least this was what Saon had said to me. As an artist, he was concerned with symmetry and balance and that I could've been beautiful if it wasn't for that unfortunate Badger trait.

It always came down to that. I didn't look like a Moon, so maybe I wasn't truly a Moon at all.

PROTECT ME

Most of the decisions regarding the village of Tall Trees were talked through in the House of Women but beneath the low roof a couple of benches were placed for any men or Others who had business to get involved in. They were strewn with furs and blankets and Silid had asked for a brazier to be provided on the chilly autumn morning that saw me jittery with anticipation, my hands clawing into each other in the desperate attempt to keep my composure.

It was obvious that Mother hadn't changed her mind. There was no reason why she would've; all the pleas I'd sent to her via my sisters had gone unanswered and time was running out for all of us. Soon, the valleys of our forests would be snow-filled and even more dangerous to travel through. A last hope I clung to was the thought that Silid would laugh at me and reveal all of it to be an elaborate prank: surely I wouldn't be expected to ride all the way to Goldenlake to represent the Moons, no one had seriously believed me capable of taking on such responsibilities when there were two other sisters who sought our mother's approval and would each have given half a finger to be named as envoys …

I waited under the dripping roof, biting my nails. It took a long time for Silid to appear. She shoved the skin that kept out the worst of the wind to one side and her long necklace of amber beads rattled against her brooches as she took her seat on the bench in front of me. She seemed exhausted, with a red runny nose and dark circles under her eyes.

"How long have you been waiting?"

"Not that long."

She huffed, because she knew that I was trying to placate her.

"Is Mother coming?" I asked, and she shook her head, drawing her cloak closer; the light of the brazier flickered over her face.

"She is tired after the discussions we had last night. But she left me with clear instructions, and she will not tolerate another plea from you. Are we clear?"

"So I'm going then?"

"You will be going, without further complaint. You may take Qes with you and Auntie Sjunil will come too. To guide you."

I felt my jaw drop. "No …"

A tired smile tugged at my sister's mouth. "You will find her to be an interesting travelling companion. I dare say she will bring her apprentice, so she won't work you too hard."

"Isn't she a bit too … fragile to travel so far this late in the year?"

"It was her own idea."

"Mother trusts her enough to attend the council to further the family's interest? After all these years of …" I made a helpless gesture, but Silid understood. She'd been at Mother's side for all of her life; she was the one Mother complained to about her own sisters.

I'd always had the impression that Mother tried to keep me and the wizard of Tall Trees apart. I breathed in, deep and slow. My head was whirling, pounding as if all our goats had jumped around on it for fun and I had to hold out a sweating hand to keep myself steady against the wall of the House of Women.

Silid stretched her fingers into the warmth of the fire in front of her. "It's going to be fine," she whispered.

"It's going to be a nightmare."

"Sjunil will be the main attraction. I thought you might like that. She will be the one who is sitting on the council and who will have to represent our general grievances. You are going to be there as a witness and will only have to speak when they ask you to attend. She was trying to protect you, Sloe."

"To *protect* me?"

"Auntie Sjunil has been in Goldenlake before. Not as an envoy, but in Mother's entourage. She knows what to do. You will be allowed to choose a horse and Mother has asked for you to be given better clothes and a haircut."

"I don't want a haircut."

"You are still going to get one." She sounded weary, rubbing at her reddened nose with her sleeve. "Three days, Sloe. Mother has called Auntie Sjunil in for tomorrow and I expect she will want to talk to you. You better start saying your farewells." She pushed herself up again and shivered. "And get out of the cold, before you …" She pressed her lips together, had a quick look around, but the village square was empty. The rain had driven everyone inside. Silid pulled me into her arms and gave me a hug so quick that it made me feel even guiltier. She'd never hugged me before. As she pulled away from me, she gave me a quick pat on the back, then ducked through the door into the House of Women.

Qes pushed the wet hood from his eyes. "She did what?"

"You heard me well enough. We're going to be the laughingstock of all the eastern families."

"Not that—she really hugged you?"

"She did."

"Wow. She must feel bad for you."

I spat into the trampled grass at our feet. "She knows what's going to happen. They'll all look at me and think that it's no wonder that the Clouds decided to break with us. She really should send my sisters."

He crossed his arms on the paddock fence. He was almost as soggy as the horses that had gathered under one of the large oaks, their coats streaked with rain and ears flopped sidewards in mute acceptance. On rainy days, no one got any work done and we

were the only ones outside, our boots muddy to the ankles and
our woolly hats squishy with moisture.

"Why are you so scared, Sloe?"

"I'm scared because …" I gulped for air. "You don't understand."

"No, I don't. It's an opportunity many others would kill for.
Your … *friend* Saon is one of them."

I blinked. "Don't be stupid."

He smiled at me, his canines sharp and wolfish. "I bet he'll
be back at your side as soon as the news is out, now that you're
an official representative of the Moons. It's an honour, Sloe. It
might not feel like it yet, but it's actually amazing that they let
you go. We need to make the best of it. There will be lots of
important people in Goldenlake, plenty of Badgers, and some of
them might've known your father."

It felt as if he'd slapped me. Why hadn't I thought of that? The
rain washed over my face, sticking my hair to it, but my skin was
burning, flaming. "You think that's what Mother has in mind?"

He laughed. "I'd never presume to expect that your mother would
like you to meet some of them, but Silid? I wouldn't put it past her."

The rain had cleared overnight and when I stepped out of the Other
House the wind was drying the leaves that carpeted the village
square, making their crisp edges flutter like resting butterflies.

"Sloe."

I flinched.

Saon waited for me, his colourful shawl wound around him in
a way that the thick folds accentuated his narrow waist, his silky
black hair bound back in a braid. He wore an amulet around his
neck: a polished stone, heavy and with a deep purple glow. "So it
is true," he said. "You *have* been chosen."

Qes was right, I thought. I wish he wasn't always right. "Why
are you here?"

His eyes glittered. "It must feel good to be recognized at last."

"Recognized?"

"As your mother's child."

"I've always been my mother's child."

The left corner of his mouth twitched. "She has never made a favourite of you before."

"A favourite?"

He sighed. "You should really stop doing this, you know."

"Doing what?"

"Repeating everything I say. It makes you look … a bit simple."

"Simple?" I bit my tongue. "What do you want?"

"I received an order from your sisters." He turned and retrieved a package wrapped in painted hide from a low stool.

The hide was soft under my fingers, a precious gift in itself, but as I pulled it apart, I saw the shimmer of a blue so astonishing that I had to gasp.

"I dyed it from the waste of Silid's own cloak," he said. "I had intended it for …"

Not for me, then. "It's beautiful," I acknowledged, unable to bring myself to thank him.

"You will tell them who made it, when they ask?" His voice had an edge to it, needier than I'd ever heard him.

I wrapped my old cloak around the package to protect it from the dripping branches above us. "If they ask," I said and left him without another word.

"It matches your eye." Qes' thick fingers stroked the fulled cloth as if he was petting a rare and capricious animal. "Even I must admit that you couldn't have asked for better. That doesn't mean that he's grown on me," he added quickly. "He is an opportunistic weasel with excellent taste, is all. You'll look great. Why don't you put it on now?"

"I don't want to get it dirty."

"Will you show it to your aunt when she comes?"

"I might."

He grinned at me. "What about—"

"I am not getting my hair cut! It's only just grown out enough."

"It's like a shaggy shrub."

I had to laugh. "Look who's talking, Qes."

"It's not my fault—all my brothers have the same hair, and some of my sisters. You could at least give it a brush, that might help." He pulled a bone comb from the bag over his shoulder, with multiple broken teeth and greasy from long use.

I slapped at him. "Get that thing away from me." It felt like the first time I'd laughed in days. We'd huddled together under one of the rocky outcrops in the valley, away from the others. It was one of the best places to meet up when the weather was fickle. Qes had brought a few fruitcakes and a skin of fermented milk, and we took turns to drink while we waited for the rain to stop again.

"Will the trees sound different in Goldenlake?" I asked him.

He knitted his brow. "I can't remember," he confessed. "I haven't been at the lake in far too long. Even if the council proceedings prove to be a nightmare, you'll be glad to have gone. Everyone wants to see the Golden Lake at least once in their lives, to come face to face with the Tall and the Small Gods …"

"Yeah, well … I hope Sjunil won't make us sit through too many rituals. I prefer my prayers like my biscuits—short and sweet."

Qes pretended to be shocked. "Don't let Silid know," he said with an unexpected hint of disapproval in his voice. We'd known each other for some time but he'd never come across as particularly pious.

I took the goatskin from him and emptied it. The last dregs were especially sour, and I used my sleeve to wipe my mouth in disgust. "I hope the food will be good."

Qes broke the last of the fruitcakes apart for us; they'd long since gone stale and were sticky to the touch. "Something to look forward to," he said.

Siw and I had never seen eye to eye, being so close in age. We'd always jostled for position, though I was sure she would've liked the burden of living with Aunt Sjunil to fall on me. Becoming a wizard had never seemed like an obvious choice for her, though she'd always been observant and quite taken with the rules the gods had once laid upon the families in the forest.

Siw resembled Silid, though they had different fathers, and she shared her taste for amber and statement jewellery. Her eyes narrowed when she saw me standing against the wall of the House of Women and her shoulders straightened. She'd never let me forget that she was the older one, whatever Silid might say.

"Sloe." Her voice was raspy, full-throated and perfect for leading prayers.

"Siw. Nice pony."

Her black mount was brushed to a high sheen, its mane braided, and the saddle cloth chosen to impress. Aunt Sjunil followed her on a fat grey mare, clean enough but without adornments. Our wizard was wrapped in a chequered blanket, the felted hood hiding her hair and the teardrop-shaped tattoo on her forehead. She looked like any other older woman of the families, tired and a bit unsteady as she dismounted in the village square. Qes stepped forward to take the reins of the mare and Sjunil stretched with a sigh.

"Come on," she said, and it took me a while to understand that she meant her apprentice.

Siw rolled her eyes, threw her own reins in Qes' direction, her spotless cloak swishing as she jumped to the ground. There'd always been a flourish to her, and she obviously liked arriving with so many people staring at her every move. She pulled at her tunic and fussed with her belt before both women went into the house I was no longer allowed to set foot in.

IF I'D KNOWN

It'd gone dark when I was finally sent for. Mother had asked for the Roundhouse to be prepared for a small gathering and they waited for me around the central brazier, everyone nursing clay bowls filled with steaming honey beer. Seated next to each other, Mother and Sjunil really looked like sisters, though Mother was almost grey and Sjunil's hair was still mostly black and pinned into a firm bun on top of her head, sporting a single silver hair needle shaped like a crescent moon.

"There you are," she said and patted the bench next to hers. Her shiny eyes raked over my face. "It's a good name," she said after a moment, and no one asked what she meant with that cryptic comment.

The line between Mother's brows became more pronounced. "They will make themself useful to you," she said.

Sjunil's hand briefly touched my elbow. "I've never questioned their usefulness. I wouldn't have asked them to join me otherwise." My mouth opened, the question burning on my tongue, but I managed to swallow it. Asked me to join her? "It is time to meet the other side of the family," she said peacefully. "Tall Trees is very nice as such but there *is* a whole world out there." She gave a signal to my sister and Siw filled another bowl, stood up, and gave it to me, the hot yeasty smell of the beer hitting me full in the face.

Sjunil continued, "I had long thought about going on another journey, so this is an excellent opportunity to school both of them." She gestured to Siw and me. "They're going to need it."

"For what?" Mother's voice was flat and unfriendly.

"For the things the gods have let me see," Sjunil said, not a little smugly. It seemed to give her pleasure to needle her older sister. As a wizard, she was the volatile element in the government of the Moons; her word could overrule if necessary and she'd used many a veto in the last years.

"Let me guess," Silid murmured. "Danger and hardship, storms and floods?"

Sjunil grinned at her, the lines around the corners of her eyes deeply etched into her brown skin. "Something like that."

My heart picked up its pace. Aunt Sjunil seldom spoke about her visions. We all knew that she had them from time to time and that they made her weak and irritable. Usually the only one who got to hear about them was Mother, when the sisters started their monthly meeting to determine the best days for weddings or other important village events.

Our wizard busied herself pulling burrs from her blanket and flicking them into the flames. Her grin slowly faded, as if she was starting to remember the things she'd seen.

Siw cleared her throat. "I have begun to work out the route," she declared, but Mother held up a hand, her fingers as gnarly as oak branches, in a forbidding gesture that made my sister turn pink with annoyance. She wasn't interested in the minutiae of our journey.

"You will tell me," Mother said quietly and Sjunil's glance shifted. She looked weirdly young and guilty, as if there were many secrets she'd kept from our leader.

"You're sure?" she asked.

Mother nodded slowly.

Sjunil shrugged. "The gods spoke of change."

"Which ones?"

My aunt pulled a necklace from her tunic: likenesses of some of our Small Gods had been formed in clay and baked to keep their shape, each one identifiable enough.

Mother relaxed. The Small Gods were known to be unreliable, to play with us to keep themselves entertained. "There is always change," she said. "This is not news."

Sjunil shrugged again. "I've decided to take it as a warning. For how many generations have the Clouds stood with the Moons? Suddenly they decide on an alliance with the west coast, after fighting the families there for generations? Something has happened to upset the balance and made them risk breaking their word."

Mother stared at me. She didn't have to say it, we all knew what she was thinking.

Sjunil spat out a bitter laugh. "No," she said. "Qarim Badger might have been a disappointment as a husband, but it was not his fault. It wasn't Sloe's fault either. The Clouds took their chance to break away, that is all."

I ground my teeth and quickly drank more beer.

Siw smiled at me, a small, mean smile that I felt in every fibre. Her own father had died honourably, on the hunt. No one had ever proclaimed him a disappointment, though he hadn't been clever enough not to provoke the gigantic boar that had done him in. Mother had cried, as was befitting, but then she'd picked my father from all the candidates the other families had offered her—someone young and shrewd, who carried many regrets with him. Siw hadn't known her father, hadn't even been able to walk yet when he died, and even if that should've made us draw together and help each other, she'd always been glad to badmouth her stepfather. Maybe I would've done the same in her situation.

In Mother's immediate family, we were both the odd ones out. Wizards were not expected to marry for political reasons, and I'd been rejected. Perhaps Sjunil had the right idea after all when she'd asked for me to be apprenticed to her. It might've made everyone's life much easier.

The prospect of travelling with my sister for at least a few weeks made me shudder. Siw wasn't someone to let an opportunity pass by. She'd find more ways to humiliate me. For the moment, she contented herself with seeing me squirm on the bench, someone who would've given everything not to confront what had happened to them, though it was my right to address the council and ask to be compensated for the damage the Clouds had done to us.

I noticed that Sjunil had watched me for quite a while, registering the dynamic between Siw and me and doubtless squirreling the information away to use against us. I'd never made the mistake of underestimating my aunt. She might've seemed scruffy and motheaten, not nearly impressive enough to be taken for what she was at first glance, but she kept score. No one else had ever dared to oppose Mother in the way she constantly did and the fact that she wasn't displaying a wealth of ostentatious jewellery singled her out even more.

She yawned, not bothering to cover her mouth. "It is decided," she said, rubbing her aching jaw afterwards. "I will take Siw, Sloe, and Qes but I will need someone who is able to fight."

"Qes can fight," I said. "He just doesn't want to."

Mother groaned softly but Sjunil nodded. "I knew that there was a good reason why you like him so much. Who else is available? Someone high-ranking enough who can handle themself with a longknife?"

"What about Julas Raven?" Siw's voice suddenly had a slight squeal to it, and no one missed it. She blushed. "He came second in last year's competitions."

Mother shrugged. "Do you want him?" she asked her sister. No question whether Julas wanted to come. He wouldn't be given a choice.

Sjunil moved her shoulders under the blanket. "At least he looks impressive enough." She glanced at me. "What do you think, Sloe? Is there someone else who might be a better fit?" She had a tone in her voice that let me know that she didn't ask me just to irk her apprentice.

"Julas is all right," I conceded. "A bit … headstrong but nice enough." Perhaps he'd keep Siw occupied so I could have a good trip after all. Julas had joined us from a Raven settlement. His Moon father had married into their family, and he'd decided to try his luck in Tall Trees instead, where the yearly competitions were held and he could find many more fighters to train with after the goats had been milked and the fleeces spun. He was a viable prospect for Siw if she wanted to claim him as a future wizard's husband, and he sure was easy on the eyes, if you liked that sort of gruff confidence in men. He'd never been mean to me, which was more than could be said for a lot of the others.

"I will expect you to be ready to leave in two days' time." Sjunil stared pointedly at the beer bowl in my hands.

"Lots of things to sort out before then," I said as I jumped up to leave the Roundhouse.

Mother held up a hand again. "Come and speak to me later," she demanded.

My throat was too dry to speak, but I managed to nod.

I asked Qes to help me choose a horse as he knew them much better than I. It was a cold morning and our breath mingled with thick clouds of steam rising from the animals. The leaf litter crunched under my boots as I followed my cousin around. All of the horses in Tall Trees were communally owned by the family and I remembered riding some of them when I'd been included in hunting parties in the past.

"You need something reliable," Qes muttered as his hands touched the hindquarters of a thickset bay gelding. "Nothing flashy, nothing excitable—a horse that is safe. He should be exactly what you want."

The gelding turned around to snuffle at his pockets, hoping for a treat. Qes fished some stale nutbread from his tunic. "His name is Yoli."

Sweetheart. "That sounds promising."

"He's one of my favourites. I'll give you a new saddle blanket for him. It's nice of your mother to be this generous."

I patted the bay's muscular neck and he started to smell my knees, then tried to get at the leaves under my boots to nibble at them. "Silid will have had a word with her. She had to offer me some perks … Have you chosen your horse already?"

Qes grinned. "Yeah. Had a spirited discussion with Julas about it. He came over first thing this morning, as soon as the order reached him."

"I hope he didn't offer to fight you?"

He made a dismissive gesture and tried to smooth his hair down. "Nah. We reached an agreement before it came to that. Of course, I'm not the runner up in any sort of competition but he saw my point, eventually."

I was relieved. At least Julas had kept his head and hadn't tried to demonstrate his strength at the earliest opportunity. "It seems Siw has good taste in men."

"Oh." Qes blinked. "Did she suggest him?"

"She did. Qes?"

He scowled. "He never said anything."

"I don't think they are together … yet. Maybe she just has a crush on him?"

He made the same weird movement again, trying to flatten his curls against the top of his head.

I stared at him. "What?"

"I wouldn't have kissed him, if … if I'd know about that."

"Oh no …"

"He seemed willing enough. Do you think Siw will turn me into a toad?"

"Not if you keep your mouth shut." I narrowed my eyes at him. "What exactly did you mean by 'spirited discussion'?"

He looked sheepish. "A bit of hand stuff."

I gasped. In all the time Qes had been with us, we'd only ever talked about my ill luck with relationships, never about his hopes and dreams. "You like Julas?"

He shrugged. "I must've mentioned it to you."

"You didn't!"

"Well, now you know."

"She'll definitely turn you into a toad. Let's hope that he doesn't blab." I stepped away from Yoli's warm body. "Was it nice?"

He blushed furiously. "It was. He's good with his hands."

I had to laugh. "It's going to be an interesting few weeks, that's for sure."

After the midday meal, I returned to the Other House to pack. The two oldest of my housemates had left for work but the youngest peeked around the corner of my sleeping platform when I stuffed my spare smallclothes into the saddle bags. Sor was all eyes and elbows, like a foal in its awkward phase before it turns into something spectacular. Their hair was gathered into a loose braid and pinned in place with a bone needle.

"I wish I could come with you."

"No, you don't." I rolled up the next items for the bag and secured them with leather cords.

In the murkiness of our house, their face had a grey tinge. "You're leaving me alone with *them*." Their chin pointed towards the opposite platform, and I knew exactly what they meant. Our housemates had married each other some time ago but were still very much in love. It was hard for me to watch and there was no reason why Sor should feel differently.

When I'd joined the Other House, it had stood empty for some time and Mother had ordered a quick round of repairs before I moved in officially. It smelled of freshly hewn wood and bracken; the blankets folded at the bottom of the sleeping platform were new as well and the pillows had been stuffed with dried grass and herbs mere hours before. The whole house was clean and inviting and Silid looked satisfied with the attempt to welcome me into my new life, though I was still not quite sure about taking that step. In a way, it distanced me from the family, but I hadn't felt myself in the House of Men and less so in the House of Women.

Silid had asked around and I was quickly joined by others from the smaller settlements; the news that the Other House in Tall Trees was inhabited again had spread through the forests and the grasslands. At some point, Sjunil ordered a celebration to consecrate the house anew, so the gods were easily able to find it should we ask them to in our prayers.

At that time, I was the youngest in the house and happy to step aside and let one of the older ones take the lead. I still remember the look Sjunil gave me on that occasion, curious and ever so slightly disappointed. As my mother's child, I should've been happy to make myself head of the house, no matter how inexperienced I was. It was hard getting used to a life between the houses and I was beyond relieved to have others to guide me. Siw had seemed especially irritated, as if I'd done it to gain an advantage over her and she was losing out on attention. I couldn't bear to talk to her for a while.

All of the sleeping platforms were filled when I was around ten summers old, and there was laughter, good food, and a fire that never was allowed to go out, warming us in the bitter nights of winter. We told stories of the ones who'd lived in the house before and gone on to make exceptionally good marriages or to find fame in other ways, all to honour the Moons of Tall Trees. We knew that there were Other Houses in almost all of the larger villages and people like us even lived at the Stoneharp, so far in the west that the salt of the sea greyed its walls. We all longed for an opportunity to travel to the coast and see it, though we knew that the families of the west would never have allowed us to reach it unharmed.

I made a few friends in those days but because they were older, they all moved on after a while, all but the two who eventually decided to marry each other and stay resolutely put. I remember falling in love with some of my housemates, mostly the ones who had made their decision a long time ago and refused to be swayed by any other considerations—but of course, they were the popular ones and eventually all of them found more promising prospects among the men and women of Tall Trees. For a while, we experienced a lot of coming and going and I felt myself going still in the midst of it, because I knew in the depths of my blood that I'd be left behind.

I loved to hear the stories of the Moons from the Other House, famed for their prowess with longknife and bow but that didn't change the fact that I wasn't particularly skilled, though I'd been taught from the time I'd been able to draw a string. Those Others had their own beauty, untamed and fierce. None of them had just the one blue eye and none of them was described as a bit awkward with people. While my housemates aspired to some sort of recognition, I smiled and sat back, because the gods hadn't picked me. Whatever their plans, I would never be a warrior to save my people; I wasn't even allowed to be apprenticed to Aunt Sjunil to become closer to the Tall and the Small Gods, the Siblings, and the Cousins. The possibility to distinguish myself had been deemed above my abilities. Though I didn't kick up a stink, I was disappointed that Sjunil, the wizard who'd chosen my name, hadn't fought harder for me.

When my housemates picked the gods they wanted to speak to, they aimed high, dedicated themselves to Sister Storm, Sister Soil, or Brother Flame, while I was ever careful and kept to the Small Gods, picking the ones that might be best equipped to help, hedging my bets so none of them was offended. It was something I did in secret and though I joined in with the communal prayers as was expected, I still preferred to communicate with them on my own.

The Cousins could be persuaded to give me a break from time to time. Some of us dedicated ourselves to only one of them and wore their symbols to signal it. I'd seen a lot of the men wear the amulets of Cousin Blade (Julas was one of them) or Cousin Quiver, while Saon switched between Cousin Skin and Cousin Pearl, to further his artistic pursuits, and Sister Stone when he needed bigger favours. I'd never asked Sjunil to fashion a particular ornament for me, never had her bless one of my own making; no one was able to see at first glance what kind of person I wanted the gods to help me be. It was a feeble attempt at being mysterious, at wrapping my wishes so tightly around me that I was barely able to breathe, while the Other House was stirring, vibrating with stories, hopes, plans, and the smells of people living close together.

I hadn't been happy when it was full up but then I hadn't been happy when it started to empty, though everyone who left did so with a smile and a hug for me, with best wishes for my own future. Sometimes Sor reminded me of this, my inability to be content and stop worrying about what could've been—they had some of the same attitude and maybe it was a family thing, coming down to me from Mother and to them from their grandmother. Sor had Mother's way of drawing their brows together, something old beyond their years, and even in the moments when I wanted to strangle them for some peace and quiet, I was aware that their anxiety mirrored mine.

"You'll be fine," I promised them.

"I won't." Sor's bottom lip trembled. There'd been days when I would've loved to boot them out of the door; they were deeply annoying when the moonlight flooded the house and they weren't able to get off to sleep.

"I'll be back before you know it."

"You will be back with a story to tell," Sor grumbled.

I sighed and considered which tunic I wanted to take with me. "There's no guarantee that the story is going to be a good one."

A BLOW TO THE BONE

"Sit down," Mother said.

It was very early and still dark in the forest, but with old age Mother had taken to rising ever earlier and I hadn't been able to sleep anyway. Someone had lit the brazier under the roof of the House of Women and next to her were the leftovers of her breakfast; she'd likely been up for hours, although no one seemed to be around but us. The village square was empty, the brazier giving off the only light in Tall Trees.

I obeyed and sat on the other bench; the furs were uncomfortably damp as if they'd been left out the whole night. Mother was swaddled in her black cloak, the embroidered moons shimmering around her, and the glow of the flames softened her face.

"It is almost too late for us to talk," she said, not looking at me as she spoke, though I felt the words hitting me deep in my chest, like a blow to the bone. "Silid says I should have paid more attention to you and might have seen how the events would affect you. I never realized you would take the affront against our family in such a personal way, Sloe." As always, my name sounded especially bitter from her lips—not the name she'd once picked for me, not the life she'd chosen for me. "The journey you will go on today is not a punishment. You are the last of my children and you deserve to be recognized by the council, to be seen as someone who is of my blood and who has my support. I have been slow to acknowledge that neither of us can be blamed for what happened with your father, for the dishonour he brought upon himself and therefore on us both. Leading the family has occupied my time for so long that I neglected to notice how much you were hurt."

I pressed my eyes closed, tears filtering through my lashes, but I knew that I wasn't supposed to reply to her yet.

"You will hear things in Goldenlake that will shock you," Mother said flatly. "Things that concern your father's past and that were not known to me when I took him to be my husband. I have tried to keep them from the family as best as I could, but there are old enemies of his everywhere, and certainly among the Badgers." I heard her take in a deep breath. "Perhaps I made a mistake all those years ago, but whatever they tell you about him, he was a good man in his own way. With all the disgrace he allowed himself to bring over us, I am sure he never intended for you to feel ashamed. He loved you, as unhappy and desperate as he was. He would have wanted you to leave your mark on the history of the families, without being held back by his memory. It is one of my deepest regrets that I was not able to see this for myself but needed my daughter's help to understand you better." She pulled a face. "Having the leader of one of the great families for your mother is an advantage in many ways but a disadvantage in others, and I have never tried to deny this. One day you might see that I aimed to do my best and that it was still not enough."

She didn't try to lean forward and touch me. I couldn't recall the last time when she'd hugged me—maybe decades ago, when I was still too small to remember. I knew why she'd waited so long to tell me. She wanted to make certain I would climb into the saddle and leave so that she wouldn't have to talk to me the day after and the day after that. The words were difficult for her to say, difficult for me to hear, and it would've embarrassed us both not to spend the next weeks as far away from each other as possible.

"Sjunil has asked me to speak to you. She was worried about all the unsaid … things between us, in case …" She didn't need to actually say it.

In case something happens.

"I am grateful to her." My voice sounded rusty.

Mother cleared her throat. "She has been by my side all our lives and served me well. She will make Siw into an adequate wizard of her own, but we both know that your sister was never the right choice for it. I was afraid. With your father's …" I'd never witnessed her struggle with words and stared at her, helplessly. So often she appeared to me like the embodiment of Sister Stone: unmoved, not one silver hair out of place. There was a fragility to her that was new and disturbing. "Sjunil will do her best to keep you all safe."

I knew I had to start responding to her, that she was waiting for me to jump in. I took a deep, painful breath. "I will follow her every wish," I promised hoarsely.

"You are not to put yourself in danger, Sloe. I need you to come back to Tall Trees." Mother's dark eyes shone like polished pebbles, and finally, finally, her hand reached for me.

I fell to my knees to kiss it, eyes and nose running and feeling like a snotty child again.

"I have charged Brother Brook with your protection." She pulled something from the folds of her cloak.

"Brother Brook?" I'd never considered him a possibility but grasped for the amulet even so. It was made from silver, one of the biggest pendants I'd ever seen, and Brother Brook's narrow face was worked with such care that it jumped out at me, each hank of hair formed into a perfect wave. It was a wonderful thing to behold. "I can't … can't accept …" I started but fell silent.

Mother shuffled towards me on her bench and pressed her lips to my forehead. "Brother Brook has always served me well and he will do as I bid him."

A ragged sob broke from my mouth, a truly desperate noise. I would never have presumed to choose Brother Brook myself. He was one of the Tallest Gods, powerful beyond measure in a forest filled with broad rivers. The silver was still warm from my mother's skin, and I clutched it to me.

"Thank you," I managed to say. "I will honour him always."

We assembled in the village square at dawn. Qes came from the paddocks with Yoli and his own horse behind him, brushed, saddled, and ready.

He shifted his shoulders as he came closer. "Everything all right?"

I was tempted to lie again, but then I shook my head. "No. Mother spoke to me. It was the best and the worst talk of my life."

Qes swallowed. "And you cried."

"Buckets."

He came closer and I took him by the shoulder to pull him into my arms. He gave an alarmed yelp but then I felt his warm hand at the back of my neck, and he held me against him, with the weird tenderness that he sometimes had when he needed to keep a horse quiet. He was firm and smelled of the animals he tended. When I pressed my cold nose into his neck, he made another sound.

"I'm sorry," he mumbled. "And I'm glad for you."

We stood that way until the others joined us and I stepped away from him with a smile.

IT HURTS

The first to pull her horse into the square was Siw and she brought Sjunil's mare with her.

She gave me a strange, calculating stare. "You look awful."

"I didn't get much sleep." My hand found the amulet hidden under my tunic and I saw Siw's gaze lingering on my fingers. She might as well guess what I'd brought with me, my new alliance with one of the Siblings. For the moment at least, I felt like I was under the eyes of Brother Brook, as if the warmth of the fire I'd shared with Mother earlier was still with me.

I heard Qes draw in a sharp breath. Another horse was led across to us, the fifth companion walking beside it in the relaxed way he had, broad shouldered and seemingly so at ease with himself. In the first light of the day, Julas' face looked older and since I'd noticed him last, he'd started a beard. His long, straight hair was pulled back in a braid that fell to his belt, where the sheathed longknife sent an unspoken message.

"Good day for it," he said. "Should stay fairly dry."

Siw went an interesting shade of red and Qes studied the tips of his boots. While all of us had wrapped up against the cold, Julas' forearms were bare, sporting a few silvery scars. Another ran over his left cheekbone, forked and not fully faded yet. I remembered seeing him getting wounded during the competition. He would've come first if he hadn't bled so much that he fainted in the last round.

He gave a nod to me, a silent acknowledgement to the fact that we didn't know each other well and would have to catch up during the next weeks. Or maybe it meant that he'd noticed that I was the only one present who wasn't visibly affected by him.

"Morning everyone." Our wizard stepped from the House of the Women, yawning like a fox and rubbing the tattoo on her forehead. "Where are the rest of the horses?"

Julas' chin pointed towards the paddocks and I saw two pack horses tied to the fence, laden with tents and provisions. "Qes prepared them," he said. "So we could leave as soon as you were ready."

Qes squirmed as Sjunil smiled at him. "Very good. Siw?"

My sister brought the grey mare closer to her master, reminded that within the group she shared the same rank as Julas, Qes, and me: we all served the wizard of Tall Trees, who pulled herself into the saddle and breathed a deep, deep sigh.

"Ah well, sod it. Let's ride."

The last time I'd left Tall Trees for more than a hunting expedition had been a long time ago, for one of the festivals, when Mother gathered all of her children and led us to the eastern caves to pray. It only happened one time and there must've been a specific rationale behind the trip, but I'd been too concerned with other things to notice. I hadn't wanted to be away from the Other House, it had rained a lot, and I became saddle-sore after the second day and very grumpy indeed.

Mother's words kept me warm on the first lengths of the journey, bits of her speech stuck in my head as if they'd never leave me again: *Still not enough … I neglected to notice how much you were hurt.* There was a chance that all of it had been carefully considered— every pause, every shuddering breath—but even if she'd only sought to manipulate me, it was so much more than she'd ever given me that I took it on with all the concerns I might choose to keep.

Siw was the first in our row of horses and Sjunil followed, the chequered blanket pulled over her head and shoulders. I rode in the middle while Qes and Julas, the muscle of the party, kept to the rear. It was cold but a few patches of mist clung to the ground, and when we came to the closest river crossing it lingered over the rippling surface of the water, almost close enough to touch. Yoli's broad hooves churned up the icy water; he snorted in mild protest as his fetlocks were soaked. I patted his bulging neck, hoping he didn't sense my apprehension. It was the first time I'd been close to a river since acquiring the protection of Brother Brook. If he resented the way in which Mother had given me to him, it was his first chance to show his displeasure. We made it to the other side without Yoli stumbling and I cast a glance back to the steep riverbank as we climbed up the other side of the valley. So far, so good.

We travelled slowly, settling into the rhythm of the horses, taking a few short breaks that were always initiated by my aunt. She was the one who knew the forest; she'd served the Siblings and the Cousins for decades and remembered the best places to stop and eat, where to find more water for the horses and maybe some rough grass for them to nibble on, while we chewed fruit breads and strips of dried meat.

Most of our conversation was weather and food related; there was an uneasiness between us five that was hard to bear. Qes seemed to expect Julas to blurt out something that would hurt Siw, Julas probably wanted Qes to acknowledge that they shared more than a passing acquaintance, Siw for Julas to notice her properly, and I waited for everything to explode around me. I should've known that Sjunil would be the one to kick the bear.

"By the gods," she groaned after Siw had mentioned the weird aftertaste of the meat for the third time. "Why don't you ask him? I can't deal with this for much longer."

"Ask him what?" Julas' brow furrowed.

Sjunil sniffed. "She doesn't appreciate that the position she enjoys comes with certain drawbacks. She's young enough and keen enough and wants to jump your bones."

A shocked silence settled.

"Huh," said Julas after a while. "That's a bit inconvenient."

Siw gave an anguished howl and tried to get up, but her master caught her by the wrist.

"Inconvenient, how?" I saw Sjunil registering the way in which Julas' eyes found Qes. Just a quick look, but it didn't escape her notice. "You're with him?"

"I hope to be."

Qes drew a spluttering breath, his round face burning.

"Ah," she said. "Why?"

It was the first time I'd seen Julas put on the spot and I must admit that I thoroughly enjoyed seeing him wrestle with how to handle my aunt. His voice was quiet and deliberate as he finally answered, surely realizing that she wouldn't let him off the hook for all the nuts in the forest.

"Because he has always been nice to me—and he is a good kisser."

"I can't imagine that anyone wouldn't be nice to you," Sjunil said with narrowed eyes.

He rubbed at the scar on his cheek, visibly pained. We all had seen what happened, how he'd lost.

Our wizard sighed. "Contrary to popular belief, I don't particularly enjoy torturing pretty young men … but I hope that this exercise has provided at least some clarification. Qes?"

My cousin sounded strangled when he finally obliged her. "I would be stupid not to want him," he said.

My aunt clapped her hands and so released my sister, who darted away from us as if something had bitten her.

"I should talk to her," I said with a sigh. "Shouldn't I?"

Sjunil nodded. "You'd better."

I found Siw between two mossy boulders, a heap of muddy cloth and tangled hair. When I approached her, she only looked up briefly. "Go on, gloat away."

"I'm not here to gloat. Maybe she didn't realize what was going on."

"She is cruel."

"She wanted to help."

"How can you think that, Sloe?" She gave a bitter snort. "You don't have to live with her, you don't know … She enjoys taunting me, because she knows that I never wanted to …" She bit her lip. "She is an old, resentful bitch."

"But she really doesn't waste time. At least now you know."

"I would've liked to be kept in the dark a bit longer."

I crept closer, wedged my hip between the rocks. "You say that because it hurts. She ripped off the bandage for you."

"Stop making her out to be a hero. She's selfish, Sloe—selfish and horrible and so very happy to torture me." She sniffled and wiped at her face. She'd gnawed at her nails until they bled. "You'll see. You'll have enough time with her."

I shivered in my shabby travel cloak. I'd never thought of Siw as lonely and desperate. It wasn't a good look on her. But then, she would've been able to say the same about me. I tried to squat in front of her and she flinched, as if expecting to be hit. "Neither of us wants to be here. It will be uncomfortable and freezing cold, and I don't look forward to travelling with a pair of lovers—the gods know I have enough of that at home. But there will be plenty of young men in Goldenlake, gawping at you, wishing they'd be good enough to impress you."

"You don't know what it's like. You have … what's-his-name."

"We've broken up. *I* have broken up with him, to be precise."

She gasped. "Why?"

"Because …" I took a deep breath. "Because he made me feel bad about myself. Or worse—again, to be precise."

Her eyes went shiny. "But he is so beautiful."

"Maybe that was the problem. I wanted him too much to realize what he did to me. At least you have better taste in men."

"I always pick the wrong ones. The ones who aren't even interested in kissing a woman."

"Julas isn't the first?"

"He isn't even the fifth, if you want to know."

"Oh, Siw."

She huffed, her breath a white mist around her chewed mouth, but she started to get up, her various ornaments clinking against each other as she shifted. She talked to all the Tall and to all the Small Gods and she wore them wherever she went. I took her arm and pulled her to her feet. We stood in front of each other, both looking sheepish.

"Siw, can we at least try to be friends while we're travelling with each other? I could use someone on my side."

Her eyes narrowed, then she smiled. "Let's try."

My aunt was careful not to say anything else to Siw all afternoon. When we joined the group, they were ready to ride on and no one talked for the next two hours, until it was time to make camp for the night. Sjunil had a place to rest in mind and guided us down a steep valley, filled with the sound of a waterfall gushing over the broken rocks at the bottom. Along the riverbank, we found a series of shallow caves that would be flooded in the spring but were the perfect spot for our first night out in the forest, with enough space to keep the horses dry and light a fire. After a quick check that the caves were indeed uninhabited, we proceeded to make ourselves as comfortable as possible.

Siw took care of the preparations for herself and her master, but she still had a notable cloud of resentment hanging around her that stood in weird contrast to the glow that surrounded the two men of our company. Of course I was more than happy for Qes, if a little jealous that it only had taken one nosey wizard for him to start a new relationship. When Qes left the cave with his mount and the pack horses to find a good watering spot on the riverbank, Julas pulled the other horses with him and followed.

Sjunil sighed. "There we go. At least it looks as if they'll be discreet about it. And thank fuck we have a second tent." She didn't turn to her fuming apprentice but busied herself with the firewood I'd collected for her.

The caves appeared well-used, with traces of earlier fires and heaps of dried leaves in the back that must've served as beds at some point. Someone had used a stick of coal to draw a few figures on the wall, maybe someone waiting for their travelling companion to wake up or someone trapped by bad weather and bored out of their skull.

As I bent over to touch the markings my aunt let out a warning shout.

"Don't!" She jumped to her feet and, as if to make absolutely sure that there was no misunderstanding, took my elbow to pull me away from the wall. "Someone went through the rituals in here," she whispered. "None of us can afford to insult the gods today." Her dirty hand gestured towards the black figures. "Someone died here—not too long ago. Perhaps the bears found them and scattered their bones, but this is their final prayer. Something to keep and honour."

Gooseflesh rippled over my back. I hadn't noticed the squiggly lines next to the largest figure but I knew who I was looking at. Brother Flame. Whoever had died where we stood had been cold, desperate, and hungry, and had spent their last moments trying to touch the gods. Someone who'd belonged to the families, maybe even to the Moons, to us.

Someone close.

TOO MUCH BLOOD

I managed to corner Qes in the morning, after I'd left the cave to pee and come back to find him standing among the horses, his face more troubled than I'd expected.

"How can you not be jumping for joy?" I hissed. "The whole of Tall Trees will give you a pat on the back when we return."

"It's not that simple," he mumbled. "I didn't think the whole thing through."

"The whole *thing*?"

"I can't relax with Siw's eyes burning down my neck." He shuddered. "She's still thinking about toads—I can feel it."

"She will get over it in time. It's not really up to her. It's Julas' choice to make and he chose you."

"But he doesn't know me very well. I'd rather spend some time with him before … before he decides."

"You don't need to marry him straight away!"

"He said it to a *wizard*, Sloe. Wizards marry people and your aunt was very excited about the whole … issue." He rubbed his eyes. "I'm scared."

"Scared?"

"What happens if I do fall in love with him, properly? And then … then he leaves, and I won't be able to breathe …"

"For months you have talked me through my own relationship, and you were right. Mostly. Why are you panicking now? I don't understand."

"I might be able to see through Saon's motives but then he isn't a particularly complicated person. And I wasn't invested in him. Julas should be so far out of my reach."

"He isn't. I can vouch for you, Qes, as many of your friends would."

"I don't have any other friends in Tall Trees, Sloe. Haven't you realized that yet? I have one friend and … now him." A soft smile came to his mouth, a smile that gave me hope. "It feels like a fluke, Sloe. I pretended that it was no big deal, kissing him, but this has never happened to me before. I didn't think he would flirt back when I tried my luck. I thought it would be the best strategy to get him off my back about the horses."

"Well, now he's really on your back. Congratulations."

He released a long breath. "Holy crap, Sloe. Holy fucking crap."

After the first few hours, Sjunil let her mare fall back to ride next to me. "How's your arse?"

"Getting sore," I said but smiled at her.

"Give it a week." She grinned. "By then it should start to feel leathery."

The night frost clung to the forest floor, washing out the colours around us, and bit into the inside of my nose. "Do I *want* a leathery arse?"

She glanced over her shoulder at the men riding behind us. "It will make some things easier, some things harder. How are they getting on?"

"Qes still needs to wrap his head around it."

"He will manage."

"Don't pressure them," I begged. "They need to sort it out by themselves."

She laughed. "There's nothing to sort out. Don't tell me you wouldn't give a tooth to be in the same situation."

"I wouldn't. Not now."

"How long will it take for you to get over the little ferret? I hear he tried to snog the head off someone else at the assembly."

"Who told you?"

"Your mother might be as old as the hills but she's still keeping an eye on everybody. She didn't appreciate the display."

"They are welcome to each other. I'm starting to see how many mistakes I made with Saon. Qes helped a lot."

"And now you want to help him?"

"It feels fair."

"You never thought of keeping him for yourself?"

"No!"

"Just saying. He seems like a reasonable young man and though I wouldn't recommend a marriage back into the Badgers for you, the heart famously wants what the heart wants."

"We are friends. The best of friends."

"Relationships change. I just want to make sure that you don't let him go if you'd rather keep him." She looked pained, as if she'd made that mistake herself, long ago.

"Julas can have him," I said and realized that I meant it. Our new circumstances had helped to define our friendship better. In fact, it was a profound relief to find myself happy for him. In the beginning, I'd worried that he expected more from me than I was prepared to give—that he'd tried to get Saon out of the way. That I would put aside the man I loved because I'd been manipulated into it and that all the problematic things Qes had flagged up about Saon really weren't all bad or might even be normal. I tried to give Qes a look over my shoulder, but Sjunil made a weird sound.

I hadn't noticed how far we'd fallen behind Siw at the front. She'd let her black mare trot down into the next valley, where the path was squeezed between old beech trees and rock formations darkened by rain.

"Siw!" My aunt's voice echoed around me. She'd shouted at the top of her lungs and with more fear in one word that I'd ever heard her express. "Siw!"

Her apprentice hesitated, then pressed her heels into the mare's belly and vanished over the next ridge.

Julas overtook us, his longknife drawn and swinging in his right hand, the hooves of his horse spitting rotten leaves and clumps of black earth. My aunt followed him, leaving me and Qes behind.

"What's going on?" I called to my cousin.

Qes had gone pale. "There's a strange smell."

"What?" I sniffed and he was right. I hadn't even noticed but Sjunil must've realized that Siw was getting into danger, so far ahead and alone. It smelled like iron and shit and ... spilled blood. Fear gripped my heart. I was tempted to wheel Yoli around and flee, but there was no guarantee that whatever gave off the smell wouldn't find me, alone and surely lost in the woods. So I stayed with Qes, who fumbled for the knife at his belt.

The bottom of the valley was churned up; a group of tents had been trampled into the mud and a large fire pit was still smoking. Bits of equipment were strewn about, fire-blackened and smouldering. A dead horse lay on its side, half buried in leaves, its guts spilled under it and—Qes made a whimpering sound—from the tallest tree hung three men, strung up by their ankles, their throats cut and bled out like pigs, their blood a congealed mass beneath them.

Siw had jumped off her mare and was beside them. She frantically sawed at the first rope with her eating knife, though she must have known—she must have seen—that there was no reason to hurry anymore. Julas was still on horseback, checking the edges of the destroyed camp, searching for traces of the people who'd killed in such a demonstrative way, but everything was silent apart for Siw's sobs and Sjunil's ragged breath as we all tried to understand what we saw.

Qes pressed the reins of the pack horses into my hand and joined Julas, to ensure that we were as safe as possible while the first of the men came loose from the branch with a sickening *splat*.

He fell like a sack of bearnuts, his limbs sprawling and his neck gaping, his head at a crooked angle and caked in blood. Sjunil knelt down next to him, careful not to let her cloak touch the ground. She said no word to keep her apprentice from cutting the others down. Siw's face was covered in tears and snot; her breath came in long rasps. The next two fell quicker, making a horrid heap of grey, dead flesh and matted hair. Sjunil bent down to inspect one of the men and as her fingers poked into his skin my stomach turned itself out.

Yoli gave an annoyed snort as I vomited down his side.

"They must have left the area," Julas concluded, his longknife now sheathed. "I'd say they killed them last night." His voice was soft and matter-of-fact.

I rinsed out my mouth for the tenth time. I'd cleaned myself up the best I could, but the humiliation still clung to me. We had all seen dead people before, had helped to slaughter animals, but it was the first time I'd seen the results of such deliberate violence. Siw was rubbing at her raw eyes, though she'd stopped crying. Qes had gone very silent.

Sjunil turned to Julas. "We will bury them, though I'm not familiar with their ways."

Julas blinked and I knew what I'd missed so far, something that had been right in front of me. Sjunil had touched their hair and skin because it marked them, or at least two of them. Only one of the dead men was of the families, though not of the Moons. From the colours he wore, and the ornaments bound in his braids, he looked to be from further west. The other two were fair-haired and bearded, their skin even lighter than Qes' and their clothes of a strange style I'd never seen before, grubby and ragged but once so finely woven that it seemed a shame to wear them travelling in the forests.

"Who are they?" Qes asked, sounding anxious and small.

Sjunil drew a deep breath. "They are men from the Eastern Cities."

"What are Cities?"

"Settlements. Big settlements, a hundred times larger than Tall Trees."

"A hundred times?" Siw gasped.

Our wizard shrugged. "Or more. I saw some of these men a long time ago, when I was at the Stoneharp." She looked at me. "When I was with your father in the west."

Memories flashed into my head. Father had told me about the Stoneharp, long ago. There'd been new words, words he had to translate and had practiced with me for a while, before he vanished from Tall Trees.

Julas cleared his throat. "There are supposedly a lot of them at the Stoneharp of late. Some came across the sea to trade and ever since their numbers have gone up."

Sjunil gave him a slow nod. "I've heard of them landing on our east coast as well, a long time ago, but no one wanted them there and the families killed them and sank the ships they had come in."

"Why are they here?" Siw asked.

Sjunil sighed. "We can only suspect that they'd arranged to be taken to the Golden Lake."

"But why?"

She shrugged. "Because they must've heard about its wonders? Because they are desperate to find a more direct way to trade with the families? Why do we do anything? How many shovels have we brought?"

"One." Julas scratched at the scar on his cheek. "I can try to make something useful from the things they left behind. The ground should still be soft enough. Just about."

"Let's get to it. I'd rather not stay here for the night. I will find prayers for them that will do." Sjunil closed her eyes for a moment. "Siw, you will help me prepare. Sloe, you will make sure that all of the rubbish is cleaned up and buried. See to the horses first, so they can rest. Take what we can use for firewood and see if you find something in the tents that gives us more information about them."

I should've been grateful that she tried to keep me out of the way but after I'd managed to find water for our horses and fastened them between the trees, far from the ground Julas had chosen to dig up, it still felt horrible to poke about in the trashed remains of the camp. There were muddy blankets and smashed clay bowls, the tents ripped and though I could probably have stitched them back together, there was too much blood on them. The attackers must've taken everything else after the raid; I found nothing that was still usable for us.

I made a big pile of stuff for Qes and Julas to bury, while I heard wizard and apprentice speak in low voices about the gods they planned to involve in the rituals. Siw sounded calmer and my heart twisted when I thought about the sounds she'd made while cutting down the men. My sister had tried to help even though there was nothing she could possibly have done to save them.

At last, the camp was picked clean, my own boot prints covering the ground. I shuddered as I turned my attention to the dead horse, its yellow teeth, grey gums, and tongue, the eyes dull and black, a saddle squished beneath it. The cut that had opened its stomach had severed through the straps and the leaves covered most of it, but a bag was still fastened to it, something that might give us an idea of what had happened here. I crouched on the back of the animal and tried to pull the bag free, gritting my teeth with the strain of it, as the leaves to my right shifted and I saw fingers—bloody, broken fingers trying to reach for me.

"There's another one!"

NOT AWAKE

He must've been thrown from the horse and left for dead. Three splintered arrow shafts stuck in his back, his left hand was smashed, and his temple covered in blood. He had obviously hit his head on the way down. His breath was so shallow that it barely moved his chest.

There'd been three men from the Eastern Cities, and he was as pale as the rest of them, his hair of the same colour as the withered leaves on the beeches around us—a light copper red. He seemed older than his companions as we all stared down on him.

"This complicates everything," Sjunil said. "Fuck, fuck, fuckity-fuck."

Siw was ready to jump into action. "We need to pull out the arrows," she decided. "See what we can do about the fingers and check what other wounds he might have. At least he can tell us—"

"He can't tell us anything," her master muttered. "He's barely alive."

I gave her the bag I'd managed to retrieve. "I suppose this belongs to him."

Sjunil grimaced. "Fine. Siw, get Sloe to help you clean him up. Qes and Julas will finish closing the graves and I …" She cursed as she fumbled with the clasp on the stained leather bag.

My sister suddenly had a weird glow around her, as if she needed something to do to keep her from thinking about the three men Julas and Qes had buried. The opportunity to save at least one life had her rifling through her own bags.

I sat down next to the man we were trying to bring back to life. Grime smeared the inside of his collar; his skin was unwashed, and he stank of old sweat and horse. He'd lived in his clothes for a long time, must've brought them onto the ship to the Stoneharp, weeks and weeks and weeks at sea, just to see another coast, to speak to other people. His shirt was grey, the jacket he wore made from leather, shiny with use and fastened close to his sides, covering his arms and hips, and almost meeting the tops of his boots. A piece of cloth was wrapped around his neck, too small and finely woven to be of any true use, embroidered with shooting stars. Maybe his wife had made it for him or someone else he held dear; it looked like something he wore to remember, to keep a loved one close. I leant over him, the temptation to touch the stars overwhelming, and as my fingers hovered over him, he gave a sudden cough and his eyes flew open. They were almost the same colour as his hair but of an even lighter yellow. They widened as he saw me and I touched him, soothingly. There was a word I'd forgotten, a greeting that my father had taught me, so many years ago, that sprung up to connect me to the wounded trader.

He stared at me, his mouth opened, and he echoed the word back to me. He'd heard me, understood me.

"What are you doing?" Siw loomed over us, a bowl in her hands that smelled so horrible that my nose wrinkled.

"My father taught me a few words."

"You can speak to him?"

"Just a few words, Siw."

Her brows drew together. My father had known the words, and it had decided how he'd been regarded by the Moons. The words were precious and useful.

She put the bowl to one side. "Help me get the clothes off him."

We stripped him as best as possible to assess the damage, moving him onto one of the clean blankets from Siw's bundle. He was covered in bruises but had no other open wounds, so Siw quickly wiped him down and covered him up to his hips with her cloak, cleaned the skin around the embedded arrows, and started to pull and cut them out of him while I held him down and he gurgled words that none of us understood.

It took some time for him to faint. Siw was on the last arrowhead. "He can count himself lucky that they weren't barbed," she commented and laid them aside. Fresh blood welled up and she wiped it off, stuffing the wounds with dried moss and cobwebs and bandaged him up, before getting to work on his fingers. My sister might've resented having been apprenticed but she made a fine healer, resolute and sure of hand. That aspect of wizardship would've suited me much less. The sight of his blood and the smell of the herbs made my stomach flutter again.

"How is he doing?" Sjunil held her arms across her chest.

"He might live." Siw got to her feet. "Can't make any promises for the hand but he had some luck. The arrows all managed to miss the important bits."

Sjunil gave her a satisfied nod. "Well done. Now we need to decide if we can try and move him."

Siw sniffed. "I think we can if we must. Give him a few moments."

"Julas will build something for him," Sjunil stated. I saw a muscle in her cheek flexing. "Fuck, fuck, fuckity-fuck," she said again.

Julas had found two saplings, long enough to be strapped between the pack horses. He used one of the ripped tents to fashion the middle part and then he and Qes pushed and buckled the man from the Eastern Cities in to make sure he didn't roll out of the stretcher. As a result, the prayers Sjunil found for his companions had to be cut short; we needed to leave the valley as fast as possible if we wanted to find another spot for us to spend the night. Her voice was firm and the words unsentimental. Sjunil had picked Brother Rain to take care of them, a choice I found strange at first. I'd expected one of the Cousins instead, for men who didn't share our beliefs—but then one of them had and that might've been the reason why. Brother Rain would take their hands and guide them gently, cleanse them of all their pain and sorrow. The short prayer made all of us cry—even Julas buried his face in Qes' shoulder. I saw my cousin kiss his forehead, tenderly stroking the nape of his neck. The gesture made my skin tingle.

It took only moments for us to blow our noses afterwards and to climb back into our saddles. The man from the Cities was still unconscious as we left, his head bobbing against the side of the stretcher, his bandaged left hand kept in place by part of the leather girth strap that had been cut from his horse's saddle.

"He will slow us down," Sjunil grumbled.

My sister bristled. "We can't leave him behind."

Sjunil shrugged. "But maybe we can dump him on the way."

"On whom? Who would take someone like him and keep him alive?" Siw's voice had a sharp undertone. "He's my responsibility— and Sloe's. They spoke to him."

My aunt's head made a move in my direction. "Spoke to him?"

"In his own words."

My aunt squinted at me. "Is that true?"

"Father … he knew some helpful phrases and he taught me some."

"Can you ask him why he was stupid enough to set foot in the forests? He and his companions must've had somewhere in mind. Goldenlake, or one of the other family settlements. It would be good to know."

"I'm hardly fluent," I protested weakly and felt my cheeks burn. I had an unexpected chance to prove my own worth, attempting communication with ten words at most.

Siw looked back to her patient. "He's still not woken up."

"Maybe the problem will go away by itself," Sjunil murmured and her apprentice seemed scandalized.

"You can't possibly hope for him to die!"

"Watch me. He's not good news, Siw."

"But he's hurt. He's in no condition to be dangerous to us."

"He doesn't need to wield a longknife to cause damage. Once we agreed to host a few of them at the Stoneharp but no one wanted to let them explore the forests. The guide they had with them might've been rewarded with silver seeds—or with an alliance. If the families of the west look towards the Cities, things have changed for the worse." She scratched at the teardrop tattoo on her forehead. "The men from the Cities are greedy. They always ask for more."

"He's not able to ask for anything now." Siw was digging her heels in.

"On your head be it." Sjunil made a gesture of disgust. "Don't come running to me if he bites your head off."

Yoli had fallen back until we were next to the stretcher. The pack horses had transported countless carcasses in their life, elks and spotted deer, braces of birds and fish; they weren't alarmed by the smell of blood and bitter sap that came off him in the chilly autumn air. I stared at the grey-faced trader with traces of blood in his coppery curls. He was a tallish man but not especially muscly, with rather knobbly wrists; the bandaged shoulder made him appear deformed. I'd spent all my life in the forests, but he'd survived a long journey at sea before someone had decided to kill him.

"Your father really knew how to talk to them?" Qes nudged his gelding close to me.

"I'd forgotten all about it. It must have been shortly before he ... went away. Maybe that's why I can still remember." Though when

I tried to bring back my father's face, I could recall nothing. I still had the words, but I didn't know what he looked like anymore. Sour spittle pooled in my mouth, and I swallowed desperately. I couldn't risk throwing up all over my horse again.

"I'm sorry." Qes sounded exhausted, and I hoped that Sjunil would lead us to our campsite before dark.

None of us was in good shape to face the night.

We had to use the tents and I helped Julas to get them up while Qes took care of the horses and Sjunil started the fire. Our new companion was shoved into the first tent that was secured, his head wobbling from side to side; Siw followed, clutching a waterskin in order to make him drink a few drops. Julas worked quickly and quietly, and the second tent was up within moments. I was starting to shake with fatigue. Qes' new boyfriend gave me a worried look.

"Sit down," he said and took me by the shoulder, bringing me over to the fire.

My aunt pushed a three-legged pot into the flames and started to boil some water for tea and tinctures. She exchanged a quick glance with Julas, rummaged through our food supplies, and gave me a strip of dried meat. "Eat."

"I'm not hungry."

"You need to eat." Her voice made it clear that she wouldn't discuss the issue.

My mouth was dry as I started to nip at the shrivelled meat that smelled strongly of its marinade, but it reminded me of the concoction that Siw had washed the patient with. My stomach contracted painfully though I continued to chew. Sjunil was still watching me like a hawk.

It didn't take long for the others to join us. Julas flopped down next to me and hid his face in his hands. He looked up as Qes patted his back tentatively. As soon as he and Siw had sat themselves down, Sjunil heaved a big sigh.

"This is not how I'd hoped to start off our travels. I must say that you have all impressed me today."

"But I puked," I said sorrowfully.

"You puked and after that you helped anyway. How is he, Siw?"

"Still not awake. I changed the dressings, and it looks as if I was able to stop the wounds from going bad for now."

"You really think he's going to live?"

"Yes." Siw's voice wavered, as if she had to talk herself around.

"I'd hoped to make it to Goldenlake before the first snow." Sjunil handed the wrapped-up cheese to Siw, along with bread and cakes pressed from berries. No one had enough energy left to cook properly. "I'm going to take first watch," she said. "You all look awful. Does anyone want to ask any questions about what happened to us today?"

Qes sniffed. "Who do you think killed them?"

Our wizard grimaced. "I hope by all of the Tall and all of the Small Gods that Sloe will be able to find out."

Siw stared at her master. "Could they have been Moons?" she asked. "We're still on our territory."

"We will find out," my aunt promised, but her face had suddenly gone very hard.

DO YOU REALLY WANT TO KNOW

The man from the Cities came to with a strangled sob. I'd just fallen asleep after waking Siw for her turn on watch and almost swallowed my tongue. The tent was dark and cold. I'd slept on Yoli's saddle blanket, and my face was stubbly with horsehair.

"Sht sht." I rolled to my knees. His face was so pale that I could see his eyes like dark pools of distress. I touched his clammy cheek. "Sht. It's going to be fine, absolutely fine." I said the word again and he relaxed. "I know it hurts." I fell into the comforting singsong I used with the goats or with Sor when they had a tummy ache. "It will be fine, in just a little while." My right hand found the waterskin and I opened it with trembling fingers. "Water will help," I promised.

His right hand shot out of the blankets and caught my wrist. "Help," he croaked.

"Oh, yes, of course. Help." I tipped water into his mouth. He was obviously thirsty. I checked his forehead, but he was cold rather than hot. "My sister will be so happy that you're still alive."

"Alive." Another important word he repeated, though his accent was thick and difficult to understand.

My legs started to cramp, and I shifted closer to him. "My name is Sloe. I am going to help you."

"Sloe." It sounded weird, so weird. He continued haltingly, "My … name … is …" He said something I didn't quite catch.

"Ileon?" I repeated softly. "Your name is Ileon?"

It seemed as if he wanted to protest against my pronunciation but then decided it was close enough.

"Eh," he said.

"Are you hungry? You must be—I'm going to get you something to eat." I tried to get to my feet, but he caught me a second time.

"Water."

I tried to push his head up, but he moaned with pain. I heard him swallow desperately. "Sht sht," I said again.

The tent flapped open behind me.

"Siw, he woke up!"

She laughed with delight. "Move over, Sloe." She brought an oil lamp into the tent that gave off a warm, fragrant light.

I slipped back out into the night to take over her shift as long as she checked the wounds. I found myself smiling, even with only a few moments' sleep under my belt.

"Did he say anything else?"

Siw mashed a handful of herbs into a pungent salve. "No, he didn't talk to me."

"He didn't? He talked to me when he woke up."

Siw seemed hurt. "He was too busy squirming when I poked around in his shoulder."

Sjunil, with dark smudges under her eyes, gave us a filthy look. "Keep your voices down. My head is splitting." She sipped her bitter tea.

"Where are the others?" Siw asked.

Sjunil shrugged. "When I left them, they were still all snuggled up. Let's give them a few moments—they won't have much time to themselves in the next weeks." She turned to me. "What did he say?"

"He asked for help and water. I think his name is Ileon or something like that."

Sjunil made a dismissive noise with her tongue against the roof of her mouth. "At least he talked to one of you."

Siw jumped up and left the fireside, the smelly bowl pressed against her.

"Don't be so mean to her," I said quietly. "She's working so hard."

"She always works hard. Sometimes it just gets on my tits."

"Because she makes you look bad?"

She drank more tea. "Maybe. It would have also been easier to ditch him." She gave me an evil smirk.

When Qes and Julas finally showed up they both seemed a bit uncomfortable—especially as our wizard gave them a toothy grin.

"I need details," she said and both blushed.

"You won't get them," Qes answered. "Even if something had actually happened."

"Such a spoilsport," Sjunil grumbled. "I can't see anyone crawling into my own bedroll soon, so I need to keep myself entertained somehow."

"Yeah—right," my cousin said and Siw laughed—the first laugh we'd heard since the incident in the valley. For the smallest of moments, I could almost forget about the three men we had to roll into the ground and cover, about the way their gaping throats had been like second, even greedier mouths, begging to be fed.

"*Nothing* happened?" I asked Qes when we readied the horses.

"We were extremely aware of our audience." A quick smile came to his face but vanished almost instantly. "We're not in any hurry whatsoever."

"Does he agree?"

"Of course he agrees. Especially knowing about Siw's feelings." He checked the last buckles on the pack horses, then we lifted the stretcher up and strapped it in place again. The tents were already on the horses. We'd been lucky to roll them up before a steady drizzle started to fall. Fortunately, it wasn't as cold as before and I even had to wipe the sweat off my face when we finally asked Julas to help with our sixth companion.

The man from the Cities had slept through our preparations, protected by a thicket of hazelnuts and overhanging branches of the older trees around. His face was buried into the blankets and the left hand, bound up to straighten the broken fingers, looked like a strange contraption, all sticks and knots. When we took him by the arms and legs the smell of herbs, sweat, and pain hit us. I saw Julas gag, though he recovered quickly and made sure to check that all precautions were in place for the man to travel as safely as possible.

Siw pulled herself into the saddle. "Are there any more caves we can use to camp in? It would be good to get him out of the rain on some nights at least."

"We might have to adjust the route." Sjunil peered down to the stretcher. "He's very green around the gills. Are you sure he's not on his way out?"

"His heartbeat is strong and even. There are few signs of infection and I have enough supplies to drug him for the next ten days."

"Sounds as if he's going to be more comfortable than me," our wizard said with a shrug. "You're the expert. I just hope you're aware that he might not be inclined to repay your kindness. The men from the Cities can be judgmental little shits."

Qes patted his horse's greasy mane. "Judgmental?"

"They tend to look unfavourably on people who reserve the privilege to pray to their own gods. I had some rather unpleasant experiences at the Stoneharp. There was even a trader who had the guts to call me 'savage'. After that I had no choice, I simply *had* to headbutt him. He might take exception to the prayers that I chose for his companions and as you're the apprentice, this might also reflect badly on you. I'm just saying, don't expect him to fall to his knees and thank you for saving his life."

"Can you tell me about your time at the Stoneharp?" I asked her.

With the stretcher, we weren't able to travel fast but Sjunil didn't seem very happy to talk while our horses found their way over the muddy road to the east.

"It's not a time I remember too fondly," she said, muffled, because she'd pulled the shawl over her nose. "I was younger and less … restrained."

"Did you get into many fights?" I asked.

She sighed. "I would have but your father kept an eye on me. Even when he'd given up his position, he still had pretty firm opinions about representing the gods with dignity."

"He'd *given up* his position? Silid always said that he lost a duel of some sort and was punished with the loss of his … powers."

"That's a romantic way to express it." My aunt snorted. "It would be more accurate to say that he was invited to remove himself. He resented it deeply. He knew that your mother wanted me to keep an eye on him later. She was worried about … some of his tendencies."

"Tendencies?"

"It's not my story to tell, Sloe."

"But no one else talks about him. They all look down on me because he fathered me, but I don't really know why."

"Once he had the most astonishing rapport with the gods— they could be persuaded to do all sorts of things for him. How could he not miss that sort of power? It made him bitter and a pain to be around. Sometimes, at least. He'd talked about going east for ages, bored the bloody pants off all of us. He always wanted to meet more men from the Cities and probably was a bit disappointed when they turned out to be what they are."

"Is this why you said all of those things to Siw?"

"I'm just trying to manage her expectations, and I can see that this connection with Ileon draws you in. He might be nice to you now, Sloe, but this doesn't mean that he will be a friend to you when he is back with his people."

"How many of them did you meet at the Stoneharp?"

"Enough of them. They landed four ships in the bay, stuffed with cloth and spices. They weren't the first but this time they knew what they were looking for. They wanted furs, birch syrup, and amber."

I stared at her, rapt, and she kept going: "Your father said he spent a lot of his youth on the road and that he often went on long journeys when he was apprenticed to his own master. We had some things in common, some of the bad experiences as well. I thought it would be a good way to help to suggest his marriage to my sister. He would never have been able to marry your mother as a wizard, but he still yearned for it, and we often talked long into the night about the allegiances he'd once made with the gods." She winced. "The amulet that your mother gave you …"

"It was his?"

"No, but he said that Brother Brook had once been the first of the Siblings for him. The one he loved most and who had shown him favour in the most distressing situations. That might be why she thought it would be a good idea to gift it to you. Blood flows as water flows." She made a gesture that I recognized from the rituals. "When we were at the Stoneharp, the men of the Cities had been there for months. They had sold most of their cargo but asked for more. And more. Your father tried to befriend them but I'm sure he soon saw into their hearts. He brought back some of their words to Tall Trees but not much else, and he never really spoke about the Stoneharp while he was with your mother."

"One day I want to go."

"Of course you want to. Everyone wants to see the Stoneharp, and everyone wants to see the Golden Lake. I'm glad to go east this time though, now that I worry that we might find some of them in Goldenlake—they're like an infestation. At some point we need to decide what to do with them." She glanced towards the stretcher and shuddered. "It could be too late to smoke them out."

"I thought it was a duel?" Qes was obviously disappointed.

"Sjunil says that's not true."

"Then what happened?"

"She didn't really explain." We stood up to our ankles in the shallow stream, the first lot of horses between us. It was after midday, our first rest, and they were thirsty. Their quiet slurping noises were almost swallowed by the babble of swift-flowing water. "She said the Sibling he felt himself most bound to was Brother Brook."

Qes shot a look back to the clearing where the others had gathered around the stretcher. "Makes sense," he said. "Do you actually want to find out what he did to make them take his powers away?"

"I'm not sure. I should know, though." I pulled the silver amulet from my tunic and looked at it upside down. "It might be a good lesson to learn before we reach Goldenlake. Before the council calls me into their midst to speak for my family."

Qes' horse had finished and started to pull away. He kept it with us, waiting for Siw's black mare to be ready to be brought back. We stood next to each other, both overwhelmed with the new situation we found ourselves in. The last hours hung between us like a thundery cloud.

He sighed. "It must be your decision, Sloe. I don't think that there is anything I can say to you that could make you more careful. Knowing him better possibly won't make you like him more. I think you already are aware of that."

Siw's mare gave a watery snort. Qes turned and took his horses back between the trees. I waited for a while longer, fingers clamped around the amulet, while my horses watched me expectantly. I shivered, my feet getting damper, and it took a wrench of resolve to move away from the water.

HE WILL LEARN

When he sat up, we all froze. He'd slept for most of the day. I'd only seen his eyes open from time to time, troubled and veiled. With the stories Sjunil had told me and the things she'd left out, I hadn't really thought about him. He'd been there, suffering, probably watching us, wondering if any of us could be trusted. Perhaps it was a good sign that he knew some of our words, or maybe that made it worse. He studied his left hand, the way in which Siw had bound the fingers. She stood up, fetched a bowl of soup from the fire, and went to him.

His eyes narrowed. "No," he said. "No sleep."

"It's just soup." Siw turned to me. "Can you come and explain, Sloe?"

I rose slowly to my feet, and he smiled at me. Without doubt Siw had saved his life, but she'd also hurt and drugged him, while I was the one who'd tried to speak to him first. I knelt in front of him and said his word of greeting. Siw rolled her eyes and left the bowl with us.

He didn't respond until she was a good few steps away. "Sloe," he said.

"Ileon."

It was the first time I saw him smile and it did something to his face, as battered and bruised as it was. I smiled back at him instinctively, took up the spoon, and ate some soup, to show him that he wouldn't be sedated again. He held out his right hand and took the bowl from me. He drank carefully, though he must've been painfully hungry; I saw his throat move up and down, the dirty skin shifting with each swallow. I waited until he'd emptied the bowl and given it back to me.

"Your friends?" I asked.

He looked nonplussed and I found the word that my father had taught me. The lines around Ileon's mouth contracted as if I'd slapped him. "No friends," he said and before I'd tried to make up my mind what he could mean by that, he drew the tip of his finger across his neck. He'd seen them getting killed.

I swallowed. "No friends," I repeated. "Who killed them? Who … did that?" I made the same gesture.

"Bird," he said.

"Bird?"

He pointed to the saddle blanket on Siw's mare, that bore our half-moon sigil. "Bird."

"Oh."

"What did he say?" Sjunil suddenly stood next to us. Ileon shrunk away from her. Even a man of the Cities could sense her authority.

"I think he says the attackers were either Ravens or Magpies."

"Magpies?" Sjunil drew breath through her teeth. "This far east? That's not likely, is it? Ravens, then. Ask him about the man of the families who was with them."

"How?"

"Be creative." She drew up her shoulders. "Go on, ask him."

I held up two fingers. "Your friends." I held up a third. "The man who was with you. The guide."

His yellow eyes widened—he had understood me. He seemed to think for a heartbeat, then he held his right hand behind his head, the fingers splayed wide, in an imitation of …

"An Elk?" Sjunil spat. "Fuck no."

"It makes sense," I said quietly. "Ravens would've attacked an Elk without hesitation."

"I know it makes sense." Her voice was filled with poorly suppressed rage. "You know what that means, Sloe? Our future council meeting just got a whole lot more interesting."

"Interesting?"

"In the sense of 'trying to avoid absolute fucking disaster'."

It was clear that the man from the Cities registered her mood, though he tried to keep his face as unmoved as possible. She hissed and stomped away from us.

"Thank you," I breathed and tried to stand up, when he touched my arm.

His eyes now had a hard glint in them, a resolve that probably explained why he was still breathing. His grip was strong enough to hurt. "No sleep," he said again.

"I will tell her."

Julas sidled up to me as the others were preparing to crawl into the tents and rest before their watch began. "Did he really say Ravens?"

I pushed at the embers to keep them closer together. "Yes, he did. At least Sjunil thinks that's what he meant."

He rubbed across his face. "Ah, shit." His voice was as soft as ever and strangely flat. "It's been some time since my own cousin exchange but even then, the Ravens spoke a lot of the Elks, of the ways of the past." He leant his wrists on his knees and stared at the thin flame that made its way to the heap of sticks I'd just put on the fire. "Ravens are not known for their restraint," he said after a few moments. "Some prejudices are based on good observation. They would have killed on sight."

"That's what I said to her."

"It might make my position at the council a bit awkward," Julas said.

"I'll ask Sjunil to keep you out of it," I promised.

"She won't if she sees any advantage in involving me."

I shrugged. "I can try."

"Thank you, Sloe." He emptied his bowl of tea, long since grown cold. "Are you happy keeping first watch by yourself?" He glanced at the knife I'd put at the ready, just in case.

I nodded. "Of course."

He smiled. "I can stay for a bit longer."

His presence had a calming effect on me; he was a trained fighter with the scars to prove it, his longknife next to him an unmistakable announcement to anyone who dared to come closer to the camp. It was weird to sit with him, without Qes present. I wasn't able to keep my mouth shut for long.

"Are you happy, Julas?"

"Happy?"

"With Qes, I mean."

"I don't know yet."

"Qes might be a bit … strange but he's just shy—like me."

"Sure." A smile hovered in the corner of his mouth. "He would be delighted to hear you say that, Sloe. I'm glad that he has such a good friend in you."

The inside of my nose prickled, a sure sign that it wouldn't take long for me to start crying in front of him. I pinched my nostrils together in the desperate attempt to hold back the flood. "He's helped me a lot. Maybe I would still be with Saon if …"

"Saon?" Julas looked surprised. "Him? Really?"

"You think he was too handsome for me?"

Julas shook his head and said, "Saon has never been good news. I went with him on exchange, and they sent him back to his village before the moon was full. I'm glad to hear that you're no longer with him."

"What did he do?"

"The master weaver kicked him out. Artistic differences."

"Sounds like him."

Julas grinned. "He always was a pretentious twat."

After Julas left me, I spent my watch listening to the noises around me: the quiet spitting of rain on the leaves and the tents, the sparks of fire, and the rustling of horses. I liked to take first watch to hear the camp settle, the first snores from our wizard, and to know that afterwards I'd be able to sleep uninterrupted. If my aching limbs and saddle-sore arse would let me.

I'd drawn the amulet out again, its sheen reflecting the small fire that kept me warm, my fingers stroking the waves, my eyes wanting to close with the prayer, but I resisted. The darkness around the camp was full of awful possibilities: maybe the Ravens had seen us leave with the last man they'd failed to kill, or they'd followed us all this way east to make sure that no one got away from them.

I hoped we'd have a bit of quiet time at the lake, so I could ask Julas to teach me at least a few more moves with the longknife.

Ileon tried to rise on his own the next morning, pulling himself to his feet on one of the tent poles. His bandages were freshly changed, his hair scraped up into a knot to keep it out of the way.

Siw made a disapproving noise. "Sit down."

He ignored her and managed to stand, his knees shaking badly.

I stepped forwards to keep him upright and Siw rolled her eyes once again, scooping up the dirty bandages and salve bowls. "Ungrateful shit. I'll leave you two lovebirds alone."

Blood rushed to my face, but Ileon obviously hadn't understood my sister's meaning. He slowly straightened his back. Something in his spine gave an audible click and he groaned. His shirt felt grimy under my fingers, but I still held him. He wasn't quite as tall as me and of much lighter build, not a fighter either. I could feel the weight of him as he leant on me; he had no scruples accepting my help while harbouring a weird kind of resentment for my sister. Maybe he really was an ungrateful shit. I was still glad to see him on his own two feet, very much alive.

Sjunil pulled back the tent flap with a flourish. "Needed to see it for myself." I could feel Ileon's muscles contract as she looked him up and down. "Ask him if he can ride. Maybe we can finally travel a bit faster. I can smell the snow coming." Without further ado, she whirled around and left.

He released a deep breath. I had the thought that he might be tense around Siw and Sjunil because they were women, but it seemed such a disconcerting idea that I pushed it away. The power of the wizard and the power of the healer could have made him nervous. They both had a special arrangement with the gods and even someone like him might be able to sense it in the way my aunt commanded respect, unmistakably the leader of our group and Siw her second-in-command. The boys and I were little more than the henchmen of the operation; we followed their orders most of the time. Perhaps it was done differently in the mysterious Cities of the East? At least, I'd never heard of a woman or an Other of the Cities coming over on the ships; maybe they never wanted to come, were happy to stay where they were, safe and snug and just not interested in any sort of adventure, thank you very much?

"Horse?"

He stared at me.

I pointed out of the tent to where Qes was busy saddling up. "Can you try and ride?" I mimicked the rhythm of a gallop with my shoulders.

He laughed and his right hand curled around my wrist, giving it a squeeze before he shrugged and said something I couldn't understand.

Dispensing with the stretcher meant separating the loads until we'd made room on the sturdier of the pack horses for a rider. Qes helped him onto the broad back but kept the reins firmly in his own hand. Who knew what the man from the Cities was planning to do? His eyes were clearer, and his face looked almost human again. Any escape attempt would rob us of some of our equipment and supplies, though for Sjunil it might've been a small price to pay to be rid of him. She'd crossed her wrists on the pommel of her saddle and kept a watchful eye on him; Qes wasn't the only one preparing to out-manoeuvre our guest. At least he looked at home on horseback, like he'd be able to keep up.

She gave me a reproachful look. "Another witness for the council, may all the Siblings and Cousins help us in their wisdom and mercy."

Siw seemed apprehensive. "Has there ever been someone like him at the council in Goldenlake?"

"Who knows? But by then he'd better be able to tell them himself."

My heart sank. "Sjunil …"

"We have enough time, Sloe. He looks like a clever one, he will learn. Ready?"

Julas nodded and we departed the camp later than ideal and eager to get going. Qes waited for me to take the place after Ileon before moving his own horse forward. He didn't need to say it, his face expressed it all—he didn't trust me around Ileon. He'd seen someone take advantage of me before, and having received the order to spend a lot more time with him would have consequences of some sort. My hands felt clammy. Was he right to not give me the benefit of the doubt? I must've learned something from the Saon debacle at least? It was difficult to shake off the memory of Ileon's face as he'd seen me wiggle about and laughed, so surprisingly boyish, and how his hand had felt on me afterwards.

A BIT DESPERATE

Ileon's vocabulary was limited to very few words of the families but he seemed to understand that it was to his advantage to learn. We started to swap words for hours, until my head started to hurt. There were some concepts he had problems with. When I tried to explain the Tall Gods and the Small Gods, he looked offended.

"Small Gods?" he asked incredulously.

"Some prayers concern the everyday problems, and it would be rude to ask one of the Siblings for assistance to fix a shovel so you can dig out the shitpit. We need the Cousins to take care of these kinds of things, so everything gets seen to—eventually."

He frowned and I tried to find fewer words to express the same.

"How many?" he asked. "How many Smalls?"

I shrugged. "As many as needed. From time to time, new ones will make themselves known to a wizard."

I'd already noticed that the word 'wizard' was one he took issue with, and his reddish brows pulled into a scowl. We'd spent the last few days riding next to each other whenever possible and it was getting easier to make myself understood and to repeat a few simple phrases in the words of the Cities: "My name is Sloe," "I'm very hungry," "I'm hurt, please help," and "Nice weather for the time of year." The way in which I pronounced them amused him endlessly and we'd gone over the dirtiest swear words right at the beginning, so I was already quite fluent in that particular department. He was much less forthcoming when I asked about his own gods. He didn't wear any ornament that could've been interpreted as a token of his faith but from the way he grappled with the Small Gods, he was clearly not used to the idea of countless deities.

"Usually we will develop a relationship with one particular Sibling over time," I said while we travelled through one of the less dense areas of the forests. Tall birches stood dotted across gentle hills, stark and white, with the last of their leaves clinging to the tips of the branches like golden crowns. The air was crisp, the grass beneath the hooves of our mounts cropped short by a multitude of deer and livestock the local families brought here to graze their fill. Sometimes we passed a few goats and Sjunil made a point of talking to the youths who were on herding duty. Most of them belonged to the Ravens and gawped at us with curiosity. Tales of the fire-haired man who rode towards the lake would make their way into the villages—Sjunil didn't even try to keep his presence hidden. I worried about her strategy, though I was the one charged with his upkeep.

He stared at the silver amulet around my neck. "One of them?"

"Yes, but you will see that Julas favours Cousin Blade, one of the Small Gods—a Taller Small God, to be precise."

He closed his eyes in resignation. "Too hard."

"Too hard? You mean, too complicated? Of course it is complicated. Life has never been known to be simple. My favourite Small God is Cousin Crumb, because I like to eat." I patted my stomach and grinned at him. "But the Sibling I talk to now is Brother Brook. My sister likes to speak to all of them, but then she has to, as a wizard's apprentice. She needs to be careful not to offend any of them if she wants to be a worthy heir to my aunt one day. You should talk to Sjunil, she will help you find your own—if you want to."

When I mentioned her name his gaze had flickered to the blanketed back of our wizard. "No. Thank you."

"She likes to come across all scary and demanding, but she has all of our best interests at heart." At least I hope so, I added silently.

He pulled a face. "Never trust … a wizard."

That made me laugh. I realized too late that Ileon hadn't meant it as a joke.

That evening the sky cleared, and we camped under a glittering dance of stars, the icy wind whirling through the group of younger birches we'd used to shelter the tents. We ate a meal of roasted deer, provided by Julas' skill with the bow, sprinkled liberally with salt mixed with dried seaweed and sour peppers that had come from the west coast with the dyes that Saon had once traded for. Qes baked some fresh flatbreads while we waited for the meat to be ready, to soak up the spicy juices. I was content to sit on my folded saddle blanket, feeling the heat of the fire on my cheeks, fed, sated, and already quite sleepy, almost able to forget that the council waited for us to reach Goldenlake and that actions would undoubtedly arise from its proceedings.

Having lost the Clouds to the western families, Sjunil needed to be careful with her accusations. Ileon had witnessed Ravens at work, but we couldn't afford to lose their allegiance, too. In a way, she'd been right: it would've been easier not to know, to leave him by the wayside. As a wizard, Sjunil was beholden to the truth—or at least, that was what the councils wanted us to believe. Most wizards were crafty enough to know when to hold their tongue and wait for events to unfold. Sjunil had always been fiercely loyal to her sister, if a little disrespectful at times. I needed to believe that hadn't changed.

I was disturbed to realize that the way in which Ileon saw people like her woke my own mistrust, when I should've been careful not to give too much credence to the feelings of a man who'd seen his companions murdered not so long ago. Murdered by people like us, people of the families. When I stood up and turned away from the camp to pee, my head started to whirl again. Qes followed me and we made our way over to the horses.

"You look worried," he said.

"You're not?"

"I need a piss."

"Qes …"

"Of course, I'm worried. But you have made a lot of progress with him. Have you found out why he is here?"

"I'm getting to that, don't rush me. I'm trying not to spook him."

"What have you found out so far?"

"He doesn't approve of wizards."

He laughed, as I had done. We split up to each find a good spot behind a tree. After I'd laced my trousers up again, I started to check the horses over in the light of the stars. They were calm and happy enough. What had I found out so far? Nothing, really. I'd talked to him about me. I hadn't asked Ileon enough questions and he hadn't offered me a lot of himself.

"What?" Qes asked softly.

"I'm *really* worried."

He patted the muscular arse of Sjunil's grey mare. "We're going to keep an eye out for each other, right?"

"Right," I said, somewhat relieved. "Can I have a hug?"

When his arms folded around me, I breathed in his strong smell of horses, damp wool, his unwashed curls. "I'm so glad that you're here."

Qes gave a low chuckle. "It will be all right in the end."

"How far down the line, though?"

He kissed my cheek and released me.

In the morning, I left Ileon alone with Siw so she could see to his injuries and helped my aunt with breakfast. We'd settled into a routine that ensured efficiency without too much hurry. Julas and Qes handled the tents while I fed and watered the horses, and put the saddles on them so that the bedrolls could be packed away.

Breakfast was the last thing we did before leaving the camp—a quick affair of tea and leftovers that gave our wizard the chance to look helpful while she hatched her plans for the next weeks. She handed me a shallow wooden bowl and I started to fill it with the rest of the cheese we'd brought with us from Tall Trees.

"How is your student?" She checked the tea and gave it another stir.

"Not sure. Learning, though."

She nodded.

"Why do you want him at the council, Sjunil? It's such a dangerous move."

"Because we can't cover it up without making it look worse. Believe me, I have tried to think my way around this problem. If everything goes well, we will demonstrate that the time has come to set the arguments of the past aside and find a way to stand against the men from the Cities together, as one family—and giving both the Ravens and the Clouds a slap on the wrist at the same time. It won't be easy to pull off, but there is no other option for us." She made a noise with her tongue against her teeth. "And I can't take him away from you now, Sloe." Her smile was small and bitter. "Trust me to make *that* mistake. Qes warned me, you know. He said that you're a bit desperate."

"He didn't."

"He did."

"He said 'desperate'?"

"Well, no. But something to that effect. I know how it feels, Sloe. You want somebody to love, but I beg of you, be careful with him. I'm not sure that he would understand it."

"I don't love him!"

My aunt pursed her lips. "You're well on your way, though. There might come a day when he will try to hurt you, when he is close enough to his own people again. None of them would be particularly accepting towards someone from the families. They think different thoughts, they don't understand us in quite the same way. Have you tried to explain to him what you are?"

"What I am? You mean, Mother's child?"

"No." Her shoulders slumped, and my heart skipped a beat. "You should try, and maybe you'll see for yourself."

The bandages were smaller, didn't need as much moss padding, and Ileon's shoulder looked a lot less lumpy, though something did itch constantly; he couldn't keep his fingers off it. He seemed exasperated and cross, though the sun had come out and glistened on the last morning dew.

"Are you married?"

This question took him by surprise. "Married?"

"Did you join your hand to someone once? Someone in the Cities?"

It took a few moments to sink in, then he nodded. "But my woman died."

So he had felt loss before. It wasn't the jolt of relief I'd expected to feel. "Any children?"

He held up one finger. "One man." Three fingers. "Three women."

"One son, three daughters." I closed the hand around Yoli's reins. "Where are they now?"

"Home."

"Not here?"

He looked astonished. "No."

"One son, three daughters—no Other?"

He blinked at me. "What?"

I needed to do this slowly. "Siw is a woman, Julas is a man. I am Other."

"Their brother?"

He obviously hadn't followed. "No, no. That's probably too difficult for now."

Sjunil had been right to prepare me for disappointment. From that moment on he looked at me differently, as if he was trying to work out all the relationships between us. Since he understood much more of what we said when he was around, he picked up on things and I saw his eyes widen in shock when he witnessed Julas kissing Qes one evening. It was a quick kiss, not especially tender, more of a greeting between them. He didn't share a tent with them, and they usually weren't exactly demonstrative with each other in the camp, because of Siw.

As soon as we'd crept into our own tent and Siw had left for the first watch he turned to me. "Are they married? The men?"

"Not yet. But they're together."

I couldn't see his face in the darkness, but his silence said enough. We didn't speak again that night.

"What's his problem?"

Sjunil sighed. "This is what I meant, Sloe. They do things differently. Here, this is the last of the fried liver. Are the horses ready?"

I nodded and lined up the drinking bowls for her to pour out the tea. "You mean he wouldn't be able to ... he said he has children with a woman back home, but she is dead now. He wouldn't be able to love me, right? Even *if* I were to tell him that ..." My tongue felt furry, tasted sour.

My aunt touched my face, her hand was warm against my temple. "Maybe he will if you give him enough time. But chances are that he has his own plans in Goldenlake and that he will leave us sooner rather than later. I wish I could make him understand for you, but he has expressed very clearly that he doesn't wish to come near me in any way. You will have to wait and see if he can change his mind about these things. If you want to. All of Goldenlake awaits you—in just a few more days."

She put two fingers in her mouth and gave a shrill whistle, her preferred sign for all of us that it was time to eat and leave.

STAND BACK

It started to snow on our last night out in the open, a thick curtain of whirling flakes that coated the forest floor astonishingly quick, though it was still too warm to stick; the snow soaked our hair and the wiry manes of the horses. Ileon shrank into his borrowed cloak until he was just a sorry heap of cloth. He coughed a few times and Siw shot him a warning glance that made him suppress any further noises that might lead her to brew more foul-tasting medicine for him.

He hadn't asked more questions about Julas and Qes, but he held back as if he feared to catch something off them, careful not to let them touch him. I knew that he'd stop speaking to me if he heard about my own relationship history. He engaged with me because he didn't understand who I was.

In the last week we'd mostly spoken about the things around us, the trees and the changing landscapes, topics that didn't hurt either of us. It had been hard not to ask about his family in the east, to find out more about the life he'd left to go on an adventure—the kind that had gone so spectacularly wrong that he was dragged along on a pack horse, not even able to control his destination and still suffering from his injuries.

We'd fallen behind a bit, and I was starting to wonder what I could say to start up the conversation again as Ileon's horse jumped into Yoli, its quivering ears pointed towards the thicket on the wayside. Ileon's bony knee punched into my thigh.

"Fuck, ow," I gritted out.

"Quiet." He tried to nudge his horse away, but the gelding pressed itself against me, squashing my leg. Yoli tried to side-step off the path and my head dislodged a shower of snow from the branches above us. Ileon hissed a curse he'd taught me at the beginning of our lessons. "Give me the blade."

"What?"

He gestured towards the eating knife sheathed at my belt. "Quickly."

"Why?"

His chin pointed towards the thicket, and I took a deep breath. Beneath the crisp smell of snow wavered a hint of musk, a stench that had been on many of the goats we'd recently lost in Tall Trees. I felt my stomach go to water. "Oh no. We're dead."

"What?"

"You can't fight off a werebear with an eating knife and a broken hand."

He straightened up in the saddle, shoved his reins between his teeth and lunged over to pull the blade from me. As he kicked his gelding forward to square off with whatever waited for us in the snow, I realized that he tried to position himself between me and the bear.

"Ileon, don't be stupid!"

His horse reared up and he yelled at it, made it push forward into the shrubs. His laugh rang out.

"What the fuck …"

He turned around to me, gesturing to the steaming pile of scat behind the bushes. The smell hit me and I saw the trail of paw prints leading away from it.

"Bear has gone," Ileon said with grim satisfaction and handed me back my knife. "You all right?"

I stared at him, at the man who'd been barely alive only days ago and had tried to protect me from the deadliest predator in the forest with a blade as long as my palm. "I'm all right—and you're … that was amazing!"

He grinned at me before nudging his horse into a trot.

We were lucky that Sjunil found an overhanging rock cliff in the forest, the best available shelter under the circumstances. Julas managed to fasten the tent tarpaulins in a way that kept out most of the wind, so that our fire burned steadily and heated up the small space the bedrolls were crammed into.

Qes had brought back a few fat birds and their grease dripped into the pot the bearnut porridge cooked in. He'd almost used up all of our dried provisions; having to feed one additional man had cost us, and Siw had depleted her own supplies to keep him as healthy as possible. As always, Ileon was quiet in the company of the others, his eyes slowly wandering from one face to the next, listening to the conversations.

"This is it," Sjunil said, tasting the porridge carefully so as not to burn her tongue. "Only a few short hours and we will arrive. Any questions before it is too late?"

Julas cocked his head to one side. "Maybe a few."

She made an impatient gesture. "Go on."

"How long will we be expected to stay?"

"That is not for us to decide. The council will let us go when the important decisions are made. By then it might be impossible to travel back immediately. There will be time to rest in Goldenlake, time to enjoy more privacy—if that is your concern."

Julas stifled a grin. "Good to hear."

"I'm sure Qes will be delighted to introduce you to his cousins. Never too early to meet the future in-laws."

Qes' cheeks went slightly pink, but he kept his gaze averted.

"Can you please stop teasing him?" I muttered.

Our wizard gave one of the birds a poke. "Crisping up nicely. We're all tired, Sloe. It hasn't been an easy journey and I'm beginning to think I might be too old to do this again. Next time, I will send Siw to represent me." She smiled at my sister. "We will find time to speak to the gods as well," she promised her apprentice. "We will do what is right and proper." She sharpened the blade of her knife against the flat stone she kept with her, then pricked the skin of one of the birds to check the colour of the juices. My stomach gave a low growl and she chuckled. "Patience. I always thought if the wizardship didn't work out I could make myself useful around the pots. You might even start to miss my cooking when we're at the lake. They eat an awful lot of fish around there."

"I like fish." Ileon's voice was raspy. We all stared at him. He cleared his throat. "Are there more wizards in Goldenlake?"

She shrugged. "It's a wizard council with lots of powerful people."

"Powerful people," he echoed.

"As we're finally talking directly to each other, I don't suppose Sloe has asked you if you are expected?"

"Expected?"

"If someone is waiting for you at the lake." She still wore a smile on her face, but her eyes had a shrewd glitter to them. "Elks by any chance?" She made the same gesture he'd used once: the splayed fingers behind her head.

He shook his head slowly, a coppery curl flopped into his face. "Not Elks."

"Who then?" She started to cut the legs off the birds, letting them plop down into our deepest bowl. "We have waited long enough. It would have been nice of you to volunteer at least some of the information, given that I allowed my apprentice to save your scrawny arse." One of her canines glinted in the light of the fire. "It would be a shame to unmake all of her good work now, wouldn't it?" Her forefinger flicked and from one heartbeat to the next, the freshly sharpened blade was pressed into the freckly throat of the man from the Cities.

A narrow line of blood ran into his dirty collar, and I called out, "No!"

"You've been our guest for many days and as you see, Sloe has come to care for you. They won't forgive me but I'm sorry to say that I can't take that into account." She nodded at Julas, who had moved into a crouch, his longknife half-drawn. It would only take a wink from the wizard to make him kill. Qes' mouth hung open in disbelief, but Siw didn't seem terribly surprised. She must've known that Sjunil would do something at the last moment, when he almost felt safe.

"No," I whispered.

"Who is waiting?"

Ileon moaned as the knife dug deeper but then he smiled back. "The rest of the companions."

"Did they manage to get away from the Ravens?" my sister asked.

"No—we split up when we left the Stonehouse."

"The Stonehouse?" asked Qes.

"He means the Stoneharp," Sjunil hissed. "How many companions?"

"Three other groups. If they all have made it this far inland, there will be more than two dozen of us. Our group was the smallest, the last to leave."

"Why?" Qes sounded squeaky. "What had you hoped to find in Goldenlake?"

"The same as you. Powerful people of important families." His left hand crept towards his neck. "There is no need for this." He used the sticks Siw had stabilized his broken fingers with to push the blade away and Sjunil let him.

"So you're an envoy?" she asked. "Like Sloe? Like me?"

He rubbed at the nick in his skin, looked at the blood smeared over his right hand. "Something like that."

"Who sent you?" Julas asked.

"My family." There was a bitter edge to this word. Ileon licked the blood off the tips of his fingers.

"Why?"

He glanced at the amulet around my neck. "Silver. Gold, if we can find some. The riches of Birkland."

"What the fuck is Birkland?" Sjunil spat.

He pointed into the snow. "This is Birkland. All of this. You are part of it, of all that is claimed by the Kings of the Cities."

"*Claimed*?" Sjunil scoffed. "Is that really the word you want to use?"

Something started to smell decidedly burned. Qes nudged the birds away from the flames to save our meal.

"You can kill me." Ileon acted strangely unmoved. "Or ask him to kill me. He might make a cleaner job of it." His yellow eyes flickered to Julas and back. "But it will have to be explained one way or another."

Sjunil rammed her blade into the ground. "You do have some pebbles on you, my friend. The council will make it their business to determine what will happen to you. We have done enough. Sloe, prepare a bowl for him, before I change my mind and send him to bed without his dinner."

"Sorry." He said it under his breath, so quietly that I almost missed it.

I put the bowl down in front of him, the inside of my nose tingling again. "Siw was right—you are an ungrateful shit."

"It was nice of you to help. I'm sure you are a good man, Sloe." He scratched under his bandages; they were due to be changed but it was more than likely that Sjunil would deny him those attentions.

"I'm not a good man." I felt my eyes spilling over but if I tried not to blink, perhaps he wouldn't notice. "I'm not a man at all."

After he'd eaten, Julas bound his wrists and ankles. Ileon groaned as his injured shoulder was put under strain but didn't protest. He glared at me, as if I'd been the one to mislead him for weeks.

I wolfed down my porridge and all the meat Sjunil allocated to me, then I crawled into the corner furthest away from him and closest to the horses. I shivered into my blankets. I'd been stupid, so incredibly stupid. My aunt had used me to make the wrong impression on him all along; I'd trusted a wizard and paid for it.

My regrets kept me awake until deep into the night. No one asked me to take a watch—perhaps the distrust had become mutual. Qes belonged to Julas and that meant that he was no longer free to side with me. In a single evening, my whole world had been dropped on its head; one single exchange of threats and inconvenient truths.

When I peeled myself from the blankets in the morning Siw was on last watch. Grey light filtered through the wet tarpaulins and brought out the lines in her tired face.

"Have you calmed down?" she asked me.

"I'm calm enough."

"Don't be angry with her. It was my idea not to warn you." My sister drew deeper into her cloak that was covered in muddy splashes and grime. "I knew you wouldn't be able to bear it. You're too soft, Sloe. Too soft and too open, and I'm sure Saon picked you because he knew that you wouldn't call him out on his horseshit. Not without help from Qes, anyway. Tea?"

I thought about refusing but I was so cold, so disheartened, that I found myself nodding. "Thank you." The small clay bowl warmed my hands and I pressed it to my face. "Maybe I wouldn't have started to feel for him so much if I'd known."

"He doesn't deserve it, Sloe. You have heard him—suddenly he knew the game was up."

"He said 'sorry'," I muttered into the bitter tea.

"Do you believe him?" Siw asked warily.

"Just yesterday he saved me from a werebear—or he would have, if it hadn't run away …"

"He's a shrewd one, someone who plans ahead. He knows how to earn trust. He didn't just stumble into our lands, searching for new friends. He would cut Brother Brook from your throat to get at the silver, you must know that now. I'm sorry too, Sloe. You asked to be friends and I did little to honour your request. But you must understand that I'm an apprentice first and your sister second."

"You have spent a lot of time on him getting better."

"We needed him to talk, and we both did our bit to make it happen."

I nodded again, rising to my feet, desperate to get away from her. The tarpaulin felt stiff and icy beneath my touch as I pulled it to the side. Sleet pelted down into the forest; all the leftover snow on the ground had gone transparent and slushy, while the trunks of the birches around us looked streaked and unclean, the mud around their roots black and trampled.

"Stand back, Sloe."

Julas had drawn the man from the Cities to his feet and was shoving him past me. With his ankles still bound, Ileon could only make the smallest of steps. He held his shoulders in a way that showed he was in pain. Sweat darkened the hair at his temples and his breath came in harsh, foggy gasps. The man I'd spent too much time talking to, teaching, who had taught me in return, averted his eyes from me, maybe ashamed of himself, or just disgusted with me. Julas' broad hand was on his back, a gentle warning. I'd wanted to like him for Qes' sake, but his presence made my skin crawl; so much violence was hidden in his every move. I let the tarpaulin fall closed behind them. I didn't need to see Ileon trying to relieve himself, bound as he was.

"Good morning." My aunt stood behind me, her face as if carved from stone. "Will we have a problem, Sloe?"

I pressed my lips together. They had all revealed themselves to me, calculating and deceitful. I glanced past her right shoulder into the corner of the camp where Qes was loading up the horses, desperate to be the bystander, the helping hand, and not the one responsible for the disaster.

"No," I said grimly, aware that Sjunil wouldn't have allowed me not to respond.

A HANDFUL OF VILLAGES

Goldenlake was famed for being the oldest settlement in the east and had become one of the largest, covering almost the entire area between the upper and the lower lake, where the land cut deep into the water, the only sensible spot to cross over to the eastern shore. It was hilly terrain with a road winding between groups of wooden houses and clumps of ancient trees, gardens, and paddocks. Goldenlake would've been called a city where Ileon came from, as if someone had squashed a handful of villages together, each with its own distinct character and population. Though Goldenlake was theoretically positioned on Badger territory, all families had representatives there, even the ones so far west that their ancestors had watched the Stoneharp being built. The different family sigils were displayed all around us, painted on leather, stitched on faded cloth. Some of the colour choices served to set one group of houses apart from the next.

Qes' family showed their presence with stripy blankets used as flaps in front of their doorways and, as expected, there were a lot of them. The prospect of travelling to Goldenlake had excited him when we'd talked about it in Tall Trees, but he seemed wary and jumpy. With every noise, his head flew around as if he waited for some sort of assault. We were bringing a prisoner with us.

Our wizard led us on, as always without visible ornaments proclaiming her position, but the people must've felt her power, known why she was the first of us; even the grey mare suddenly had a spring in her step, her wide neck rippling, her eyes fiery. Siw had brushed her cloak out to regain some of its past glamour, and the masses of amulets around her throat gave off a sound as they moved with the steps of her black horse, her hair pinned up for our arrival. None of us others had prepared ourselves to impress, but Julas managed even so. I tried to keep my head down, though some of the people we passed on our way to the centre square stared at me. Maybe they noticed the eyes and the half-moon sigil on Yoli's saddle blanket—two things that didn't belong to each other in a place filled with Badgers.

Riding between the trees and houses, the lake itself glided back and forth and further away from us, though a distinct smell of water was in the air and boats were everywhere: being repaired, built, sold, and wide nets laid out across constructions made from bleached branches. We passed smoke huts and the whiff of preserved fish pulled at my guts. People sold food at every second corner—nutcakes and honeyfudge and stuffed roasted apples, reminding me that breakfast had been an even more hurried event that morning to ensure Sjunil could fit the prayers in before we left camp. I hadn't eaten enough, anyway.

We followed the wide road eastwards until we reached the biggest square in Goldenlake, still a fair bit away from the boat station. The houses stood further apart, their roofs freshly thatched with a new coat of dried bracken the same colour as Ileon's hair. I could finally see the water, grey and restless, behind the houses to the left— my first glimpse of the Golden Lake, framing the Roundhouse of the council, a gigantic structure festooned with garlands made from thousands and thousands of yellow birch leaves. The people around us kept under the low-hanging roofs, out of the worst of the weather, where the food stalls were lined up at the right-hand side of the square, their patrons watching our every move.

The striped flap of the Roundhouse snapped aside and another older woman stepped out to meet my aunt. Her hair was even more dramatic than Siw's, silver braids fashioned into elaborate coils, gleaming with clusters of freshwater pearls. A heavy necklace was draped around her thin neck, of badgers running snout to tail, made from silver: a demonstration of the wealth the man from the Cities had hoped to find.

"Sjunil."

"Qerla."

"We expected you days ago." She leant on a staff carved from bleached wood, inlaid with more pearls. No one in their right mind would've doubted her being a wizard. Her beady eyes settled on us, and a shiver swept through me. One brown, one blue.

"We ran into some difficulties along the way." Sjunil gestured towards the pack horses. "They slowed us down somewhat."

Qerla's right brow moved a fraction upwards, as if she understood. "Welcome to Goldenlake. We have ordered a house to be prepared for you in the Quarter of the Moon. You are the last one to arrive and the assemblies will commence shortly. Rest, eat, and freshen yourself up." Her staff moved in the direction of the people watching and a young woman stepped forward to bow to us. Her hair was bound into fluffy bundles along the top of her head, with discs cut from mother-of-pearl sewn to the leather strips keeping everything in place. One of her apprentices; I saw Siw's shoulders shift. She'd never reacted well to competition.

"Qor will see to your needs." Qerla Badger gave a small smile. "She is my youngest apprentice—one of four."

Sjunil snorted. "We are grateful that you can spare her for our convenience. Julas?"

Julas urged the pack horses on to follow the apprentice across the square. I saw Ileon staring out from under the hood, his eyes searching the people of Goldenlake for signs of deliverance.

"I didn't know that she chose you." Qes walked next to Qor, pulling his horse behind him through the narrow streets on the eastern side of the settlement.

"It's still quite new." Self-satisfaction radiated from her.

"This is Sloe from Tall Trees—our cousin."

"So I gathered." She barely looked at me. "We heard you had made friends in the west, Qes." It sounded like an accusation.

"That's the point of cousin exchanges."

"And who's he?" Her chin pointed towards Ileon.

"Someone we picked up on the way." Qes sighed. "Are there many of them in Goldenlake?"

"Of *them*?" She shrugged. "How should I know? They have been popping up everywhere recently. Goldenlake isn't any other six-hut mud pit, in case you hadn't noticed—there is no way of telling who comes and goes."

The hairs on the back of my neck were standing on end. Whoever the fourth apprentice to the mighty Qerla was to Qes, I started to dislike her intensely.

The Quarter of the Moon lay close to the boat station, one of the oldest and a warren of bracken-thatched buildings, all with the half-moon depicted in mussel shells on the walls. The house we were brought to stood next to the lakeshore, its narrow windows shuttered, with a stable attached. I wondered how many empty houses there were all around Goldenlake, kept ready for visiting travellers. With the families living in separate quarters, there must be many Houses of Women, Houses of Men, and Other Houses at the lake, filled with people I'd never met before—even Moons who served my mother but hadn't been to Tall Trees itself.

It smelled differently than home. Like a place where many people live close together, mixed with the slight brackish tang of the shallow bank behind our guesthouse, where a thicket of reeds prevented boats from coming close and the remnants of birds' nests lay empty and blackened, their inhabitants having left for the winter.

"It's a bit snug but the biggest we have for you." Qor led us into the dusty interior where blankets were piled on the sleeping platforms, as well as firewood and a basket with fresh provisions. "We will expect you to be at the Roundhouse for evening prayers. Qerla will officially welcome you then, when everyone smells a bit better." She looked at me again as she said it, but then she bowed to Sjunil and retreated. My aunt turned to face me.

"Whatever did you do to her?" she asked sourly. "Help Qes with the horses, Sloe. We will try to make this house into a home."

"Is she your sister?"

Qes grunted as he pulled the last saddle off and hung it over one of the wooden dividers in the stable. "First cousin. But she still has the same hair."

"Wait. So she's my cousin too?"

"Yes and she's always been insufferable and hasn't improved with age."

"Why does she pick on me? She doesn't even know me yet." I drew the brush over Yoli's hindquarters, trying to dislodge as much mud as possible.

"She's afraid."

"Of what?"

He pulled another set of brushes from the pack and started working on Siw's black mare. The horses were chewing on armfuls of sweet-smelling hay and leather buckets filled with water stood ready for them. "Because you have Qerla's eyes, Sloe, isn't it obvious? As I said, for the Badgers they're not a bad thing. They are a sign of belonging. It goes with the overall sense of ... stripiness, I guess. Usually, they are seen as an indicator of certain talents. Two of Qerla's older apprentices share this family trait with you and it surely is no coincidence that Sjunil had her heart set on you before your mother intervened. It's a mark of wizards. Qor needs to kick downwards if she wants to stay afloat." He sighed. "I'm going to find out if more of my closest family are in town when we're finished. Do you want to come with me?"

My heart felt as if he'd squeezed it. "You're sure? I mean, why wouldn't you ask Julas instead?"

"Because he's going to be busy, and because we are in a fight." He cleaned his brush against the wall. "You and I haven't spent much time together recently, not really."

"I've noticed," I muttered and gave a little cough as the salty dust was patted from the brush. "Why are you fighting?"

There was a stubbornness around his mouth that I'd missed. "You might not believe me, but they didn't talk to me either. Maybe they thought that I wouldn't be able to help myself and warn you straightaway."

"Would you have warned me?"

He shrugged. "Probably. It wasn't a very nice thing to do to you. I know, it's what I should have expected from someone who prays to Cousin Blade, from someone so obsessed with his longknife that he can't even go to sleep without it. I thought it was a sweet quirk of his." He rolled his eyes. "I never should've gotten so much on your nerves about Saon—turns out I'm just as stupid. Can we try and forget about the last few days, Sloe? I miss … *this.*" His smile was shy and hopeful.

"Let's try. Let's make the best of it, whatever plans the others work on. Deal?"

"Deal."

He looked relieved.

"You're going to do what?" Siw sounded scandalized.

"Explore a bit. Just wanted to let you know so Auntie doesn't bite your head off when we're nowhere to be found for the next few hours."

"You'd better be back in time for prayers, washed and dressed."

"Thank you, Siw."

I tried to slip away as quietly as possible. Qes waited at the next corner for me.

"The last time I was here, I never made it into the Quarter of the Moon. Where do you want to go?"

"Can we follow the shoreline to the station? I want to see the lake properly, maybe get something to eat that doesn't taste of Siw's favourite herb mix. Something sweet and sticky, like … ooooh, like honeyfudge or berry cakes, or …"

Qes put an arm around my shoulders, pressed his face into my neck. "Sorry," he said. "I'm sorry that you were hurt."

I kissed his forehead, still dirty and gritty under the curls. "Will you forgive him?"

"If he asks very, very nicely, maybe. But not today. I promise you, not all of my cousins are like Qor. We will find someone interesting to have a drink with."

"But first …" I pulled him with me to the water's edge, where we had to get used to balancing on the pebbles until we found a sandy patch snaking around the shore, passing empty drying racks, more nets and fish and a row of boats in various stages of disrepair, one of them so smashed that it could only be destined for scraps. Not many people seemed to check the bank on that side; I found quite a few shattered bowls, a ripped cloak half-buried, and even a shoe, sodden and broken apart, as if a dog had chewed and left it, and then there were a lot of boats on the water, even on such a cold day. We saw a jetty built into the lake, beleaguered with bigger boats, bigger than I'd ever seen, sleek, with many spaces for rowers and passengers to sit. Boats with which the Golden Lake could be crossed, and after these nothing else. Only water, endless water.

I stood for a long time, staring, until the sleet came down harder, biting into the grey surface at my feet, puckering the waves. From that point the shoreline lay behind us, with only the space of the lake at our feet, gradually opening out until it touched the sky, so far away from me that the gods seemed to swallow the water.

✤

WEAK ENOUGH

Evening prayers in Tall Trees were seldom a formal affair and I'd
given silent thanks to Siw and her warning. After discovering a
vendor selling sweet curd at the boat station, Qes and I had hurried
back to the guesthouse only to find it already empty and managed
to join the others after a quick scrub and change. Qes looked
strange with his sleet-wet hair pulled away from his face, older
and nervous as he arranged my new sky-blue cloak around my
neck. We were almost the last ones stepping into the Roundhouse,
where three massive braziers were positioned in a triangle, with a
whole group of wizards sitting in-between: Qerla Badger, Sjunil,
and five others, mostly older women but one youngish Other,
their brown hair falling in a thick braid to their ankles, woven
through with stylized leaves made from finely hammered gold.
Their cloak touched the ground around them, heavy and lined
with the spotted coat of fawns.

Qes caught me gawping. "Oh no," he groaned. "This would
really be your next disaster, Sloe."

"Who are they? Another cousin?"

"No. They are not of the Badgers. They must be from further
east." He pushed me onto one of the benches, quite far at the back.
"You can ask your aunt to introduce you later."

The doors were closed behind us, with many people having to
stay outside and pray in the cold—all the curious inhabitants of
Goldenlake, who loved to see seven wizards wrangle for centre
stage. Behind the seven sat their apprentices, charged with tending
to the fires and the incense that spread a fragrant haze through the
Roundhouse. I saw Siw next to Qor and knew that she hated

it; her face was carefully blank, but her hands were scrunched into fists. Apart from the leaders of the prayer in the middle of the house, no one was easy to spot in the darkness, though Julas must've brought Ileon with him to attend—likely his first official prayer ritual in the lands he sought to claim for his kings.

"We thank Brother Brook for making the council complete." Qerla Badger's voice was deep and resonant and the flames around her seemed to waver with the words. "For granting safe passage to our siblings from other families so we can declare the assemblies open upon the morrow."

One of the apprentices pushed a bundle of dried herbs into the brazier at the front and a bluish flame leapt up, almost singeing off her eyebrows. The smoke thickened and a cloyingly sweet smell wafted over the congregation. I immediately felt weird, as if my thoughts tried to jump in a dozen directions at once, making me dizzy.

"We welcome our sister of the Moons, the last arrival." Qerla gestured towards my aunt who nodded gravely and with ill-concealed annoyance. "We thank Brother Rain and Sister Storm for granting safe travel." Her two-coloured eyes roamed over the front benches. "We welcome the news from the western forests and the warnings brought to us of great upheaval. Let us pray." She hugged her staff to her. Maybe it was the dancing firelight or the herbs, but for a moment I saw sparks running from the pearls in her hair to the pearls decorating the staff, and a low hiss came to my ears, reverential and awestruck.

As was our custom, everyone prayed in silence for a while, perhaps even Ileon, wherever Julas had placed him, before the next batch of incense was released and the Other from the east offered their hands in the old gesture of surrender to the earth beneath their feet. The glossy cloak pooled around them, and the end of the gold-adorned braid fell to the floor. When they straightened up again their cheeks were streaked with tears. I caught my aunt's disgusted sneer. Then the younger wizard started to sing and her expression changed abruptly, fell into a softness that I'd rarely ever seen on Sjunil's face. The voice was even deeper than Qerla Badger's and the song haltingly beautiful—a prayer set in melody, a prayer to Sister Soil and Sister Sun not to forsake us during the coming winter. When it ended and the wizard came back to their feet in one fluid motion, the Roundhouse was buzzing like a bee skep.

After the performance, we heard prayers from the other wizards present; the last one was Sjunil, who looked exhausted and bored. She stood, hitched up the chequered blanket that covered her shoulders, and for a few heartbeats she said absolutely nothing.

"Sister Courage," she said then and a shocked murmur ran through her audience. Sister Courage was not of the eight Tall Siblings. "Brother Fear," Sjunil added wearily. "We will soon find reason to call on you more and more. Give us the strength to face the challenges that are coming to us from far in the west, from the feet of the Stoneharp to the knotted roots of our forests, to the pebbles of the golden shores. Grant us sturdy hearts and superior cunning against our enemies." She crossed her arms and for a moment she seemed to sway in an embrace. "We will need new allies and we will need new resources. If the teachings are true and the gods keep a special place in their hearts for the prayers of Goldenlake, then show us your favour—sooner rather than later."

Voices erupted as Qerla Badger rushed to her feet, her face livid. "The gods will not be ordered about," she spat, probably louder than planned.

It promised to be an interesting first council meeting.

"Glad to see you managed to come, too." Sjunil gave me a bowl of honey beer. We'd returned to the guesthouse, where a platter of roasted meat and fresh nutbreads awaited us, as well as a bowl of salted cheese mixed with chopped water mint. Someone had seen to our fire, probably instructed by Qor herself, though it was to be expected that her diligence would soon find its end if Sjunil continued to piss off Qerla too publicly.

I took a careful sip; my head was still swimming from the smoke. "Why did you do it?" I asked.

She broke off a piece of bread, wrapped it in a slice of pink meat, and chewed. "Because I won't be humiliated in front of all of Goldenlake without kicking up a storm. Qerla loves to assert her authority in unhelpful ways. Being the wizard of Goldenlake is not some special achievement—technically, we are all of the same rank. She might be older and richer, but she can't make me pretend that we don't have pressing concerns to discuss. And poking the bear is to ensure its attention." She gave Julas a sign. "Let him eat," she ordered. "Over there, I really don't want to look at him."

Siw pushed some food into a bowl and brought it over to the sleeping platforms where our prisoner sat huddled against the wall, the bandaged left hand pressed against his chest. I also didn't want to look at him and was grateful that he'd decided to remain quiet. He was likely biding his time, maybe even waiting to be rescued. I emptied my beer bowl with a big second gulp and started to gnaw on a goat rib slathered in a delicious sauce of honeyed apples and juniper berries.

"Who was—" I didn't have to finish my sentence as my aunt exchanged a glance with Qes.

"Werid of the Far Side. Don't, Sloe—just don't. They are talented, I grant you, but oh so dramatic. I'd hoped you'd had enough of the artistic types for a while. They have the advantage, what with being all dressed up to the teeth and beautiful. They too will grow old one day and their voice will croak and roughen and the playing field is levelled. We were all young once. Even

Qerla could have stopped your heart with a well-calculated smile, and never forgave me for not accepting her hand so many years ago."

"She wanted to marry you?"

"Don't sound too surprised, Sloe."

"I've never heard of two wizards getting married to each other."

"It wasn't the best idea she'd ever had, believe me. It has been done but usually these marriages don't last for long. Too much rivalry, too much envy. We would've had a few nice years and a very messy divorce at the end of it. And I knew what your mother would've had to say—not another Badger."

It didn't happen often that Sjunil was so generous with details of her own past and I found myself feeling sorry for her, for having to make that decision against someone, but then Julas brought Ileon's empty bowl back and the way she took it from him, without a word, hardened my heart again.

I cleaned my fingers on the seat of my trousers. "I'm going to check on the horses one last time."

My aunt let me go without protest and as I turned around before closing the door, I noticed yellow eyes staring at me from across the room.

I gave Yoli the crust of nutbread I'd squirreled away, made sure that all the water buckets were well-filled, and hoped that Qes took the hint and followed me. He didn't and so I found myself alone among the animals. I could hear the lake lapping against the pebbles, a steady rhythm underpinning the shuffling and deep breathing of our horses; perhaps it would help me sleep. Would I still be expected to keep watch or were we safe in Goldenlake? I took the oil light with me and had barely pulled down the latch when someone came up behind me.

"Qes?"

Julas stepped from the darkness between the houses. "Can we talk?"

"Why?" I didn't want him so close to me.

"Because … because I need you to help me." His voice was unhurried and in the small light the forked scar on his face was much more prominent, a reminder of what he was capable of.

"Is this about Qes?"

"No, it isn't about Qes. It's about what is going to happen when Sjunil accuses the Ravens at the meeting."

"Excuse me?"

"Our guest might not have had the best of intentions in travelling to Goldenlake, but the lives of his companions were not theirs to take. Sjunil hopes to call for unity among the families, but she doesn't understand how the Ravens will react. She can't ask them to forsake their grudges—they have nursed them for generations, centuries. It will be an awful muddle and we will find ourselves in the middle of the wreckage. You have seen how easily she manages to enrage the other wizards, how she *enjoys* stepping on their toes. You are the only one who can talk her out of it. You are your mother's child and not her apprentice. Siw would follow her master to the land of the dead if she had to, despite what she says. Sjunil respects you, loves you even. She is going to make a dreadful mistake and we will all suffer for it." His gaze held mine, his handsome face deadly serious.

"You're afraid of her," I realized.

"She's a wizard. Of course I'm afraid of her."

"And this is why she let Siw bring you. Because she needs someone strong she can boss around. You would kill Ileon in a heartbeat if she asked you to."

"Yes," he admitted without a moment's hesitation. "He is a dangerous man and I dare say he has done enough bad things to warrant the command. He has tried to play with you too, but you don't seem to take offence. You'd rather blame your friends for not explaining the obvious to you."

"For Qes' sake I'd hoped you were as gentle as I thought you were, and as kind. But you are a coward, like me. A coward with a longknife."

He smiled. "There are different kinds of courage and there is one that makes you ask so many questions of her. She couldn't react with grace if I started to resist her. Please, Sloe. There must be another way about it." He touched my cheek and I wanted to recoil, shake him off, but instead I stepped into the light between us. It was a dare, the stupidest kind of courage, every fibre of me aching—not for him, for *someone*.

His right hand closed around the small bowl that held the light, moving it away. His hips pressed against me. I could feel him harden and I pulled him even closer. My mouth was on his, the light sputtered into the mud, my fingers slid deep into his hair. He moaned as I closed my fist, his beard much softer than expected on my neck.

"So you think you can bribe me?" He tried to get away, but my fist was cruel and I hissed in his face, "Because I'm lonely and you have decided that I'm weak enough to risk a friendship, just to be touched? You must've laughed at me time and time again, when I wore my heart so openly and ready to be kicked."

He yelped in pain as I yanked my fingers free. "No, Sloe, don't … don't take it like this."

"I wish there was another way to take it. Fuck you, Julas—and fuck off."

I STARTED TO FOLLOW

"You don't understand. I was so tempted to give in."

We sat at the shoreline between the broken boats. It was barely light enough to see where the water began, and the pebbles ended.

"I'm glad that you told me about it." Qes scratched at his right ear with his left hand, an awkward movement. "He is ... he is the worst. At least that tells me that I did the right thing. It will be easier to forget a short fling, I suppose."

Our shoulders touched and I shuddered. "The gamble almost paid off and I hate myself for even considering it."

"He's clever and he had enough opportunity to observe you. He thought he had found a way to tempt you. We all do stupid things when we are unhappy."

"Do you think we can blame some of it on the lake? Weird things happen so close to the water."

He gave a soft laugh. "That might be something to ask Brother Brook about, Sloe. He might not have a particularly clear answer for you, but he is much more qualified to consider this than I am."

"I never want to hurt you again, Qes."

"We will hurt each other from time to time, even if we don't want to. It happens with close friends, but that doesn't mean that we can't find a way to deal with it. You just need to know that I love you, Sloe."

I hugged him to me. "I love you, too."

A boat glided out of the dawn, two fisherwomen at the oars, pulling in steady strokes to push their vessel further out. To them we might've looked like a heap of rubbish left on the shore or maybe they didn't notice us at all. I breathed in Qes' half-awake smell, slightly musty and dog-like, and for the moment it was almost enough.

We'd just finished breakfast when the drumming started.

Sjunil yawned. "Here we go. Wish me luck that I don't fall asleep in the first session."

Her knees cracked as she stood up from the guesthouse table and she rubbed them mournfully through her trousers. Siw hoisted up a bag filled with her paraphernalia and left the house first.

My aunt looked at me. "Sloe? Come with me."

I turned to Qes, but he simply shrugged. I didn't want to leave him alone with Julas and our prisoner, but in the end I followed my aunt's command.

It was a cold, dry day with the smell of ice in the air and we pulled the hoods over our heads. There was almost no wind, as if all of Goldenlake held its breath, anxiously waiting.

"What happened last night?" Sjunil took me by the elbow and steered me towards the centre of town.

I almost stumbled over a small heap of stones, perhaps left by one of the playing children, and caught myself at the last moment. "Nothing."

"Learn to lie a little better." Her grip around my arm was relentless.

"I got into a fight with Julas."

"What about?"

"If it's my responsibility to help you avoid the next communication breakdown between the families of the east and the families of the west."

She blinked. "And you found yourself on which side of the argument?"

"I think you're entitled to make your own mistakes. None of us is as experienced as you are."

"But you still expect me to fuck it up?" A slow grin spread over her face. "I guess you know me pretty well by now. Would the Moons profit from a big argument?"

"It depends on who is arguing with whom, right? We want to keep the Badgers and the Ravens bound to us, but only the Ravens hate the Elks enough to agree on organized strikes against them and none of them knows what to make of the Clouds' new direction yet. Are there any western deputies at the meeting?"

"It doesn't look like it. Qerla said it multiple times—we were the last to arrive."

"How can we come together if half of us are missing?"

She reached out with her forefinger and booped my nose. "That is an excellent question to ask, Sloe."

The benches had been cleared out of the Roundhouse and it was enormous and empty, apart from the table built in its centre, flanked by four braziers and folding chairs strewn with deer pelts. Bowls and jugs were grouped in the middle of the table and a few platters heaped with refreshments that were easy to eat during the talks. The seven wizards stood at the ready: Sjunil would speak for the Moons, Qerla and two others for the Badgers, two for the Ravens and Werid of the Far Side was probably there as a more independent observer. They were dressed in a simple smoke-grey tunic and their hair spilled loose, only held back from their brow by a silver circlet, all understatement and careful elegance, while the other wizards had gone all out; one of the Ravens wore so many bone bead necklaces that they looked about to strangle her. My aunt exchanged a nod with Werid and drew me closer.

"There's someone I'd like you to meet. This is my sister's youngest child, Sloe."

"Slow?" Werid's deep voice sounded mildly astonished.

"No, not 'slow' Slow but 'sloe' Sloe, like the bitter fruit."

Only the gods knew how often my name had been explained in similar fashion. Werid's eyes were of a warm chestnut brown, a shade darker than their skin. They focused first on my blue eye, then on the other. "I see. Another one of your apprentices?"

"No, no." Sjunil made a dismissive gesture. "Believe me, one apprentice is more than my nerves are prepared to handle. Sloe will be involved in the meetings at a later stage. They are here as a witness. It is their first time in Goldenlake, their first time to leave Tall Trees, and as you have travelled so far and you seem to have a few other things in common, I thought it would be nice to introduce you properly."

"So this is an educational journey for you, Sloe?"

I blushed under Werid's gaze. "In a way, yes. Don't hold it against my aunt—I asked her about you first. Which family do you belong to?"

They smiled. "I am a Wolf."

"I've never heard of the Wolves," I breathed, entranced by the spicy scent that clung to them.

"I don't blame you. It is one of the oldest families in the eastern steppes, but we are few in number. Nice to meet you. Perhaps later we'll have more time to talk—it looks as if the meeting is all set to begin." They turned away. I was still smiling at their back when Werid faced me once again. "Find me after. I will wait for you."

The door of the Roundhouse closed before me. Only the attendants were allowed to remain and so I found myself in the centre square, overwhelmed by the prospect of an evening in the illustrious company of a Wolf. Maybe Sjunil had done it to distract me? To keep me from yapping at her heels and begging for scraps? Or she realized that I was too awkward to manage on my own? But Werid had promised to wait for me after a gruelling day of seven wizards trying to yell over each other …

I decided to take the long way back to the guesthouse, but first I wanted to stare some more at the lake. The sky mirrored itself in the waves and faint ripples tickled the pebbles with every other heartbeat. Quite a few boats were out and had joined the two fisherwomen Qes and I had seen that morning. More people were about on the roads, the dry weather brought them forth and the streets suddenly turned into markets.

I cut through the Quarter of the Badger. Though the families of the west didn't have representatives attending the meeting, they all kept their houses in Goldenlake. I noticed Magpie banners strung up between two huts and a few people with feathers sewn onto their tunics. I thought I might meet some of them later, when it was my turn to speak of the discourtesy the Clouds had thought to inflict on me—something that felt so far away that it was hard to remember why I should still feel angry about it. So much had happened in the meantime, so much that held my attention—the gaping throats of the men strung up in the trees and the kiss I'd taken from Julas. That particular memory burned. When I closed my eyes, I could still feel him, smell him, our thickening breath. Maybe a part of him had actually wanted me in that moment, not just anyone, but me, while I had simply failed to rein in my reaction to the closeness of someone. I had still balked at the thought of him laughing at me after he'd managed to take me against the stable wall. Such an easy conquest to make, a doddle, so weak and willing to betray—

"Hey! Watch where you're going!" A hand grabbed my shoulder, pushed me to the side.

"Sorry—gods, sorry!"

Green eyes met mine, then the face turned away; another man from the Cities, hooded but not quite hidden. I blinked. He wore clothes like a member of the families, and his shoulders were hunched up to make him appear smaller, but there had been an unmistakable accent. An accent I knew all too well.

I started to follow him, though he went the way I'd come from. Swaddled up against the cold, it was easy to overlook him. He wore a chequered blanket like my aunt and his boots resembled mine in their make. How many were living in Goldenlake in such a way? He knew the town, walked quickly, purposefully, as if he had somewhere to be. At least the hood he wore restricted how much he could see, and I tried to keep far enough away. He didn't stop for food, he just walked, passed the centre square and continued into another quarter. I noticed the sigils nailed to the houses: Bears. He stepped into their House of Men without hesitating. The door woven from hazel rods closed behind him and I heard voices raised in greetings, with words I'd learned not too long ago.

"You're sure?" Qes put the brushes aside and used his fingers to pull the last knots from Yoli's mane.

I nodded breathlessly. "Perhaps these are the men Ileon spoke of, the ones he was supposed to meet? Or there are even more? What should we do? I don't really want to tell Julas, but maybe we should?"

"We'll wait for Sjunil to come back. If the Bears are involved, she should know. Could be that this isn't even a big secret, and they have permission from the Badgers to stay in town. Whatever we do, none of us should get themself into a panic." He took his leave of my gelding with a pat to his nose. "Now you're pretty enough."

"Maybe Goldenlake is just too big to keep scores on everyone?" I worried at my thumbnail. "When Julas brought him to the evening prayers none of the wizards said anything, did they? They must've noticed that he wasn't there because he wanted to be. Should I talk to him again? I've been trying to stay away, but ..."

Qes' warm hands settled on my shoulders. "Don't rush into any assumptions, please. Everything might be much more complicated."

"More complicated? These are the men we need to stand against and they're already here!"

"But not all of them might have come with the same agenda. Breathe, Sloe, please breathe."

"Can you do me a favour? I need you to distract Julas for a bit."

Qes crossed his arms in front of him. "I don't want to."

"Please. You don't have to offer him anything … like that, that's not what I want. Talk to him, divert his attention."

He growled. "This is not a favour I'm likely to forget."

"Of course not. Just … please, Qes."

When we went into the guesthouse, Julas sat at the table, re-fletching some of his arrows. Qes shot me a filthy glance and went to him, while I turned towards the sleeping platforms.

Ileon was bound to the wall, his arms uncomfortably drawn up, his hair a tangled curtain across his face, legs sprawled in a position that looked as if he'd tried to find the least painful way to sit. He stank of piss, sweat, and pus. I waited until Julas was focused on Qes, then crouched down, close enough to whisper.

"Have you ever had dealings with the Bears?"

A hint of a smile appeared behind the coppery hanks of hair. "You've come back to me."

"For information."

He used his forearm to move the hair out of his face. A few moments before he'd crouched as if he was in pain, but his eyes were clear and sharp.

He said the same hateful words I'd used: "Fuck off, Sloe."

CARRY HIM

Sjunil's gait was stiff. She pressed her palms into her back and groaned. "The most uncomfortable chairs I've ever sat on. I bet this is by design. I tend to make quick decisions when I'm in agony." She noticed my burning face. "What's wrong?"

"I saw more men like Ileon in Goldenlake." She nodded and disappointment flooded me. "You knew?"

"Qerla mentioned it when I spoke about the matters I wish to raise in the next days. They have been here for a while, though. The Bears asked to host them, and the guide Ileon spoke of was an Elk, was he not?"

"That's what he said. He might've lied." I recalled the glittering eyes in the darkness. "He probably lied."

She sighed in exhaustion. "You could ask for permission to speak with them directly? Find out if they have any connection to him?"

"Why would they talk to me?"

"Because you wish to learn more about them, don't you? They might be happy to teach? I'll ask Qerla," she promised. "Tomorrow. Right now I need a bowl of very strong tea and someone who is willing to walk on my back for an hour." She left me standing in front of the Roundhouse, which had the same smell as the day before, the same intense herbs, as if the apprentices had tried to cleanse the air after the meeting.

"There you are." Werid of the Far Side looked just a little bit tired.

"How was it?"

"Do you know what happens if you buy a new hen and on the first day there are feathers everywhere and a lot of noise?" They grinned at me. "That was a good approximation. And to think that it was such a lovely day outside." They squinted up to the sky. "Will you walk with me?"

I nodded, desperate for them to take my arm, but instead they clasped their hands behind their back, drawing up their hair and draping it over one elbow to keep it off the ground. I let them lead me towards the water until our toes touched the waves.

"Your aunt has added a few very interesting items to our list," they said after a few heartbeats of silence. "Is it true?"

"Which bits of it?"

"Are you here to accuse the Clouds?"

"Yes."

"What happened?"

I hesitated. "I will go through all the details at the meeting."

"But I want to know how they could possibly arrive at such a bold decision, to snub the youngest child of a leader."

"They wanted to avoid association with my late father and I'm his only child."

"Your father? Who was he?"

"Qarim of the Badgers." It was the first time in years I'd actually said his name out loud. Their brown eyes went wide, and I knew that they understood. "So you have heard of him?"

They reached for me, inadvertently dropping their gathered hair. "I think we all have and I'm sorry, though I'm sure that no one would assume you are responsible for his conduct before you were even born." They bit their lip. "But they might have made assumptions about yourself, based on the information, you're right. Did you want to marry?"

"Doesn't everyone?"

Their smile was sad. "No, not everyone. There are other ways to serve your family than leaving your village to take a spouse. Did you know the person you were supposed to marry?"

"No, I didn't."

"You don't think this could have been for the best?"

"It wasn't my idea to come here. My mother made me. And then … then absolutely everything went wrong and now I feel like a fish out of water, like that time, before …"

"Before?"

I stared at my feet and at Werid's hair swirling around them in the calm surge of the lake. They didn't seem to notice. "Ehm …"

They followed my gaze. "Ah shit, not again. It just got properly dry." They started to wind it around their head, squeezed out the ends and tucked it in. "There once was a time when my family had a pretty bad reputation."

"Really?"

"There is a reason why there are only a few of us left. A lot of Wolves were killed in the wars and after we lost, we were forbidden to use our name for a long time. For hundreds of years my ancestors tried to keep the stories of the Wolves alive and one day … one day the family was reborn. I'm trying to live up to this legacy, but it can be hard work. I'm not saying that I know exactly how it feels but … I know how it feels. Maybe Sjunil wanted us to talk, because—"

"Because she has a mean sense of humour." I kicked at the water and regretted it instantly. I needed Brother Brook on my side and that was not the way to keep him happy. I clutched at the amulet and noticed Werid's glance to my chest, registering the movement.

"Good choice," they said.

"Actually, not really my choice."

"My wife belongs to him."

I closed my fist so hard around the amulet that it cut into my palm. "I hope he serves her well."

"He does, but he always asks for a little more than she expects."

"Is this why she's not with you now?" I forced myself to open my fingers. "How did you meet her?"

They turned towards the horizon. "She is one of those weird people who knows exactly where she belongs. She has no interest in anything that lies beyond the steppes and she cursed the day she fell in love with me, because I've always had terrible trouble staying put. Neither of us wanted to marry, but in the end there was no other way to make sure of her and keep her family off my back. I came to the lake to pray that I will see her soon. Have I disappointed you?"

"No. I'm happy to hear that there is someone who is waiting for you to come home after the council decisions are made."

"But you still hoped for more?"

"There are no longer a lot of Others in Tall Trees."

"I heard. So you say that you need a mentor?"

"Just someone who knows. What it can feel like sometimes."

Their hands were cold as they took my face between them. "The Clouds did not reject you, Sloe. They would have declined whatever offer was sent their way. It was an excuse, no more than that."

"How could you possibly know?"

"Because as you are standing here with me and I'm speaking to you, I'm getting to know you. Even the most disreputable parentage does not make you unworthy. Ask Brother Brook. He knows." Their hands dropped. "He has his own secrets."

I slept in the stable that night, curled up in the hayloft, not able to stomach being near either Julas or Ileon.

Qes woke me when he came in to feed the horses at dawn. "They're preparing to take him down to the council today. I think you should come. Help them translate for him, just in case."

I climbed down the tree trunk lashed to the upper floor, its crudely hewn steps. "Why today? What changed Sjunil's mind?"

"She had some time to think about what you said yesterday, about the Bears and their guests. The Badgers might have given their permission, but that doesn't mean they actually know what is happening around them. The quarters are quite self-sufficient, more like independent villages. You have a lot of hay in your hair."

I tried to rake my fingers through to get rid of most of it. When I pushed the door to the guesthouse open with my left shoulder, I almost ran into Ileon. Julas had bound a rope around his neck, so tight that it bit into his skin; his wrists were tied to his ankles, and he couldn't do much more than shuffle along.

His eyes latched on to me. "I suppose you like to see me like this?"

Julas grabbed his neck and shook him like a puppy. "Shut up and walk. Unless you want me to carry you like a sack of nuts."

"Carry him," Sjunil said behind us. "Put something over his head and carry him." She bit into an apple, spat out a pip.

"No!" Ileon writhed like a snake.

Qes held out my travelling cloak, still stinky and encrusted with mud. "Cover his clothes as well, not just the face."

When Julas put him down in the Roundhouse, Ileon's mouth and nose were bloody. He collapsed to the stamped clay in front of the council table, his bandaged hand pressed to his body in a desperate attempt to avoid breaking his fingers again. Julas bent down, his right hand clasped around the nape of Ileon's neck, in one of the deceptively tender gestures he was capable of. He pulled him to his feet.

"No need to be dramatic," I translated without thinking, and Ileon glared at me.

The doors opened again and the first wizards joined us. Werid of the Far Side was the second to step into the Roundhouse. When they perceived whom Sjunil had brought with her, their face closed off. "This is your guest?"

They had gone for outlandish; their floor-length gown was embroidered with golden wire and their wrists covered in bejewelled bangles. Their hair was wound with shimmering strips of cloth and pinned into a glorious heap with needles topped with golden snail shells. We all were transfixed by their presence—even Ileon's eyes were glued to them.

'Guest?' he mouthed.

"For now." Weird's voice was icy. "The gods will decide if your status changes."

"Your gods or mine?" He tried to wipe the blood from under his nose.

"Your gods have no place in Goldenlake."

The other wizards formed a disapproving half-circle around them and Qerla Badger used her staff to close the door behind her with a *bang*. "Enough. The meeting has not officially started." She glanced at the other attendants. "No time to lose. We will find a bench for the others." She made a gesture to Julas to leave, which meant that I would be the only one sitting next to the man from the Cities, feeling more than a little useless after he'd demonstrated his understanding of our words for everyone to hear.

Qor dragged a bench closer to the largest of the braziers. At least we wouldn't freeze to death while we were waiting for the wizards to let us speak. They took their well-cushioned seats and Qerla Badger opened the day's meeting with a short address to the Tall Gods before the first lot of incense was burned by her eldest apprentice. The list of discussion points was read out and suddenly all eyes were on me.

Sjunil stood up. "Sloe Moon of Tall Trees comes to the council of Goldenlake and wishes to be heard."

The six other wizards responded in unison: "We will listen."

After the formalities were dispensed with, my aunt seemed to relax. "Tell them what happened, Sloe. Tell them what we saw in the woods that day."

At first my voice was shaky, and I hated that Ileon watched me from the side, trying to keep up with my words. When I described how his companions had died, I saw him flinch, but when I talked about the days we'd spent tiptoeing around each other and repeating phrases and names, he listened with a strange little smile on his bloodied lips, as if he was disappointed in himself for not realizing that he wasn't the only one playing a game. I stopped my retelling before I'd reached the moment when everything changed for me. As I breathed in deeply to continue, Sjunil held up her hand.

"The rest is quickly told. He was expecting to meet more men from the Eastern Cities at the lake. They travelled in smaller groups to avoid drawing attention, but the Ravens intercepted his group and decided not to wait for explanations. We suspect that there are more of them here than we know of. Men who keep themselves hidden, some with the help of the Bears, some with the help of the Elks, and other families in the west might also be involved. It would be a good idea to ask them to attend the council."

The two Raven wizards shuffled in their seats but didn't interrupt her.

Qerla Badger's brow was furrowed. "This is speculation. Men from the Cities have traded with the families for many years to everyone's satisfaction."

Sjunil scoffed. "It's about time that they realized that everything is twice the price at the Stoneharp. This is merely the beginning—they will flood our forests. They will push the families out of Goldenlake, maybe in five, maybe in ten years. Silver and amber and the softest of furs. Pitch and timber and birch syrup. Beads and cloth and gold. They are a greedy people, deaf to the voices of the gods. We don't know how many ships they will launch to the west. The families are many, but we used to be more. The Cities are overflowing with hungry men, eager to seek their fortune in our lands. We need to stop it. We need to resist." She paused. "Together. That means Ravens together with Elks, Moons together with Clouds—Badgers together with Magpies. It's time to let the past lie and decide how we can survive our immediate future."

✿

NOT MY STORY

"They really hated that." Ileon chuckled. "I thought at least one of them would explode."

Sjunil hissed at me, "Shut him up, Sloe."

"No. I'm not prepared to hurt him." We were the last delegation left in the Roundhouse; the fires had burned down and I shivered into my sky-blue cloak. "You can ask Julas to take care of that. I'm sure he'd be happy to bloody his nose again."

"Eh." She looked at Ileon. "They will question him tomorrow and then there will be enough blood."

"They have heard everything today." He shrugged in my direction.

"It won't be enough to convince them. The Badgers can't very well forbid the families of the west to worship in Goldenlake, but they'd rather not give them any opportunity to be involved in real decisions. Goldenlake exists in a fragile balance. By your standards this town might not be up to much, but it is a very special place."

Ileon scratched at his healing shoulder. "It's dirtier than I expected."

"It's not about the mud, it's about the water," Sjunil said. "I need at least a full skin of honey beer and a shitload of bacon pancakes to forget about this particular day. Wait here, Sloe. I will ask Julas to come and collect you both." She wrapped the chequered blanket tighter around her and left us alone.

Ileon watched her, then held his bound hands out for me. "A little help here?"

I tried to ignore him, but he edged closer.

"You don't need to do this. It's not in your nature. I heard you talk about my friends. You mourn them almost as much as I do. And you must be clever enough to know that it is already too late. There are many more of us than there are of you. Your aunt is right to be alarmed, but even someone as suspicious as she can't imagine what has begun. More ships are on their way, hundreds of them, all dispatched under the banners of our kings. Each day more of us arrive—on the west coast, on the east coast, and we are making our way across. Even if the Badgers can be convinced to allow for a full council, there are many more families who will not be represented, who have profited from their association and won't be so easily persuaded to join arms with the families they have hated for generations. This is where we came from, once. This is exactly how it was in the Eastern Cities—tiny kingdoms squabbling, trying to expand and failing, until the Alliance of Kings was brokered. The east has seen more wars than any of us can recall and one day we finally learned. We are still seeking to expand, and we will prevail. Perhaps the gods need me to die by your hand so that others will come and take their revenge."

"Will you *please* shut up."

He laughed. "Make me."

I stared at him. "You won't die by my hand, and I won't let Julas kill you either. You need to see that you're wrong." I took his left elbow and pulled him to his feet.

"Ouch, careful—you might not want to hurt me, but you still do." He tilted his head. "Why don't you want to hurt me?"

"Maybe you're right and it's not in my nature."

"But it should be." Suddenly he sounded sad and tired. "If your aunt wants to take up the fight, you will have need of anger. You can't even give me a clip around the ear. Sometimes you remind me so much of my son that I want to scream in your face."

"I hope he is a kind person."

"He is useless."

I stepped back from him in the same moment Julas arrived. He stopped in the door. "What happened?" he asked softly.

"Nothing much." I watched him bundle Ileon into my filthy cloak again. He didn't struggle this time and when Julas hoisted him over his shoulder, I made room for him, still stinging from the words.

"Am I really so useless?"

Qes let a flat pebble skip into the lake. "You know he only said it to get a reaction out of you."

My right hand was cramped around the silver amulet. Ice had started to form on the shoreline between the larger stones and thin slivers broke under our heels as we made our way from the centre towards the boat station. "He succeeded. I think he wants to die."

"Nobody wants to die." Qes picked up more pebbles, gave them a tentative stroke, before discarding most of them.

"We don't know what he lost on the day we found him. He might long to join his friends. I think he wants to make it mean something. A spark to start the flame. You should've heard him speak. More words than in all the days we spent together. He tried to persuade himself—at least, I hope that's what he wanted to do. Otherwise … But I don't understand why he chose me, if he calls me useless moments later." The wind bit into my face.

"He lives in your head, Sloe. Everything he does to you makes him burrow in deeper. Leave him to Julas and Sjunil."

"Will you help me with something, Qes?"

"Sloe …"

"I want to go back to the Quarter of the Bear. Talk to the other men of the Cities."

He froze. "This is what I feared you would say. Sjunil will rip your head off."

"The council will keep her busy. They can question him without my help."

"If I say no, will you go by yourself?"

"What do you think?"

The door opened just a bit. "What?"

The man who stared at us was not from the Cities and I let go of my breath, already disappointed. "Ehm …"

"Qati?" Qes took me by the shoulder and pushed me gently aside. "Qati—is that you?"

"Qes?" Suddenly the door was flung wide open and with an exuberant laugh the man pulled my cousin into his arms. "What the fuck are you doing here?"

Qes gave him a kiss on the cheek. "We came from Tall Trees to attend the council. Sloe, this is another cousin of mine. Why are you staying with the Bears?"

Qati pulled the door shut behind him, nervous again. "Cousin exchange. They asked me to come because I have been in Goldenlake before and know my way around." His eyes narrowed. He had a long face and straight hair. He looked so unlike Qes that it was hard to see how they could be related at all. His association with the Bears made it likely that he was half-Bear at least, like Julas and Saon were connected to the Ravens. "Let's walk for a bit," he said quietly. "Seriously, Qes— why are you here?" He gestured to the buildings around us. A flock of brown chickens made their way across the leaf-covered square, their outraged clucks followed us as we walked through them.

"We're here because of the guests hosted by the Bears."

Qati looked uneasy. "Guests?"

Qes gave him a pat on the back. "You may have heard that we brought one of our own."

"Is he as disagreeable as ours?" Qati's narrow face twisted in distaste.

"Probably yes. Though I suppose it's worse if you have a few of them to entertain."

"Ignorant bullies. Every morning the house looks as if the pigs have gone through and none of them lifts a finger to clean it up again. The number of times I have swept under their arses this week …" he grumbled.

"Why are they here?" Qes asked.

We stood next to the main road, huddled together against the wind. Qati shrugged. "Don't know, don't care. They have been here for a while and are an absolute pain in the pebbles." He rubbed his face. Close up he seemed terribly tired, his eyes surrounded by dark shadows. A sloping set to his shoulders made him look older than he probably was. "Most mornings we draw straws on who has to wait on them for the day and the gods weren't with me for a couple of times now. Sorry about the rant."

"How many of them are here?"

Qati scratched his nose. "About a dozen. The Elks have some as well."

Qes shot me a quick glance. "Do they meet up?"

"Sometimes. The last time they got really drunk and trashed the place. They are always bickering, but I had to pick up the pieces. Can't wait for all of this to be over." He smiled. "I guess your cousin exchange is proving to be more enjoyable?"

Qes grinned. "Sloe and I have become good friends."

"How good?"

"Really good. I'm thinking about extending my stay."

Qati sighed. "How nice for you. Maybe I'll come and join you in Tall Trees, though knowing my luck, they won't let me get away easily. I better get back, can't risk getting another reprimand after yesterday's disaster."

"What happened yesterday?"

"You don't want to know. Let's meet up for a drink soon?"

"Sounds good."

"Has he always been so … moany?" I asked, watching him go.

Qes shrugged. "Yes. But it can't be easy for him, having to clean up after the men of the Cities every single day. If they are half as bad-tempered as Ileon … Sloe?" He sounded worried.

"He said there are more of them with the Elks."

"We're not going to the Quarter of the Elk—someone will notice us snooping around. I suggest we ask Qati to join us for a beer and let him talk for a bit longer. With a few drinks in him there is absolutely no stopping him." He studied my face. "We can trust him, Sloe. We used to sleep on adjoining platforms for most of my life. It's hard to get him to shut his trap but he's not here because he chose it. You'll get used to him."

"Do I have to?"

We returned to our own house for the evening meal. There were pancakes, as Sjunil had hoped, as well as goat cheese rolled in the dried purple flowers of ground-ivy and preserved apples dusted with the aromatic bark that must've come from the Stoneharp, a wild and exciting taste that I'd encountered only once before, when Mother had splashed out on Silid's wedding feast.

My aunt licked her fingers, already slightly the worse for wear. "You're late. Julas brought him back ages ago." She shrugged towards the dark corner of the house, where Ileon was leaning against the wall, tied up as usual.

Julas knelt next to the stack of firewood, loading logs onto his left arm to bring them over to the brazier. He glanced up briefly but kept his face carefully blank. He didn't look as drunk as our wizard.

"Sit with me, Sloe." My aunt patted the empty seat on the bench next to her. "Talk to me."

"Why? I don't think you actually want to listen to my concerns. I don't understand the game you're playing with the council. If you provoke them too much, they'll kick us out of Goldenlake."

"Qerla wouldn't do that to me. Not after …" She bit her lip.

"Not after what?"

"After she helped to strip your father of his powers."

"That was here?"

Sjunil pulled up her left shoulder. "It couldn't have happened anywhere else—not if it was supposed to be official."

"Were you with him?"

"It was before he married your mother, Sloe. I was back home again and thought that he probably deserved it." She sloppily filled another bowl and held it out to me.

My fingers shook as I took it from her. "Why did he deserve it?"

"That's really not my story to tell."

"Who else?" I gulped down a mouthful of honey beer. "I need the story to be told." I noticed that Qes had edged closer to us, his round face lined with concentration. "Do you think he was a good man? After you got to know him better?"

She laughed. "He would never have called himself a good man. He knew he'd made mistakes and he knew that the gods would struggle to forgive him. It doesn't happen all that often, a wizardship being taken away from someone—only in the most unusual of circumstances, and to the most extraordinary people. The cheese balls are really good, we left you some."

I felt for the amulet around my neck. "I wish I knew if he died in the grace of the gods."

I thought to detect a wet shimmer in Sjunil's dark eyes. "I'm sure Brother Brook was merciful in the end."

"But you can't know for sure."

"As I said, your father was an extraordinary man, Sloe. If someone could have found a way to attain forgiveness, it would have been him."

ASH

No one tried to wake me in the morning. When I crawled down from the hayloft the guesthouse was empty. My aunt had taken Ileon with her again and even Qes wasn't around. The house was cold, the brazier filled with soft ash and all the plates were clean, put back into the basket our last meal had come in. I would have to find something to eat in town if I didn't want to skip breakfast altogether.

I had a slight headache from too much honey beer, but my stomach was rumbling impatiently. I decided to forego the blue cloak and found my old one stuffed behind the sleeping platforms. It smelled pretty bad but would draw much less attention. I'd just fastened it around my neck when someone knocked on the door. Maybe they'd realized that no one had dropped off anything for us to eat. I pushed the latch up and staggered back as the door hit me full in the face. I barely had time to scream as a hand closed around my throat.

"Where is he, you fat fuck?" The green-eyed man I'd seen in the street, the one I'd followed, squeezed my neck, and next to him, sporting a split lip, was Qati.

I clawed at the fingers and Qes' cousin started to try and drag the man away from me. "No, no! You're not supposed to hurt them!" He was slapped away.

"Get off me you …" A string of curses followed that I'd learned from Ileon. At least the grip loosened sufficiently for me to draw a desperate breath.

"Coun …" I managed to croak.

Realizing that he was hindering me from speaking, he shoved me hard against the brazier. It toppled over with a deafening noise. I stumbled and he released me at the very last moment.

Qati fell to his knees next to me. "I'm so sorry—are you all right?"

I rubbed my elbow, though my ribs hurt much worse, and I had to close my eyes, bile rising into my mouth, burning my throat.

"Where … is … he." The man was towering above me, his long brown hair hanging from his felted hood, his teeth bared and sharp.

"They took him to the Roundhouse."

"What for?"

"The council had questions for him."

"Where are the others?"

"Others?" asked Qati, confused. "They only spoke of one."

He was slapped again. "The ones he travelled with from the coast."

"They were killed." I tried to move my legs under me, but they shook so hard that I gave up immediately. "We found them already dead."

He looked stunned; pain flashed across his face. "Already dead? Killed by whom?"

"You knew them, then." My voice sounded odd through my crushed throat and the nose that started to swell up.

Qati stared at me open-mouthed, his face flaming.

The green-eyed man took a step backwards. "Killed by whom?" he repeated, quietly.

"We weren't there. We were too late, and they'd been left, strung up."

"Strung up." It wasn't a question. "One of them was my brother."

I had another go at moving my legs. I made it to my knees, pushing myself up from the bowl of the fallen brazier, its ashes spilled across the floor. "We buried them."

He fought against the onrush of grief; his face was distorted. "Buried them where?"

"In the forest, where we found them."

A strangled sob broke from the man of the Cities as the door swung open again. A gleaming blade pressed against his neck.

Qati squealed in fright and ran out of the house as Julas pushed the green-eyed man against the table. "Not a good idea," he said calmly.

The man's face was streaked with tears, and he closed his eyes as Julas' elbow went up, angling the longknife.

"No!" I was on my feet without noticing how I'd managed to jump up. "Don't."

"He hurt you. Sjunil will want him killed."

"She can't have him killed—not without causing a shitload of problems. He knew the men we found hanging from the trees."

Julas didn't budge. "That makes sense."

"Please … please don't. I'm fine—there's no need for this."

"You're bleeding, Sloe."

"Still not a good enough reason to kill him. Please," I said again.

Julas scowled. "I should have never left you behind."

"You couldn't have known." I dragged my sleeve over my face to mop up some of the blood spilling from my nose. "What is your name?"

The green-eyed man was still crying.

Julas pushed him again. "They have asked you a question," he growled.

"Tjal na Tialin."

I took Julas' wrist and pulled it away. A thin red cut became visible in Tjal's pale skin, breaking into tiny pearls of blood that started to run down his neck. "My name is Sloe. Sloe Moon of Tall Trees. I'm sorry to have given you such bad news."

Julas cleaned the longknife against the leg of his trousers but didn't sheathe it. "Don't be stupid, Sloe. He came here to attack you."

"But now he is clearly distressed."

Julas rolled his eyes. "I don't know why I bother. You are set on getting yourself killed."

I spat out some blood. "I can deal with it. Step back."

He conceded after a moment of hesitation.

The man from the Cities stared at me. "He's right—this is stupid."

I touched his arm. "I don't care."

He crumpled against me as if all the air had gone out of him in one single exhale.

Siw blanched as she saw Tjal na Tialin sitting on the edge of the sleeping platform, his head in his hands, still not able to face us.

"Are you mad?! One of them is dangerous enough!"

"He came to us."

My sister looked at me in disgust. "What have you done to him? What happened to your nose?"

"Long story. Where is Sjunil?"

"Still at the council meeting. I slipped away when they started to yell at each other again. What does he want from us?"

"He wants to speak to Ileon."

Tjal flinched as I said his name.

"But Ileon isn't here." Siw crossed her arms in front of her.

"So he decided to wait."

"Sjunil won't like that one bit."

"She doesn't have to like it."

Siw glared at Julas. "Why didn't you do something about this?"

He shrugged. "I tried."

"You could at least have bound him!"

"He is a guest in Goldenlake," I reminded her. "A guest of the Bears. I assume that Sjunil wants to avoid getting on their bad side right now."

She stepped closer and hissed, "What do you think will happen when he sees Ileon treated like a prisoner?"

"He will probably be very angry. But he has been in Goldenlake long enough to understand that Ileon's status differs from his own in a few important aspects. One of the men in the forest was his brother."

Siw drew in a sharp breath. "That makes it worse!"

"Does it? We did the right thing when we buried them. We didn't leave them dangling from the trees, and he is grateful for it."

"Grateful?" She shook her head. "Sometimes I don't know how we can be siblings. You look at the world and … you never see how easily it can destroy you. You seem to wait to be …"

"Killed? Julas said something similar."

"What the fuck." Our wizard was framed by the door, the blanket around her making her broader than she was, taller than she was.

"I knew she wouldn't be happy," my sister whispered.

Tjal struggled to his feet, his eyes red-rimmed but staring straight at Sjunil. "I have come to see him."

"Qes is bringing him." Sjunil's gaze swept over the house, the brazier that stood in a different place, the ash on the floor. "I suppose it was only a question of time until the news got around. Qes?" She stepped aside.

Ileon's hands were still bound, and he wore Qes' hood pulled over his face. As he shook it back, Tjal fell to his knees in front of him. Ileon didn't look in the least surprised, as if he was used to that kind of behaviour, as if he expected it.

"It took you long enough to find me," he snarled in his own words.

"We only heard about it this morning."

"Get up, you fool."

Everyone but the two men from the Cities were staring at me, because I was the only one who had understood their exchange.

Tjal struggled to his feet, his trousers covered in ash. "I come for you now."

"You should have brought the others."

"I thought …"

"You thought you could make a name for yourself." Ileon's voice was cold. "I have been subjected to this undignified treatment for days and you come here without so much as a sword."

"I had a boy with me, but he ran away."

"Your brother would have handled the situation much better. They will not let me go." His yellow eyes found me. "They are not finished with me yet."

"How did he die?" Tjal was shaking again.

"They cut his throat and he bled out like a pig, the same as my cousin and the guide. They left me for dead, but I could hear them die. This one—the odd one—found me and for a while, I was treated well enough." He gave me a bitter smile. "You will have to negotiate my release with their wizard, and she is a crafty old bitch. Have the others arrived?"

Tjal nodded.

"Olas as well?"

Another nod.

"He will be the best to take this in hand, and not add to the mistakes that have been made today." Every muscle on him expressed deep disappointment. "Go, lest they realize what they have allowed to happen."

Tjal bowed and slipped through the door, before Julas could so much as blink.

Ileon turned to me. "He has always been weak." He sat back against the wall, waiting for Qes to tie him up again.

Julas watched him while we conferred in the stable.

"They will try to talk us into giving him up?" I asked.

Sjunil snorted.

Qes bundled hay down from the loft to make use of the time we spent there. "They will probably offer quite a bit of silver for him. Do you think he might even be a king?"

"A king in the Cities." Sjunil grimaced. "He must know that this counts for nothing in Goldenlake."

"If we let him go, he'd be in our debt," I said.

Sjunil shook her head. "A debt that would never be repaid. We need to be careful, he's a crafty old bastard."

"He said something similar about you."

"A match made by the gods. I've always admired their sense of humour."

"There are a lot of them in town." Qes pushed the last armful of hay to the ground and the horses started gobbling it up. He wiped his hands on his trousers. "If we consider letting him go, do you think he would hold a grudge?"

"This one will hold a grudge until the gods call him home. Maybe even after." Sjunil ground her teeth. "We should've let him rot."

Siw cleared her throat. "Will the council call him again?"

Our wizard nodded. "Probably. The Ravens were decidedly unhappy with what he had to say about their family members, but he is sure they were Ravens, not Magpies or Owls."

"Would he lie?" Qes asked.

My sister huffed. "What would be the point of that?"

"If we quarrel amongst ourselves, we don't look too often in his direction," Qes said.

"But he stuck to this story from the very beginning. He must have known about the alliances back then if this is what he wanted to do." Siw shrugged. "I don't think that's plausible."

Sjunil scrunched up her nose. "Why would he *not* know about the alliances? He has likely spent some time at the Stoneharp before setting out to the east and he might even have obtained this information from the guide. We don't know if one of the men he had with him was fluent in our words. We don't know anything about what happened before Sloe found him. I would much rather over than underestimate him."

PROMISE TO RETURN

The man they called Olas was expected at noon the next day. They'd sent Qati ahead to prepare us and Sjunil had asked Qerla Badger and Werid of the Far Side to be present, with the consequence that the day's council meeting had been officially postponed. The guesthouse had been cleaned, more benches turned up, and a very grumpy Qor had laid out a spread of various breads and drinks to ensure that her master was never kept waiting for a snack. It would've made more sense to hold the assembly at the Roundhouse, but that would've sent the wrong message. Qerla was present as a favour, not as a representative of the Badgers, and had tried to dress down, though her glittering staff did little to dispel the impression of her being the most powerful person present.

Sjunil allowed Ileon to sit on his own bench. Julas had made an effort to clean him up and he looked strange in Qes' spare trousers and tunic that were much too big for him. His coppery hair was bound up in a knot so that the faded bruises on his face were visible to all. He should've been nervous, but he seemed calm to me. Sjunil fidgeted with her blanket, probably praying silently that none of us would make too much of a twat out of ourselves. Siw's face was positively green with apprehension and at one point, Julas took her by the shoulder and whispered something in her ear that made her blush, but she grew noticeably quieter. His hand lingered and a sharp sensation made my heart stutter. He'd known since the beginning of our travels that she had a thing for him, and I probably wasn't the only one he would try and bribe with affection. I still felt his mouth on mine and had to press the back of my hand against my swollen face to make me wince and forget about it.

We'd propped the door open. When Werid came to join us, their shadow stabbed into the guesthouse like a blade. It had been days since I'd seen them and while Qerla had tried to fade into the background, they'd piled up their hair under a net beset with garnets glinting like dried blood. Their cloak was held in place by a monstrously big clasp, fashioned into a running wolf and made of gleaming gold. Only the gods knew how many chests they'd travelled with to treat us to an ever-changing display of wealth. Given the men of the Cities' reputation for greed it could've been a wise choice—or a very bad one.

"Are you still waiting for them?" Werid sounded resigned as their gaze flickered around the house we'd been assigned. It was all too clear that they were used to better accommodations.

"Did that ruin your great entrance?" Qerla mocked.

The younger wizard sighed. "It's a shame for all that effort to go to waste."

"It's not wasted on us," I said.

"Trust you to find a silver lining."

"You mean we don't count?" Sjunil asked acidly.

Werid gave me a pointed look. "You are too nice for your own good. You would never say something horrible to me, Sloe." They smiled at me sadly. "And it will be the death of you one day."

"Enough," Sjunil interjected. "I have better things to do than listen to you two flirt the pants off each other."

Werid looked amused. "I can't see any of them queueing up yet. They will keep you waiting as long as possible, just to rub it in. You should have insisted on meeting them in their quarter."

"But it's not their quarter, is it? We don't need to piss off the Bears any more than strictly necessary. Here, we are in control."

"Or not, as they so clearly demonstrate."

"Shut the fuck up." Qerla Badger poked Sjunil with the gnarled end of her staff. "Save it for the council."

A shocked silence wavered across the room. We were used to our own foul-mouthed wizard, but hearing someone as dignified as the old Badger swear made us all stare at her. Even Ileon's brows had shot up to meet his hairline.

Someone knocked politely on the door frame.

The man they'd sent to negotiate was short and unusually thin, his skin almost as dark as Werid's and absolutely not what any of us had expected. He had nothing imposing about him; his greying hair was cut short and stood up in a tangled quiff. He was clean-shaven and disturbingly neat in general—even his fingernails were trimmed.

"I assume I have come to the right place?" His voice was rich, like spiced honey. I would've given my little finger to be able to hear him sing. He bowed before us. "Olas da Ozanil."

Sjunil introduced Qerla, Werid, and herself—we others were incidental. Olas hadn't come by himself. There were other men standing outside, but it was Tjal he gestured to. Compared to their negotiator, Tjal looked rough around the edges. His eyes were blood-shot, as if he'd spent the night wailing into his pillows, and I was annoyed to feel another compassionate twinge for him. Both he and Olas sat down on the bench that had been prepared for them.

Sjunil started off the discussion. "This is an unfortunate situation."

Olas smiled. "We deeply regret the circumstances, but you must understand that we have to confess to be somewhat attached to the man you keep trussed up like a chicken." For all the honey in his voice, it carried a sting with it—a warning that he was prepared to be civil as long as the meeting promised a result he could consider.

"He could have had it worse," our wizard replied with a calculating smirk. "I was all for letting him die under his gutted horse. But my apprentice is a nice young woman, desperate to prove her healing skills, and now he is as good as new. He owes her his life and we won't let him forget."

"No one expects you to be overly charitable." Olas' dark eyes glittered. "Though we don't take kindly to our men being mistreated. There must be compensation."

"... and the silk gloves are off," Ileon mumbled, with an unmistakable air of self-satisfaction that made Julas grip the hilt of his longknife so hard that I heard his knuckles pop.

"He has been compensated—with his life. We, on the other hand, have fed him, used precious supplies to treat his wounds. We are well within our rights to expect payment."

"Payment?" Tjal asked incredulously. Olas bared his teeth.

Sjunil beamed at him. "For now, he will pay us with information—a cheap price. We keep him safe. I'm sure there are certain *elements* in Goldenlake who would rejoice if given the opportunity to get their hands on someone this important. We have him under watch day and night, we still feed him, and we put up with his awful personality as best as humanly possible. You must have noticed that he's a bit of a cunt."

Two men tried to jump into the house, probably the ones well-versed enough in our own swear words.

Olas tilted his head. "All important men are in some way or other. And I dare say, so are all important women."

They stared at each other, then Sjunil broke the tension with a snort of laughter. "Oh, I like you. You're *fun*."

"Ten years married, I'm afraid."

"That has never stopped me before."

Werid cleared their throat. "Who is flirting the pants off each other now?"

Ileon looked irritated, an expression that matched Qerla Badger's.

Sjunil sucked at her teeth. "We're all grown-up enough to handle this situation. The council will request his presence for a few more days and we won't let him out of our sight until the decisions have been made. But we can agree to releasing him, if there is an accord that guarantees that no retribution will be sought after."

"What?" Qerla barked.

"We can't keep lugging him around, and who knows what the consequences will be if we kill him after he has stopped being useful? I'd much rather get rid of him and gain something in return. Something that serves to keep the peace for a few days longer, if possible. What is one man in the great scheme of things? We are a reasonable people, we are an honourable people—if it serves our purpose."

"You would give up your only leverage?" Qerla asked flatly.

"If it serves our purpose," my aunt repeated, her face like stone.

"This is madness!"

Sjunil shrugged. "This is diplomacy."

"The Badgers will oppose this plan." The older wizard stomped the end of her staff into the clay.

"The Badgers have no voice in the Quarter of the Moon."

"If you're quite finished," the negotiator interrupted, "we agree to listen to a proposal of how this accord could be achieved."

Qerla shot him a warning glance. "Could you be more pompous?"

Tjal gasped but Olas seemed unperturbed. "If it serves our purpose," he said pointedly.

"Do you have a proposition?" Ileon asked, the first time he spoke loudly enough to join in with the discussion around his person.

Sjunil sighed. "We will promise to return you to your friends as soon as possible. Until then, you will live unrestrained among us, as just another inhabitant of Goldenlake. You will agree to keep the peace and will not be allowed to enter the quarters of the Bears and Elks. As soon as we officially release you, you will gather your entourage and leave town. In return for these shockingly generous terms, you will offer us full immunity from all future retributions."

Tjal threw up his hands. "Full immunity? How can something like this be guaranteed?"

"Written. Sealed. We need to make sure that there are no loopholes when dealing with men from the Cities."

Ileon screwed up his face. "This is acceptable."

That was apparently not the answer Olas had expected—it took him a moment to regain his controlled demeanour. "I appreciate that you would like to resolve this matter as quickly as possible, but is this wise?" he asked in his own words.

"I am not in a position to quibble," Ileon said calmly. "It is only a bit of wax and parchment. It will not mean much when the time comes." Maybe he didn't care that I was able to understand him. He forced his face into an exhausted smile. "We agree to these terms."

Sjunil pursed her lips. "But …"

"We agree under the following condition—as long as I am your honoured guest in Goldenlake, you will send someone to live with my own companions to ensure that your promises are kept."

Qerla jumped to her feet. "Absolutely not!"

"You mean … like a hostage?" Sjunil's brows knitted together.

"Yes. It is a tried and tested arrangement."

"You can't seriously consider this?" Werid looked flustered.

Sjunil inspected her nails. "I might."

"Who would be stupid enough to …" Werid's voice faltered. "No."

"I want it to be the odd one." Ileon's bandaged hand gestured towards me. "Him."

"Them," Werid corrected angrily.

"Whatever—them."

My skin crawled as every single pair of eyes turned towards me. Sjunil bit her lip and stepped closer. "No one will force you to do this," she said. "You don't need to agree."

"I don't?" It felt as if a cold hand squeezed my throat again.

"No one will think less of you for refusing."

"But it needs to be me," I rasped. "You have trained me for this. Can I bring Qes?" I asked Ileon.

He sneered. "If he is happy to join you."

"Of course I am." Qes came from the darkness next to the sleeping platforms, his face aflame with purpose. I'd never loved him so much as in that moment.

Qerla groaned. "As Sjunil has made so abundantly clear to me, I have no say over what happens to Sloe Moon, but I can't allow Qes to go. He might be part of this fellowship, but he is still Qes of the Badgers."

"Try and stop him." Sjunil took a deep breath. "We should drink to seal the deal." She gave a wink to Siw, who started to fill up the bowls, but my mouth swam with sour spit as an uncertain future unfolded before me.

WHEN WE FAIL

Tjal brought us across town. We'd been given little time to pack our bags, but they were heavy enough and none of the men of the Cities offered to help. Most of them still looked stunned and I knew exactly how they felt. Suddenly all the pieces had fallen into place, and they had two additional mouths to feed. Qati stood in the square of the Bears, surrounded by the brown chickens that obviously expected something from him. His mouth was hanging open in confusion.

"What ..."

Tjal pushed him aside. "We need blankets and more mattresses. You need to make up another platform."

"But we're squeezed as it is!"

"Find the space."

I stared at the door in front of me. "This is the House of Men."

Tjal frowned. "And ...?"

"I can't sleep in there. I'm not a man."

For a moment, all the men of the Cities were dumbfounded. "What?"

Qati came to the rescue. "The Quarter of the Bear doesn't have an Other House."

"A what House?" Tjal sounded unfriendly.

"That's not a concept they feel comfortable with," Qati explained.

"Then we need another solution," Qes insisted. "If there is another house available ..."

"Of course there isn't," Tjal said, deeply annoyed. "You will stay in the House of Men."

"But that is not allowed," Qes protested. "The gods—"

"The gods will learn to live with the situation," Tjal growled. "Like everybody else."

The hairs on the back of my neck seemed to burn. I'd never been made to feel so ashamed. Qes took my hand. "I will be by your side," he promised. "I will bear witness to what happened here today if you need someone to back you up."

Then we both took a deep breath and I stepped into the House of Men, closer to tears than I'd been all day.

The house smelled weird to me, like unwashed feet and mould. Every platform was covered with more than one bedroll; the building had obviously never been meant to serve so many people. I understood why Qati had complained so bitterly: the men were living in chaos. Everywhere lay heaps of gear, saddlebags, discarded boots, baskets stuffed with supplies, and dirty bowls were strewn across the table in the middle of the room. Only the gods knew how Olas kept his nails clean in such squalor.

Tjal gestured to Qes. "He will share with you, Qati, and … they will share with me."

It made sense for them to split us up, but the cold dread that bounced around in my stomach and made me go all sweaty intensified. When I'd agreed to be a hostage, I hadn't thought the details through. Qati seemed relieved that there were no further protests from my side. I didn't envy him. He was in the most difficult position of all—at least Qes and I knew exactly where we stood and had somehow managed to get half a town between us and Qes' ex-boyfriend.

Qati cleaned and cooked but wasn't particularly gifted in either department. Apart from Qati, there were only two other Bears to keep an eye on the guests and share his responsibilities. They kept their distance but from the way they glared at me, I felt their revulsion. I was not supposed to be in their house. The men from the Cities didn't only hurt my sensibilities, they'd also affronted their hosts.

The house did not receive the generous allowance of meats, fresh bread, and cheese that we from Tall Trees had enjoyed as part of a wizard's entourage. Our evening meal consisted of soup thickened with ground bearnuts and not much else; everyone was given a hunk of bread with their ration and an apple that had started to go wrinkly.

I managed half my soup and let Qes eat the rest of it. At least the apple was sweet, if a bit mealy. "Thank you for being here with me," I whispered.

Qes lowered his spoon. "I would never have let you go on your own." He gazed mournfully into his bowl. "Although it's starting to be a bigger sacrifice than I expected. Even if they keep their word in the end."

"I'm not counting on it," I admitted. "They'll give Sjunil an important looking scroll and nothing more."

"It must mean something to Ileon that you were prepared to do this for him. Maybe he thought he could get you out of harm's way."

"He despises me. Almost as much as his own men do." I looked around us. "Why do they need to be so stinky?"

Qes giggled and everyone stopped eating to glare at us for amusing ourselves in their presence.

Olas came back to the quarter after dark, like a thin shadow gliding across the room. There only was one single brazier for all the men and in its golden light, his face was taut with displeasure. He pulled Tjal aside to talk to him in private.

"They really don't want us to be here," Qes said. "Maybe that's to our advantage."

I took care to squeeze myself as close to the wall as possible. The blankets Qati had found for us were clean enough, and I folded my blue cloak into a soft square to use as a pillow. Tjal seemed to balance himself on the edge of the platform, loathe to even touch me accidentally. I'd hoped for Ileon to understand our ways someday but based on the attitude of his followers, that was an impossible thing to achieve.

It took forever for me to drift off to sleep. Two of the men snored so loud that the rafters shivered, in addition to the usual sounds of shuffling, groaning, farting, and mumbling that come with cramped sleeping arrangements. It had been a long time since I'd slept in the company of so many people and when I finally nodded off I dreamt of Saon—of the last time we'd lain together out in the woods, on the softest bed of dead leaves, and his warm hands around my face. He breathed into me, filling every sense of me with him, his weight on me and I stammered words of love, but then he kissed me and his face changed—I tried to get away from him, but Julas held me close, even as I struggled. I cried out and woke myself up. Tjal was pressed into my back, his breath feathered over my neck. I turned around and pushed him back to the edge of the platform.

For the rest of the night, I stared at the roof, sweaty and desperate for dawn to save me.

From the way the other men from the Cities behaved around Olas, it was clear that he possessed a different status, much closer to Ileon himself. He was the only one who'd been given a whole platform to himself, and crude curtains had been fashioned from a pair of riding cloaks to allow him a small measure of privacy. Everyone tiptoed around him. It looked as if he'd been one of the last of them to arrive in Goldenlake and always had at least two men following him wherever he went.

It was fascinating just being among the group of people; to observe the unspoken dynamics between them. Some of them clearly hated each other but tried hard to get along for the greater good. Others almost seemed joined at the hip, and a lot of them were related. The brother Tjal had lost in the forests hadn't been the only sibling on the adventure so far from home. They often discussed the politics of the Cities, and it took me a long time to figure out that they all hailed from a particular place on the south coast—not an old town, but recently established and hungry for fame and riches.

Tjal was in a strange position. He was clearly their second spokesman, with an excellent understanding of our words, but no one was very respectful towards him; in fact, they behaved as if he stood a mere step above Qati and the other Bears of the quarter. He took care of the details, while Olas was left to handle the general questions that barely required any actual work. From morning to evening, Tjal was on his feet, running around Goldenlake, sometimes just to ensure that food rations would be delivered to the house. He flung himself into those tasks, as if he hoped to gain their regard one day. The others lounged about, sharpening and oiling their knives, fixing saddle straps or mending their clothes, leaving disorder wherever they sat.

Qes dealt with our new situation by making himself useful; from the first day, he started to cook, swept the house, sorted away the rubbish on the table, and fed the chickens. We weren't allowed to leave the quarter square and they seemed to be under strict instructions not to let me do anything at all. I was to be treated as Ileon's counterpart and he was someone who delegated, not someone who worked, even if I had absolutely no say in what was going on around me. For the first two days, it was painfully lonely. Then Olas sat down next to me at breakfast and the house held its collective breath.

"How are you adapting?" he asked.

With Qes' help, Qati had produced a quite edible bearnut porridge—something that elevated my cousin's standing among the men. I stirred a blob of honey into it. "There are still so many things I don't understand. How is he?"

Olas was the only one of them who asked for tea to be prepared each morning and he poured out a second bowl for me. "He is well. Your sister is very happy with how his hand is healing. He will be able to take off the bandages soon, though it remains to be seen if he will ever regain full use of it. I will tell him that you asked after him. For some reason, he takes an interest in you."

I felt my heart glow. "He asked after me?"

"He did. That makes you someone important. It is not that easy to get on his good side, as you may have already noticed."

"What is he?" I took a big gulp of the rapidly cooling tea.

Ileon's negotiator blinked, but then a slow smile spread across his shaven face. "He is our leader."

"A king?"

"Not quite. You could call him a prince, I suppose."

"You must have been very afraid to lose him."

Olas winced. "We were. We desperately waited for him and his guards to arrive. He had insisted on travelling with the smallest group."

"So Tjal's brother was one of his personal guards."

"Yes, he was. A talented young man, stout-hearted and noble. His loss is a terrible tragedy for the company."

A death that had shaped my own life. "Tjal seems to try and walk it off."

Olas scoffed. "He feels he has to step up, but he knows all too well that his brother is irreplaceable. Everyone mourns in their own way."

"I feel for him."

The lines around his mouth became more pronounced. "I think you feel for everybody, Sloe Moon of Tall Trees. Some men may believe that this makes you weak, but I see someone who will leave their mark. Perhaps not today, but in a few years' time when we know how the mission has ended for us all. When the fate of Birkland has been decided."

"Does its fate need to be decided?" I asked cautiously. The men of the Cities used the name 'Birkland' a lot, and I bristled at the sound of it.

"The gods have their plans."

"Which gods? Yours or mine?"

"Both sets, I expect. I must admit, I am not a pious man. Too much has happened to me."

"Bad things?"

"Very bad things. None of the men who came with us to Birkland have been given this mission as a sign of favour. We were selected because we won't be missed much when we fail." He saw my eyes widen. "Even him," he confirmed. "He has enough brothers to firmly secure his father's succession."

Olas wasn't the type to surrender information without the hope of results. There was something he wanted me to do or just *feel*; maybe he tried to stoke my love for them in case I ever came to be in a position to make an important decision.

"He chose me to come with him because he knows that I have a certain talent for languages. He knew that I would pick up your words quickly and that this would be most helpful to him. But he also knows that I shouldn't be the one he trusts too much. You need to be careful, Sloe. Nivael is not someone who forgives easily, especially his friends."

"Nivael? I thought his name was Ileon."

He blinked. "No. His name is Nivael da Nileon, Prince of Crooked Hill."

WHO YOU ARE

When I woke, Tjal was curled up against me. It was still the middle of the night and the house as silent as it could be with our two snorers (Olas was one of them and surprisingly loud, considering his slender frame). I sleepily stroked Tjal's back and he pressed his head deeper into my chest, mumbling something in his sleep. My fingers tangled in his long hair, cold in the air of early winter. For a while, I was able to forget that I came by the closeness in such a dishonourable way.

I made myself release him, but he edged closer, his body unconsciously following the warmth of mine. I gave in. It wouldn't mean much to him or maybe he'd be shocked when I decided to tell him that I'd held him, even if it served to keep us both comfortable. I pulled the blankets over us, and he settled with a deep sigh, his breath on my cheek. It only took moments after that for me to slip away and when I opened my eyes again, he was already gone. The house was almost empty, as if they'd all decided to run after him—even Olas—but they'd left two men to guard me and Qes, who was busy grinding herbs into a paste with goat milk butter. The pungent smell wafted across to me.

He smiled. "You still look tired," he said.

I pulled the blanket around me, fished for my boots next to the platform, and put them on, yawning. "I have trouble staying asleep during the night." I came over to him. "What is this for?"

He pointed to plucked, gutted chickens, laying sprawled in a shallow bowl. "Qati was persuaded to kill two of them and I'm trying to improve on his cooking."

"You don't need to do this, Qes."

His brow wrinkled. "Yes, I do. I need to give them a reason to keep me around. Otherwise they might get ... unwholesome ideas."

"Where have they gone?"

"To see their leader speak in the Roundhouse. Today is his big day."

"I wish they'd woken me up to join them."

"They wouldn't have allowed you to go, Sloe. Qati tells me that you are now the most famous person in the whole of Goldenlake. Sloe Moon of Tall Trees, who let themself be taken hostage to serve their wizard. An act of devotion that many people admire."

"Devotion?"

He grinned. "Just go with it."

"Maybe this is what Olas meant when he said ..." I shook my head to get rid of the thought. "No. Can I help, Qes?"

"I'm almost finished. You should go back to bed. Keep your strength up for later." He lowered his voice. "What is happening with you and Tjal?" he asked.

"I'm not sure. He ignores me all day but at night ..."

"No one should know," he said, sadly. "It would be dangerous for both of you."

When they came back to the quarter after dark, none of them was particularly forthcoming about what had happened at the council meeting. As the hostage whose life depended on their prince, I was the last to know what was really going on. If Sjunil or Siw tried to get any messages to me, they weren't coming through, but I figured they probably tried not to alarm me too much. I wanted to ask Olas but after he drank down a bowl of beer in one gulp, he retired behind his curtains and left the other men to brood.

Tjal didn't come back until much later. I was tucked into our blankets and impatient to talk to him, but he seemed so exhausted that I thought better of it.

I waited for him to come close to me in the night; I was getting used to him, yearned for the moment in which he jostled against me in his sleep and I woke up entwined with him. He kicked the boots off his feet and crawled into bed. He smelled of icy rain and wind and a dampness came off him that made us both shiver. I heard his stomach rumble in the dark; he was obviously hungry but had decided not to eat. I knew that he'd push me away if I tried to hug him while we were awake—me squashed to the wall and he on the edge. It was a weird illusion we both tried to keep alive.

"You can tell me what went wrong," I offered at last.

He flinched. "Oh—I thought you were asleep."

"What happened today?"

He secured the blankets around him, pushing them under his sides and feet. "Olas has asked us not to speak about it while you and Qes are around."

"Is it that bad?"

He sighed. "Please don't, Sloe. I'm … so tired tonight."

I turned away from him. The situation felt oddly familiar, me asking for attention from someone who wasn't prepared to consider my needs. Things with Saon had been different—we hadn't been exactly well-suited, while everything was much more complicated with Tjal. With him I longed for something else, something much less definable. It probably was as fundamental as my body fearing to freeze to death overnight—a desperate bid for survival that awoke memories.

Sure enough, when I came to later, his knees were snuggled into the back of mine and his arm was around my waist, holding me against him. I could feel the slow movements of his chest against my spine and even if I tried to rationalize what was happening, it didn't change the fact that I felt hungry for him, for another one who made me feel bad about myself when his friends were around but used my softness to his advantage when no one else was paying attention. His fingers were burrowed into my belly, holding on to me as if he was scared of drifting away.

During the next few days, the weather changed even more. The men spoke of the lake starting to finally freeze over, dark ice forming on its gentle waves, trapping the last of the golden birch leaves. In the mornings, when I inevitably woke up alone, I tried to make it a habit to pray but Brother Brook felt far away from me, even if the edges of the amulet cut into my hands. I waited for Olas to speak to me again, but he avoided me like the rest of them. The game between me and my bedfellow continued: he ignored me during the day and held me at night. When I left the house to relieve myself, carefully watched, I noticed the snow building up around me. The chickens had fled and tiny icicles began to grow on the edges of the roofs where fires heated the dwellings from within. I started to wear both of my cloaks on top of each other, bound strips of cloth around my hands to keep my fingers as warm as possible, and spent most of my days huddled close to the brazier, feeling incredibly useless.

They'd started to trust Qes enough to let him help Qati and the Bears run errands in town, so he was gone most of the time. The men who kept an eye on me were often the ones least interested in communicating and maybe that was why my thoughts latched onto Tjal and made it into a much bigger deal than it actually was. It was likely that all the men around us slept in a similar way—apart from Olas, who might start to wish for a bedfellow of his own, as the snow lay thickly around us and was starting to creep higher where Qati and Qes swept it between the houses in an effort to clear a narrow path for the men who came and went in the quarter.

One night, the wind howled across town and caught itself between the buildings. The whole quarter whistled with it, and the House of Men shook ever so slightly. I tried to push away from the wall so I wouldn't feel the vibrations as much. Tjal grunted softly. His lips briefly touched an exposed bit of my shoulder. I realized that he was *awake*. I tried to turn but his fingers dug in and steadied me. He kissed me again, on the base of my neck. I pulled one of his warm hands to my face and pressed my mouth on the knuckles. I expected to be grabbed and used after giving him that much, but he just caressed my cheek and buried the tip of his nose in my collar.

All night I waited for something to happen, but it didn't.

"I think we need to talk," I said to him when he let go of me at dawn and started to dress.

He closed his eyes. "Not in the house," he whispered. He waited for me to wrap myself up, then he brought me outside. The night's storm had rearranged the snow and blocked some of the quarter's passages completely, so we stepped further away from the house than I'd been allowed for all the time I'd been with them.

We stood close to keep our voices down. He wiped at his face with the back of his hand. "I am sorry," he said. "I thought you liked being held."

"I do—and I want to be with you properly."

He went pale. "They would kill us."

"Why?"

"Because the laws of the gods forbid it."

"No, they don't."

"All right. *Our* gods forbid it."

"That's the stupidest thing I've ever heard. Anybody can get married to anyone."

"Not where I come from." He was shaking. "Can we not just carry on as before? This is the best part of my life, now—getting ready for bed after another horrible day and knowing that you will allow me to sleep in your arms." The smudges under his eyes were so dark that he looked as if someone had hit him in the face and bruised the skin.

We stood, both with crossed arms, both of us holding ourselves. "You are very far away from home," I said to him, my voice raspy. "I know that you don't understand who I am, but this is ridiculous."

"I would lose all the respect they have for me."

"They don't have a lot left as it is. You shouldn't have kissed me. That changed it." I glanced over my shoulder. We were alone. It was early, around sunrise. I touched his wrist, trying hard not to spook him. "I wish you would let me be with you."

"But I don't deserve it."

I was reminded of the conversations I'd had with Qes. They felt like half a lifetime away. The man standing with me was so close to breaking down that it hurt me not to be able to soothe him. "Why?" I asked gently. "What makes you so special that you don't deserve to feel good?" He wasn't the only one my question was directed at. It was obvious that we both struggled with it.

"It should have been me, having my throat cut like that. My brother was the better man, the best man. He had the favour of the gods—he had been chosen to join the guard." A tear spilled from his left eye.

"When Ileon—I mean, when the prince talked in the Roundhouse, did he describe what happened again?"

Tjal nodded. "In detail."

That explained the weird mood all of them had been in on their return. "And did he tell you that he wished you had died instead?"

Another nod.

"Has he always been so cruel to you?"

"He loved my brother almost as much as I did. He grieves for him."

"But that doesn't mean that he should take it out on you."

"It is his prerogative. He is the Prince of Crooked Hill."

"And you almost kill yourself to serve him, every day. I see you running about, Tjal—I haven't much else to do but watch what happens in this house. Every single person in it is desperately lonely, including me, but I think you might be the loneliest of us all."

His green eyes were brimming but he dashed the tears away before they fell, sniffled loudly, and squared his shoulders. "I don't know how I can go on without him, and I think I may even be falling in love with you, because …" His voice faltered. "Because I know that you can't simply run away. Not until the exchange takes place at least. I know that you will be there when I come to the house. I don't want to depend on this but it's keeping me alive. I'm so sorry that it's you, Sloe. I don't want to place this burden on you, I really don't." He pressed his hand over his mouth as if he had to physically stop himself from revealing more.

I stared at him, shocked. "You're falling *in love* with me? You called me all sorts of names when we met."

"I know, and I'm sorry …"

"By all the gods, stop apologizing!" I grabbed him by the cloak and pulled him towards me. Our mouths met in a first awkward kiss.

"They will kill us," he said again.

"No, they won't. Not here in Goldenlake, not where the wizards control the law and speak for our gods."

He clutched at my face and our foreheads touched. "Please make me understand," he whispered. "Please make me understand who you are."

PLEASE

"Fuck." Qes looked truly, deeply scared. "*Really*?"

"I hadn't realized he felt like this. I was thinking about getting our baser needs met. Making the most of the situation, that sort of thing."

"It looks as if you've bitten off more than you can chew, Sloe." He grimaced. "Has he promised you anything?"

"No, he hasn't. He's afraid of them noticing it."

"Yeah, no shit. You're supposed to be the hostage here. It's an impossible situation, but you like those, don't you?"

"What's that supposed to mean?"

He gave a little snort. "You know all too well what I mean. What happens now?"

"Not much, probably. He can't really ask Sjunil for my hand in marriage, can he."

"You're not seriously considering this?"

I shrugged. "In all the time I had with Saon he never once said that he actually loved me."

"It's not enough for him to just say it!"

"I know, Qes. Believe it or not, I have learned a fair bit since Saon."

He looked so doubtful that I slapped his arm, and we both laughed.

It turned out to be the day that Werid of the Far Side chose to visit. When they appeared in the square, accompanied by a jittery apprentice, it was Olas who came to fetch me, his face openly curious. I'd spent my last hours trying to distract myself from the night to come by cleaning my boots with snow and lard, repairing the laces and a seam that had started to split at the top.

"What do you think they want?" he asked me excitedly.

"Probably check that I'm still breathing."

"They could have sent their apprentice to make sure of that." Olas was the only one of them who had a firm grasp on the whole pronoun issue, the only one who'd actually paid attention while travelling from the coast to the lake. "Don't keep them waiting." He almost manhandled me through the door.

Werid was in full splendour, their cloak sewn from strips of alternating short-haired pelts—some silver, some in pale gold—and they wore their running-wolf clasp again, a not-so-subtle hint to the exceptional position they held in town. The silver circlet sat on their brow, their hair streaming out behind them like a glossy cape. Their hands were warmed by fur-lined gloves embroidered with spiral patterns and their breath was like a shimmering cloud around them.

"Sloe Moon of Tall Trees," they called to me, their deep voice silencing the men privileged to witness their display.

I bowed and went across the trampled snow to meet them in the middle of the square.

They took my wrists in a greeting that was clearly meant to look ritualistic. "How are they treating you?" they asked urgently. "Are you well?"

"I am well. Apart from the fact that no one tells me anything and I haven't had news from town since I arrived here."

They kissed my left cheek, then the right. "The Ravens have left the council," they muttered under their breath. "Qerla is very unhappy with your aunt."

"But if the Ravens left, why am I still here?"

The ring of spectators closed in on us and they decided not to answer me. "I am here to summon you to attend tomorrow's meeting to testify against the Clouds. We will send someone to collect you."

"The Clouds? I almost forgot about that."

"This is why you are here in Goldenlake."

"Why did you summon me, Werid? Why didn't Sjunil come to see me?"

"Because she didn't trust herself. She was quite upset when she found out that they make you live in the House of Men." Their gloved fingers closed around my naked hand. "I can only imagine how you must feel. The gods will understand that you had no choice in this matter."

I felt myself smiling at them in relief. "I had hoped for this."

"The gods can be pragmatic when it suits them," they promised. Their left hand slipped into the cloak and pulled out a necklace woven from golden wire, a thick rope from which dangled a single freshwater pearl. "To bind you even closer to Brother Brook," they said. "Kneel, Sloe."

The snow crunched underneath me when I obeyed their command. It was the most extravagant of gifts, a reminder to my captors that I was of worth to the families around them. They pulled the chain over my head and clasped it shut. The gold was still warm.

They kissed me again and bade me to stand up. "I will see you tomorrow."

"I heard about what happened." Tjal moved slowly as he opened the pin that kept his shabby cloak fastened, took off the felted hood, and put it on a hook to dry off. "Can you show it to me?"

I pulled the pearl into the last light of the dying fire.

"It's beautiful," he said quietly. "The tale spread through Goldenlake within the hour. To be honest, it's smaller than I expected. Are you worried about tomorrow?"

"Of course."

"Olas will go with you. He can't wait to see the wizards again."

"I would rather you'd come."

"I have a whole list of tasks to do, but I wish I could hear you speak to them." He arranged his blankets, then put his left elbow on the mattress and supported his head while he studied my face. My heart picked up its pace. I wished for nothing more than to not have to wait for full darkness to descend, until everyone else was fast asleep. I pushed my left hand under his blanket and touched his side. His right hand found mine, hidden from view. Our fingers folded into each other.

"What did you do today?" I asked.

"Found someone willing to sell us bacon and nuts. Tried to buy some goats to keep us going over the winter. Checked that the smoked fish we ordered is ready to be packed and sent over and that the horses are kept well and exercised while we wait. Nothing very important."

I squeezed his hand. "And still the most important thing of all—taking care of your companions, even if they don't have the manners to be as grateful as they should be. Have you eaten?"

"There wasn't much time."

"You will run yourself into the ground, Tjal."

The last flame in the brazier went out as I spoke, leaving only the embers aglow, and a deep shadow fell over us. He pulled my head under the blanket, and we finally kissed again, so tenderly that my skin began to tingle from the toes to the tip of my nose. I could feel him burning with want, but he didn't try to put his hand down my trousers. Instead, he groaned as my tongue touched his, when my fingers fumbled at his tunic and managed to push it up enough to reach his bare skin. We had to be quiet, we had to wait, but I felt him shiver against me. I tried to slow my breathing, to not catch fire just yet. He caressed my back, over the cloth of my own tunic, a steady movement as if he wanted to calm me down, but his left hand reached his smallclothes and loosened them just enough. I found him hard and ready as I cupped his pebbles. Our kiss broke apart as he gasped. I left my hand there, but didn't try to excite him further. It was painful to stall our coming together, every heartbeat rattled me, every breath shook me. He started to move against my hand, pressing into me in desperation.

"Please." He said it so softly that I almost didn't hear him. "*Please*."

I started to stroke him. He only lasted a couple of moments. His spine tensed as he came but he didn't make a single sound. I'd spent the last years sharing the Other House in Tall Trees with a married couple; I knew the noises and their specific meanings, and Saon had always been rather loud in his enjoyment. It felt weird not to hear him at all. I wiped my fingers on the inside of his trousers and held him against my chest, not expecting anything else from him but to feel him fall asleep. After a few moments, I noticed that he tried to pull away enough to move his hands over me; he touched the inside of my thigh, dangerously close. I had to bite into my lips not to cry out, guided his hand. It was all too apparent that I was the one bringing more experience into our bed, but he let me show him and he kissed my neck as he finished me off almost as quickly as I had him.

When I woke up later, as I'd become used to doing, I found him waiting for me again and wiggled out of my trousers to give him access. He fucked me with as little movement as we could manage, his hand clamped around my mouth, his face buried in my hair so that his breath steamed into me.

Of course, I could hide nothing for even half a day from Qes.

"Tell me," he said at breakfast when I waited for Olas to appear and take me to the Roundhouse.

I felt the blood rush to my face. "Later."

"You look as if it was fun."

"It was fun," I confirmed, and his eyes lit up. I held up two fingers and he smiled approvingly. We'd never had that kind of coded conversation about him and Julas, and I was glad of it, given how that interlude had worked itself out. But Qes and Julas had been two young men without other attachments and free to follow their wishes, and I wasn't, if I wanted my throat to remain un-slit and to keep Tjal out of trouble.

I'd combed my hair and bound it back in a braid. The pearl shone enticingly against my blue cloak, but Olas just had to top it. When the curtains were pulled back, we saw him in a carefully brushed cloak of the deepest, most expensive black, even finer than the one Saon had dyed for Mother, sporting a bejewelled clasp fit to rival Werid's wolf. We all understood that they were the one he competed with, though maybe he wanted to impress my aunt as well, ten years married or not.

"Are you ready?" he asked, pulling on his black gloves.

"Yes." I put the rest of my porridge down and followed him out into the snow.

Goldenlake seemed impossibly clean with all its dirty, untidy corners hidden by white drifts. We picked up quite a few followers on our way across town, people who knew who I was, when no one had given me a second glance before.

The lake itself was buried under ice and a thin blanket of snow, moved into patterns by the wind that rasped at my skin and bit into the tips of my ears. I kept behind Olas. Two other men from the house walked after me. One of them was the second snorer, built like a boar, all shoulders and no noticeable neck. Though he only came up to my chin, he could've broken every bone in my body, and it didn't make much sense to try and get away.

Werid had been right: it was why I'd come to Goldenlake in the first place, before everything had been changed by unforeseen events. If I'd had the opportunity to marry into the Clouds, I would have never found myself folded into Tjal's embrace, feeling him wrapped around me, so I was ready to accept a heartfelt apology and move the fuck on. Sjunil would never have allowed me to shrug off the affront, however. We'd both taken too much on to ensure that I would be heard and compensated accordingly.

As we reached the centre square, other people were lining the road and with a jolt I recognized the prince, standing unbound next to Julas, who looked more than ever like his personal guard. Ileon—no, Nivael—wore a cap of white fur, his long hair hanging around his face, and he held the bandaged hand up against his chest in a gesture that almost looked like a wizard's blessing. He didn't smile; his eyes were narrowed and his whole expression unfriendly. Julas nodded at me, but I ignored him. I'd spotted Werid next to the Roundhouse, with Qerla and a new wizard, a tall man of austere demeanour who wore a pin made from mother-of-pearl on his silver-grey goat hair shawl. A shiver ran down my back.

I hadn't expected a wizard of the Clouds to be present.

A BETTER CANDIDATE

The smell of incense was so overpowering that I had to suppress a sneeze when I entered the building. Sjunil stood at the side of the central table, her arms behind her back, and I suddenly realized that she held herself because her first instinct had been to rush over and hug me. Instead, she stepped towards me slowly.

"Did you see him outside?" she asked.

I nodded.

"There will be more of them, just so that you are warned."

"Why?"

She looked angry. "Because the Ravens made such a stink about leaving the council that the Clouds must have gotten worried about being misrepresented in their absence. It won't be a problem," she promised.

"He didn't seem too happy to see me."

"He just hates everyone."

"That doesn't help!"

My aunt pulled up her left shoulder. "What makes you think I was trying to help?"

"Because it is your job?"

"Is it?"

"Why would we need wizards at all if they weren't helpful in calling in favours with the gods?"

Something slipped in her face, an unfettered expression of endless dread. "Have you had the impression that they've regarded me with kindness lately?" she asked, barely audible.

I took her shoulder, more muscular than expected under the chequered blanket. "They will again."

"I hope they'll listen to you, at least."

We both turned around as heated words were exchanged behind us. A group of men had tried to enter the house and been stalled by the apprentices. They all wore silver-grey cloaks and their hair clipped close to their skull, like five versions of the same person. The effect was striking. They all carried a single amulet cut from bleached wood: the likeness of Brother Rain. The tallest of them pushed through and came closer, handsome but for the severe haircut.

"It is our right to present our own arguments," he growled at my aunt.

She held up her hands, palms turned towards him. "Be my fucking guest," she said.

Qerla Badger, astonishingly quickly for someone her age, came after him, lifted her staff and tapped him between the shoulder blades. "You will wait your turn, Cathil Cloud."

I stared at him in dismay. But for a few twists and turns, he could've been my husband.

Taking a step back, I couldn't resist mumbling a quick 'thank you' to Brother Brook. From the way he sneered down at the elderly wizard, it was all too clear that he was a proud man, even arrogant, and my gaze was drawn down to the longknife strapped to his belt. Next to him, Julas looked like a frightened piglet. Cathil Cloud was what a warrior was supposed to be, and I couldn't help but recoil from him.

"Off to your seat," Qerla directed, not backing down. Her staff pointed at a couple of benches prepared by the apprentices.

I noticed that the tables had been arranged differently than the last time I'd attended; they were laid out in a half-circle. More people streamed into the Roundhouse, all the wizards and the other four Clouds, probably Cathil's brothers. The Cloud wizard took Cathil by the elbow and steered him away from the tables.

Urgent whispers came from his lips, as if he was scolding the young man for his misconduct. For a heartbeat, Sjunil touched my wrist.

"Good luck," she said.

When we'd started our journey, I'd spent a lot of time thinking about how to best present my case to the council, how to explain the situation without sounding insulted and bitter, pushed aside and rejected. But then I really had forgotten about it. I clasped the pearl Werid had fastened around my neck the previous day and sought them out.

They sat next to my aunt, quite far away from me, and nodded encouragingly as I started to speak to the council, desperately wishing that Qes were with me, or Tjal, or even the Prince of Crooked Hill, just to have someone around me I actually knew.

Most marriage negotiations started off in the same way among the families: an offer was prepared and brought before the head of the other family, usually without the prospective spouses being aware of the process. But I was my mother's child, someone with the chance of joining her government one day and rising to a position of influence. No one had expected the negotiations to fail; it had been a surprise for everyone, a shock that an offer so profitable could be refused.

I tried to keep my voice steady and ignore the displeased expression on the face of our wizard, to convey Mother's words without negating the insults she'd hissed at the messenger. "We fear that the consequences resulting from these actions will put many of our cousins in the most awkward of positions when the Clouds will force them to choose between honouring the ancient alliances and falling prey to false promises from the western families. We wish the council to decide on how this unfortunate situation could best be avoided to maintain the peace in the east and please the gods who, in their wisdom and mercy, have been known to be somewhat impatient with our tendency to ignore the bigger picture. Therefore, we ask to be considered for compensation, to prove that the many marriages between the Moons and the Clouds that were once forged, are still being celebrated as the closest of bonds, and loyalties will not have to be divided from now on." My mouth was as dry as ash as I bowed and stepped back.

Qerla sniffed. "It is unusual to send the person whose hand was refused," she said. "But the council appreciates the difficulties arising from these circumstances." She looked around. "Any thoughts? Cirvi?"

The Cloud wizard sucked at his teeth. "This decision was not rashly made. It was well considered."

"That's even worse!" my aunt yelled across the table. "If you meant to cause hurt and confusion, how can you not see that this is worse?"

"The Moons have lost their good name," Cirvi replied stiffly. "There comes a time when even the oldest of ties have to be cut and new ways found. A better candidate was offered."

My aunt was completely still. "A better candidate?" she repeated. "Such as?"

Cirvi made a gesture towards the benches behind me. I heard the wood creak and then Cathil Cloud stood next to me. "I was married a month ago," he confirmed. "To a Mouse." He looked at me. "He is very beautiful."

"Congratulations," I managed to choke out and for a weird moment he smiled at me, before continuing.

"It will not be long before we will join his family at the coast. They are offering new possibilities for the Clouds to increase their influence over this land with their network of contacts."

"You mean their network of contacts among the men from the Cities," Werid said.

He shrugged his broad shoulders. "They have made camp at the coast, but this is hardly news."

Sjunil pressed her palms into the edges of the table. "But it tells us how they wish to play the game," she said, her voice scornful. "It tells us what the Clouds consider to be an advantage in the years to come. They will make themselves rich and push us others out of their way, ashamed of the traditions kept in the east."

"We will be in good company," Cirvi said. "They have been with us for a while—they will not go away."

"They won't think twice to sell you out if there is profit in it for them. Ask Sloe themself—they have experienced life among them."

Cathil Cloud rubbed over his cropped hair. "Have you really?" he asked me, and I nodded without turning to him. "And is this what you think of them?"

I had to close my eyes. "It is what I fear from them," I confessed. "There are certain things they don't understand, some things their own gods don't allow them to do. They won't approve of your choice of husband, for example."

"They will when they see him."

"No, they won't. They will feel revulsion and distress. They will call you unnatural and perverted."

A deep line had appeared between Cirvi's brows. "They would not dare."

"They are not interested in the laws of the families—they accept only their own gods and will despise everyone who is not prepared to follow them in their faith. I don't think they even realize what wizards do."

A shocked silence spread over the room, but I saw the sly grin that Sjunil quickly hid behind her hands.

Qerla stomped her staff again. "The council will decide on an appropriate compensation for the Moons, now that Cathil Cloud has been married and is no longer available to right this wrong. We will meet again late this afternoon—just us wizards," she added, and I felt my shoulders relax.

Cathil Cloud grunted. "For fuck's sake." He gave me a little shove. "It wasn't personal, you know."

I tried to take a deep breath. "That's not what this is about."

"What then? I would have bedded you, no problem." His eyes slid down to my boots and up again. "If that's what you're fretting about."

I felt the tips of my ears pulse. "Thanks, but no thanks."

His eyes narrowed. "I have won our summer competitions in all recent years."

"And I'm sure your husband loves you for your prowess." I had to bite my tongue. Sjunil certainly was a bad influence on me.

He scoffed. "Why all this … whining? This is a tremendous waste of time."

"It's the principle. And it wasn't my idea to come, if you must know. Mother sent me to complain."

"You certainly made the most of your mission."

I laughed, mainly because I was relieved that it was over. "Given that you expect to profit so much from your husband's connections, you won't miss a few bags of silver," I said. "It's probably for the best after all."

The sky had cleared while I'd spoken to the council and when I came into the centre square, the sun glittered on the snow drifts and icicles around me. Children were building snow lanterns between the houses—a whole row of them; they'd let water freeze overnight between wooden bowls and stood oil lights in the transparent domes. My heart felt strangely elated while I watched them, as if I'd escaped from a trap at the very last breath. I only noticed then that Olas was waiting for me a few steps away, standing next to his prince, and my stomach twisted. For a few precious moments, I'd believed myself to be free.

Since I'd spotted them, the two men from the Cities came across the square to meet me with Julas not too far away. The negotiator turned towards the prince. The man I still thought of as Ileon wiped his hair out of his face with the bandaged hand.

"How was it?" he asked me.

"Exciting. I met the man I would have married." I said it to scandalize both of them, but the prince managed to keep his expression blank while Olas looked positively horrified.

"And how did you find him?" the prince asked.

"He's *so* not my type."

Ileon grinned at me, something I hadn't expected. He suddenly looked a lot younger. "All is well that ends well," he said.

"Is it?"

The prince cleared his throat. "You look fine. I hope they treat you as one of our own."

"They try." I shrugged. "How's the shoulder?"

"Your sister is happy with it and so I must be as well." He poked at his cloak. "Though I feel the cold, especially at night. There will be scars to boast about once I have returned home."

Olas made a little noise, as if he wanted to bring him off this particular topic, and I squinted against the sun. "Can we go to the lake for a bit? I think I need to pray."

Ileon pointed his chin at my chest. "Your Brother Brook?"

"I need to offer him my gratitude for today. I never realized how deeply I'm indebted to him."

"I will come with you." The prince held up his hand as Olas prepared to talk him out of it. "Without discussing it any further."

THE BEST OF THEM

"He did what?" Qes and Tjal asked at the same time.

"He stood next to me and watched me pray. I tried to make it quick because the wind was so bitterly cold, and he started to get a bit antsy after a while."

We sat around the table in the House of Men, sharing a platter of cold chicken and cheese-filled flatbreads. Qati had brought a packet of honeyfudge that had already been plundered by the men, a rare treat. I'd snuck a few bites into my mouth, a reward for all the things I'd survived that day.

"Why would he do that?" Tjal sounded distressed over the possibility of his prince taking an interest in gods that didn't belong to him.

"He is of the curious sort," Qes said and gulped down some tea, long since gone cold.

"None of you have known him long." Tjal started to scratch at a splinter sticking up from the top of the table. "He never does anything just to satisfy a whim. If he wanted to see you pray, he had a very specific reason for it." He winced and pulled the splinter from his finger. "Fuck. Ouch." He put the finger in his mouth to suck the tiny drop of blood from it and I felt my whole body react in anticipation.

Qes looked worried. "Do you really think they will ask the Clouds to pay you off with silver?"

"To be honest, I don't care. Sjunil will name her price. I bet Mother instructed her thoroughly before we left." My eyes were fixed on Tjal. Something was bothering him.

Later, when we found each other in the darkness, he made me come with his mouth and hands but declined when I offered the same to him, though I could feel his cock prodding me for a long time before it eventually softened. I waited for him to talk to me, but he kept stubbornly silent.

In the morning, I saw him speaking to Olas while he was pulling on his boots. It was one of the days when all the men were restless and constantly running in and out of the house, so that the floor became muddy from the snow they dragged in. The heat coming off the fire in the brazier had no chance against the gusts wafting through the open door. Qes and Qati were included in those activities, and it didn't look as if anyone was preparing a shared meal anytime soon, so I grabbed an apple and a bit of stale bread and crawled back onto the platform. At least the blankets smelled of Tjal, of us, even if something had changed, something I didn't know about. I fell asleep, wrapped up in everything I could find.

Qes woke me up at dusk, when they returned to the house. "The stew is almost ready." His hand was cold as he touched my face. "You feel feverish."

"I'm fine," I mumbled, though my head felt like a basket of greasy wool clippings and I had a bad taste in my mouth. "I need to go for a pee."

"Someone will take you before we eat."

"Where is Tjal?"

"Not here yet."

The second snorer was on watch duty when I left the house. The wind slapped me. It would be a clear night; I already saw stars glimmering in a sky that wore stripes of different colours bleeding into each other, golden and blood red and purple and blue. While I laced up my trousers again, I leant my forehead against the wall, desperate for something to hold me up. The snorer took me by the shoulder, as if he'd seen how much strength it suddenly cost me to keep upright. As we turned around, two men were walking across the square. One of them was Tjal. Frost covered his hood.

"What's wrong?" he hissed at the second snorer.

"I don't feel so good," I sputtered, before doubling over and puking over his boots.

"How much beer did you let them have?" he barked at my guard.

"He slept all day."

"*They* slept all day," Tjal said and even with ropes of bile and snot hanging out of me that felt good. Tjal's fingers pressed into my neck, trying to hold back my hair. "And this didn't seem odd to you?"

"We all had better things to do than to keep an eye on your fat …" and then he used a word I didn't know, but I felt Tjal's body tense.

I picked up a handful of snow to wipe my face. The inside of my throat and nose were burning and my stomach gave another lurch, though I was able to keep it down, while the two men glared at each other in the twilight.

"We were charged with keeping them healthy and alive," Tjal said.

"I suppose that includes fucking his brains out? Good for some. Not all of us are as blind as Olas. You're lucky that no one really gives a shit about you, Tjal." He turned away and left us alone.

Tjal's fingers were still at my neck but he had frozen in place.

"It will be fine," I said around a bit of snow to wash my mouth out.

"No, it won't."

"It didn't sound as if he was planning to do anything about it."

"He will come up with a lot of favours he needs me to do for him to keep his mouth shut."

"What was the word he used for me?"

"I'm not going to repeat it. I never want you to have to hear it again." He tenderly tucked a strand of sweaty hair behind my left ear. "How are you feeling now?"

"A bit better."

"Have you felt ill all day?"

"I don't know. Something was off, though. Probably something I ate."

"I thought you didn't eat."

"I don't know, Tjal. What can I say to make you feel less afraid?"

"It's my fault," he said. "I should have never allowed myself to start this."

I didn't even try my luck on the stew but went straight back to bed; at some point Tjal crawled in as well but kept his distance. Maybe he didn't want to come too close to me while I was feeling unwell or perhaps he was too aware of the others listening. I might have just smelled bad. I wanted his arms around me but was too tired to do anything about it. At least my stomach kept its peace, and I didn't have to dash out again.

When the men started to move around the house, I noticed that Tjal was still there, his back turned towards me, with careful space left between us. When I leant over him, his face was flushed and I saw a puddle of puke on the floor beside him. I climbed over him, stumbled to the water bucket, and smashed the ice that had formed on its surface during the night. I wet a cloth and pressed it to his flaming cheeks.

"I must've made him ill," I said and Qati appeared next to me, trying to scrape the vomit off the clay.

"His eyes are all shiny," he remarked.

I nodded. "He's burning up. I want someone to fetch my sister and her herbs."

Qati looked unhappy. "But this is the House of Men."

"If I can live here, Siw can come visit," I snapped back. "She is the best healer I know."

It took a while for Qati to find her in town and she was deeply annoyed when she arrived.

"I had to talk myself out of today's meeting," she said. "You look fine."

"It's not me." I took her by the arm and pulled her into the house. She gasped in dismay when she saw the chaos around us. "How can you live like this?"

"Not voluntarily," I reminded her. "He's over here. I was feeling horrible yesterday but today I'm much better. I don't think I was as feverish as he is now, but I must've given it to him. He's the one I share my bed with."

She pushed me aside and told Qati to drop the basket he'd carried for her next to the platform. "Open his tunic, Sloe."

I fumbled with the laces. His chest was deeply flushed, and she sighed. "Just as I thought. They're not used to the illnesses that we can shrug off," she explained. "I've seen a few other cases around town, but they recover quickly, like you. Apparently, it happens every winter, when everyone stays mostly indoors and close together." She snapped her fingers at Qati. "Hot water," she commanded. "Sit down, Sloe," she added, as Qati left us. She lowered her voice. "They said you would be cared for, treated like an honourable guest, and I find you living in filth and sick. Do they give you enough to eat?"

"I'm eating as well as the rest of them," I said diplomatically.

"They don't misuse you?" She stared down at Tjal who was buried into our grimy blankets. "He doesn't ... doesn't hurt you?"

"No. He's the best of them." I wiped the sweat from his forehead, and she seemed alarmed by the gesture.

"You can't fall in love with him," she hissed. "Not again—you need to keep your heart in check, Sloe, only for a few more days, until you will be able to leave this house and hopefully never see them again."

Qati came back, carrying a bowl of steaming water. She went to work, steeping the herbs, mashing dried fruits, and mixing them up with lard to make a plaster that she stuck to Tjal's chest with a piece of ripped cloth. "Turn him over so I can knot the ends." She grimaced. "How can you stand the stench of them?"

I stroked Tjal's neck to soothe him, his hair lank and greasy beneath my fingers. "I hated it at the beginning, but I've become used to it. He's lovely, Siw—really."

She huffed in the older-sister-who-always-knows-best sort of way she had and that I'd hated as long as I could remember. "You should be more sensible by now." She pushed him onto his back again and he shivered in my lap, sweat beading his naked shoulders. "You'll want to marry one day, won't you?"

"What's that supposed to mean?"

She turned around to rummage through her basket. "Only that you don't want to get stuck on a man who will jump back on his ship and leave next year. He's not someone who you could ever consider."

"Ah, fuck off."

She prepared a mixture of herbs, divided into portions. "Have him drink this, morning and evening. I would expect him to get better tomorrow but if he keeps throwing up, you need to make him drink plenty of water." She looked thoughtful. "I heard that the Clouds had someone sick in their quarter. Maybe you caught it off them?"

"This quickly? I only spent a little while with them."

She shrugged. "But he came quite close to you at one point."

I tasted bile again. I'd been so glad to get away from Cathil Cloud... I felt Tjal's fever through my clothes. "Do you think he'll die?"

Siw took my chin in her hand and made me look at her. "Do you really love him?"

"I might come to do so," I confessed.

"In that case, I'm sure he'll recover."

I stared at her in horror. "What would you've said if I'd lied?"

She stood up and pulled the basket into her arms. "That there is no way of telling. He's the first of them who caught it. If there are more in the next few days, you can let me know and I'll send more herbs for them."

The others kept well away from us; suddenly we had the luxury of space. Even Qes seemed nervous when he approached the platform with a bowl of cabbage soup and a spoon.

"How is he?"

"He's quieter than before. Is that bad?"

"Here—eat."

I gratefully pulled the bowl towards me. "Thank you. Did you speak to the others?"

"They are afraid. If Tjal isn't able to run around, they will have to learn to fend for themselves—no one is particularly keen on that. Let me know if you need help." He left to let me eat my soup.

With Tjal out cold, our situation would quickly become worse and the supplies dwindle. Maybe they'd learn to respect him, but chances were that they'd just resent him for getting ill. I continued to wipe him down, trying to get him to drink Siw's evil-smelling concoction. She'd probably added something to make him sleep; he didn't shift all night. I monitored his breathing constantly, for fear he might just slip away. The thought of him dying an arm's length away kept me awake and when the first light crept into the house, I was so exhausted that I could barely hold the drinking bowl steady to dribble Siw's medicine into him. When I pressed my hand against his skin, he felt a bit cooler to the touch.

"Is he still alive?" Olas stood at the other wall, as far away from us as possible.

"Yes. He might even be doing better."

"We will not forget this," the negotiator promised, but it sounded more like a threat.

THE DEBT IS SETTLED

Tjal didn't speak for five days. Siw's tea kept him eerily calm. However, none of the other men fell ill, which meant on the one hand the relief was palpable, and on the other I was identified as the source and no one wanted to come too close to me anymore. I felt safer among them and at the same time worried about being considered cursed by the men I lived with. Siw visited once more. They all gave her a wide berth, murmuring fearful words behind her back.

"What is wrong with them?" she asked while making the ingredients for a new plaster.

"They think you're a very powerful woman, Siw."

She pressed lard into the paste with more force than was strictly necessary. "I'm not planning on turning anyone into a toad. Yet." She glowered at the men who huddled at the other end of the house. "You looked after him well," she said. "I think he might survive after all. To be honest, I didn't hold much hope when I left you to it." She touched Tjal's forehead. "He feels much cooler. I won't make the next batch of tea as strong, so he'll be able to move and eat more." She reached her stained hand across to me to squeeze my fingers. "I'm happy for you, Sloe."

I felt my bottom lip quiver and wasn't able to stifle a sob of relief. Staring at Tjal's silent face for five days had given me ample time to understand that I didn't want him to die, even if my heart hadn't quite followed his yet. Siw kneaded my shoulder as I wept for him, drawing uncomfortable looks from the other men.

"Bad news?" Qes asked, coming over to us.

She shook her head. "No, good news. At least, it seems like that today. Let them know, would you?"

Qes went away without hugging me.

I heard him speak to the others and then Olas appeared, still with a fair bit of distance. "We should reimburse you for your troubles," he said to my sister.

She made a dismissive gesture. "Don't worry about it."

"There is a saying we have in the Cities, 'never owe a debt to a witch'." He bowed to her.

She looked at me. "What the fuck is a witch?"

"I think he means a wizard."

She flushed with pleasure. "I'm just the apprentice and still need to work for years until they promote me."

"Will you accept a token of our gratitude, even so?" He held out his palm and three coins glinted in the dim light, stamped with faces and wondrous to behold.

"Are those your gods?" she asked suspiciously.

"No, our kings. This is the father of our prince." His index finger stabbed at the biggest coin of them, at a broad, bearded face. Not pretty, but powerful.

"Thank you. They will make a beautiful necklace."

He nodded approvingly. "The debt is settled?"

"It is," she confirmed, not a little smugly.

He bowed a last time to her and retreated.

She let the coins click against each other in her hand. "I understand why Sjunil likes him so much. He is the only one of them with manners. I should go. She acted weird when I said I would stop by and see you. Take care, Sloe, and get some sleep. You look like shit."

"Sloe?" His voice was raspy from disuse, his cracked lips rough against mine. He waited for me to stir, then kissed me properly.

He felt thinner, his ribs much more pronounced as I wrapped my arms around him, neither of us caring what our housemates heard and thought about us. He smelled like herbs and hot lard, and his skin was sticky from the plaster treatments, but I held him, rocking him against me.

"I couldn't bear the thought of losing you," I said and we both cried.

When he slipped out of bed in the morning, the others stared at him as if he'd come back from the land of the dead. Qes stirred an extra lump of butter into the porridge and Olas ruffled Tjal's hair as he passed by.

"He will be pleased," he promised and Tjal nodded, his mouth full of buttery porridge, the spoon already back on its way for more. When he left the house for a short walk to the bucket, Qes slid onto the bench next to me.

"It needs to stop," he said bluntly. "They won't tolerate much more of this. Everyone knows now—Olas tried to argue for you, but they won't listen to him. This is how they explain the fact that none of the others fell ill, Sloe. They won't risk more bad luck." He moved his broad shoulders as if to shield me. "I know that this isn't what you want to hear, but we need to be sensible about what they can accept and what they can't. You're putting yourself in danger. And him, most of all."

"Why can't they just learn? It's not that hard to grasp, surely?" I punched the sheep's fleece I sat on.

"They haven't come here to learn. Did Siw actually accept their money?"

"She did."

"Did she say anything about the others? I can't wait to go back to the guesthouse, even with Julas around. I wish they would bring us back. As soon as the worst of the snow is over, we could ride home. Do you miss Tall Trees?"

"I think so. I haven't really thought much about Mother and Silid lately. I haven't figured out what to tell them about this experience. Do you think they will be very angry?"

He smiled. "I think they will be proud."

They allowed me to take Tjal for a stroll down the road the next day, when the sun was out again.

"I want to see the lake," he said when we left the Quarter of the Bear.

"They didn't give us permission to walk that far."

"Fuck them."

It took us a long time to get there and Tjal, who'd spent most of his stay in Goldenlake hurrying through town on never-ending errands, became slower and slower, then had to take a pause at a corner and wait to catch his breath. Around us stood snow lanterns, though it was too early for the lights in them to be lit.

"I love these," Tjal panted. "I will never forget them, even if I'm back in the Cities."

"When do you plan to leave?"

"I don't know. There are still so many things that can go wrong. If you haven't noticed by now, our prince is a very stubborn man, and he doesn't appreciate having to wait for the snow to melt. I'm not looking forward to it, Sloe." He pressed the inside of my arm. "Let's go on."

All along the shoreline the boats had been lined up, turned over and built into a low wall, but there were people on the ice, pulling narrow sledges behind them with axes and fishing rods. Some had strapped filed bones to their boots and glided over the frozen lake, and a long line of snow lanterns pointed towards the horizon. There might even be people adventurous enough to try and cross the Golden Lake on foot. I wondered how long it would take them, how long it would've taken me if I'd just started walking towards the east.

We heard drums and flutes and Tjal buried his face in my cloak before he said, "I need to sit down."

I brought him over to the wall of boats and he collapsed, his knees visibly shaking.

"This is my favourite time of the year."

I spun around and saw Werid of the Far Side pick their way over the frozen pebbles. They wore a silver fox fur cap and their hair in a long braid down their back, closed with a golden clasp. I already knew their cloak; it was the stripey one.

"I hadn't expected to meet you here, Sloe."

"I'm not alone."

"So I see." They took my wrists and kissed my cheeks. "How's the invalid?"

Tjal managed to hold up a hand but didn't answer.

"He needs to gather his strength for the way back."

"You know that someone followed you both?"

I shrugged. "I expected as much." But my shoulders prickled. I hadn't even thought of that.

"You won't come with me? Out onto the ice?"

I shook my head. "Better not. They might think I wanted to escape across the lake."

Werid laughed. "They probably would. But it won't be long until they will release you. I could use your help with your aunt. Did they tell you what she said to Cathil Cloud?"

"What did she say?" I asked, horrified.

"I think she wanted to provoke him into doing something stupid. I won't repeat it, not with all those people around. Let's say she wasn't very happy with their first offer of compensation."

"I'm missing all the exciting stuff," I grumbled.

"I almost wish the Ravens were back. As far as I remember, none of them liked Cirvi Cloud very much the last time he attended the council. It will be so boring when I am back home."

"But you will see your wife again."

They smiled at me. "That is the silver lining." They used their right thumb to point at Tjal. "What's going on with you two?"

"He says he's starting to fall in love with me."

"Oh." They took a deep breath. "That is nice. But you know that things will be difficult for you?"

"They are already difficult. Qes tells me every day that we can't keep doing it. I just want a few more days with him. Why does nobody understand that?"

Werid pulled their right glove off and touched my face. Their hand was so warm that it felt as if it was singeing me, and their smile sad and small. "I understand," they promised. "But you need to live your own life again, even if you feel guilty that you brought sickness into their house." They turned around. "I will see you soon."

We didn't speak much on our way back. We'd come roughly halfway when Tjal started to limp. "I can try and carry you," I offered.

"Don't you dare—I would never hear the end of it. It will be fine, I just need to slow down a bit more." He leant heavily on me, and I kept him upright as best as I could. We made a spectacle of ourselves. Children started running up and down the road, trying to throw snowballs at us, until the second snorer, who had indeed followed us, lost his patience, closed in on us, and took Tjal's other arm to drag him into the Quarter of the Bear.

Tjal didn't thank him when the man let go of him in front of the door; he looked flustered and ashamed. Inside, we sat close to the brazier to warm ourselves and dry off our cloaks and caps, but we still didn't talk. We listened to the others, to their jokes and complaints about the food, how much they longed for dishes served only in the Cities, extraordinary fruits and a spice so hot that it burned right through your tongue. They played that game from time to time, when they tried to imagine the best meal of their lives, but they didn't ask Tjal to join in with them.

Dinner was cabbage soup again, though Qes had managed to find some bacon for it, and everyone dreamt of cakes and roasts, nut pastes and honeyed fruits, baked eggs and fresh herbs tossed in a sweet sauce. They talked themselves hungrier and even the skin of fermented milk couldn't find their favour. Qati, Qes, and I finished that off between us and I had to burp a few times before going to bed. Tjal followed a short while after.

He didn't even wait for the fire to die down before he pulled me close, his face in the back of my neck. His hands crossed over my chest, though we tried not to move too much until the others had turned in. I burrowed my hand between his legs and when I finally decided to roll over him it was so dark that I could barely make out his face.

It took me a few tries until my mouth had found his. His hands were under my tunic, travelling up and down my naked back, his tongue far less gentle; I could feel his teeth against my lips and moaned. We went still, both afraid that I'd been heard, but nobody stirred around us and so I started to unlace him, my hands greedy, desperate for him after so many days. He let his head sink back, both hands pressed over his mouth as I found him, working around his pebbles until his hips bucked and I finally managed to get his trousers off, at least down to his knees. I saw his pale chest rapidly falling, heaving, falling as I spat into my hand to prepare him.

He yelped as I touched him, startling me enough to stop and he struggled up, panicked, to push another man off the bed. He wasn't quick enough, not strong enough, and then the pommel of a longknife hit me across the back of the head.

BOOK TWO

SHADOWS AS DEEP

The first thing that floated past me was pain—a curiously detached pain, as if it happened to another person. My back was bent at a strange angle, my wrists bound around the neck of the horse carrying me away from Goldenlake. They'd strapped me to the saddle; with each step my head was thrown against the shoulder of the sweaty animal, its coat poking into my mouth in salty tufts. Starlight glittered on the snow. We were moving slowly through the night, and probably in a direction no one expected. It would take time to discover what had happened and we'd be far away from the lake by then.

"Stop," came Tjal's muffled voice. "Stop, they are awake."

The horse came to a halt, and I heard someone jump to the ground, coming closer. Qati Badger loosened the rope that bound my hands in place, roughly pulled my arms behind me, and lashed them together. I could barely make out his face in the darkness as he pulled me down again and dragged a strip of cloth that had been fastened around my neck over my mouth.

On the horse next to mine, Tjal was trussed up in a similar way. Blood had dried on his face and held his own gag in place. His eyes were wide as he stared at me; fear steamed off him like breath. Qati gave me a pat on the leg and shoved me upright again. It was impossible to see if we'd brought Qes with us; there were trees all around and shadows as deep as the night skies. My head was throbbing where they'd hit me. I could feel the clumps in my hair where blood had run into it and caked the strands together, and my mouth felt sore. I'd bitten my tongue at some point.

The horse started to move again, and I had to press my eyes shut. We pushed on for hours and hours, until the first light crept through the forest and I could see a lot of horses in front and others behind us. We were among more men than I'd ever seen grouped together in town, but from what I could tell, Tjal and I were the only ones bound to our mounts. It was difficult to orientate myself—every bit of forest looked the same to me. Pack horses laboured through the snow, roped together and laden with supplies. My horse was fastened to the last of them, as if I was no more than luggage to bring along.

Tjal swayed in his saddle beside me; they'd wrapped him up in the blankets they'd caught us in. They'd hurt him. He'd been in such bad shape already, before the attack, that my throat contracted in fear. At least it looked as if he wasn't the one who'd betrayed me.

We moved southwards, that much I was able to make out; as far as I knew, there'd been no talk of them turning up on the south coast. Perhaps it was a distraction, and we'd correct our route to go westwards soon enough. Whatever they'd planned for us, it made little sense that they'd thought to bring me along. It would've been much easier to kill me and leave me behind. Maybe that was what happened to Qes? My throat tightened again as I tried not to cry. Qes would have never joined them without resistance; he would have never let me be hoisted into the saddle without trying to fight them, after all he'd done to feed them and keep the house clean …

The day developed a dull grey sky; tiny flakes of snow were blown from the trees around us and melted into the cloth covering my mouth. Every step the horse took was agony. All the men must've been utterly exhausted and I was praying to Brother Brook to let them rest before long.

We entered a steep valley, where cliffs of rock jutted from the soil. The path climbed downwards, almost too difficult for the horses to manage, and then we arrived under a long stony overhang, as sheltered from the weather as it was possible to be in the forest. It was difficult to imagine that the men from the Cities had found the place by themselves.

As the horse finally stopped, I slumped over its neck. Qati came to help us dismount, and the second snorer was with him, rough-handed and sneering. It was obvious that he would've been prepared to see both of us dead. My legs were shaking so much that I couldn't help falling against him and he stepped back with full deliberation, to let me collapse in the dirty snow. Tjal fell down next to me. He'd fainted, and I tried to pull him up.

"Get your hands off him." The man's boot caught me full on the chin and I heard my teeth smash into each other before the darkness jumped at me again.

When I came to, there was a fire not too far away from me; someone had dragged Tjal next to it but left me sprawled on the ground. The horses had been brought to another part of the shelter. A line of small fires stretched out before me, each serving a handful of men. My sight was a little blurry and I squeezed my eyes together a few times until I could be sure that the men who'd settled around the biggest fire weren't a hallucination.

The Prince of Crooked Hill noticed me staring at him in disbelief and came to his feet. He took his time to walk over, dressed in clothes he must've obtained from his followers; they were no longer in the style of the families, but he still wore the furry cap. The men at the fire closest to me made space for him to pass through. He went down on one knee before me, his yellow eyes never leaving my battered face.

"I hope I do not have to explain it to you," he said.

I tried to dislodge the cloth bound around my face with a shoulder. He bent forwards and pulled it down. It hurt because so much blood had dried into it.

"What did they do to Qes?"

"He was left behind."

"Dead?"

He shrugged. "I don't really care, Sloe. He never was part of the plan." He glanced over his shoulder and Cathil Cloud pushed one of his cousins out of the way to join us. He looked triumphant, as if all of it had been his idea alone.

"Still alive?" he smirked.

That had to be how they'd found the place; he must've led them all the way from the lake.

"Just about." I spat as much blood onto his boots as I could manage. "You know, this was a mistake."

"Was it?" The prince pulled the cloth back over my mouth. "I cannot see how, but I do not want to hear it from you." The crusts on the gag scratched my skin. "Get them to the fire," he commanded, and Cathil Cloud took me by the arm, nearly dislocating it until I managed to bring my feet under me. Whatever unholy alliance they'd entered into, the prince was sure to expect to be in full control. My head still wanted to make sense of it all but a lot of information was missing; I needed Qes, I desperately wanted him to tell me that he would always stand with me, even if I knew that his love for me had probably cost him his life.

I was pressed down next to Tjal again, who was little more than a heap of cloth on the ground. They must've kept him alive because he still held some kind of value for them. His dead brother had probably more to do with that, but it was strange to think that Ileon might have gone sentimental over me. I watched Cathil Cloud escort him back to his entourage and saw Olas standing up for him, glancing over at me. He seemed suitably troubled. If they'd bought the Elks, the Bears, and the Clouds, there was little chance for my own family to avenge me. As if anyone wanted to risk their life for the child of Qarim Badger.

Rations of dried meat were shared out and they tried to shake Tjal awake, but he stayed where he was; one of the men dropped my own allowance on the ground in front of me. I was able to push the cloth over my head, leaning forwards to try and pick the leathery strip up with my mouth. Someone laughed in disgust and shoved the meat between my teeth, so violently that it made me gag. I chewed my ration as slowly and thoroughly as possible. If Ileon wanted to let me feel as he'd felt when he was travelling with my aunt, I must bear it.

At some point one of them would have to start talking.

Thankfully, the second snorer didn't sleep around our fire and Qati, who'd been charged with watching over us, didn't object when I crept closer to Tjal to keep him warm. Qati's face was closed off, and I didn't hear him utter a single complaint. They changed watch a few times that night and always managed to wake me up so that I felt ready to drop when the next torturous day dawned. I was allowed to drink a little water and helped to keep Tjal upright enough so they could squirt some into his slack mouth. For breakfast, we had stale nutbread and more dried meat while the horses were made ready. The group operated with dreadful efficiency. The sun had barely risen as the horses were brought over.

They strapped Tjal down with his hands around his horse's neck. His head bounced up and down as if he was dead. It started snowing heavily almost as soon as we'd made our way out of the valley and back onto the ridge, where the path widened enough for three horses to walk abreast. The howling wind made everyone crouch in their saddles, and the horses stamped along with their heads held low. It was not the season to travel; no wonder that no other people were around, or maybe they went off the road and hid as soon as they realized the nature of the fellowship that approached them—the number of men with longknives buckled to their saddles. Anyone would've identified me and Tjal as prisoners.

I tried to keep my horse as close to his as possible; he'd watched over me, and I had to return the favour. The way he was bound to his horse made it harder for the animal to carry him and it snorted in irritation, continually trying to side-step and shake him off. Qati cursed and hit it with a hazel switch to subdue it. I started to hate Qati Badger even more. The fact that he was here and not clubbed down and left to die like our cousin said quite enough about him. No one held a knife to his throat; he'd followed the men from the Cities because he was hoping to be rewarded. As the horse bucked violently, I started to scream at him around my gag, trying to make the others aware of what was happening.

One of the Clouds turned his horse around and trotted back to us. "Put them on one horse," he barked at Qati, "then change horses every few hours." He helped to transfer Tjal in front of me, so I was responsible for keeping him up. At least my body would shelter him, and my arms were around him once again, even if the saddle was too small for us both and we were uncomfortably squashed together. I folded my right arm across his chest and held on to the horse's mane with the other.

"All will be well," I whispered into his neck. "I won't let you die this time, either."

NOT A LOT ELSE TO DO

We were on the road for two more days, Tjal slipping in and out of consciousness the whole time, with frequent changes between horses to allow the other one to recover. On the fourth day, we kept going for longer than before and, at dusk, reached a small settlement nestled in a narrow dip in the forest. It sat within a clearing and was little more than a longhouse and a handful of outbuildings. People were waiting for us, sporting the same hairstyle as the Clouds who'd come with us. They took care of the horses and one of them pointed at one of the smaller dwellings, where Qati proceeded to bring Tjal and me. He called on the second snorer to handle Tjal and I was shoved in the back to follow on my own two feet.

Not long ago, the house had been used as a pigsty—an unmistakable smell hung around it. My wrists were lashed to an iron ring fastened to the wall and they even bothered to secure Tjal, though there was absolutely nothing he would've been able to do in his state. Qati stayed with us for a while before he was relieved by one of the resident Clouds, who brought some soup for us. I spooned as much as possible into Tjal before drinking the rest myself; a difficult task given that my movement was so restricted. The Cloud watched me eat without uttering a single word, took the empty bowl from me, and proceeded to work on a piece of wood, whittling at it with his knife. The noise of the blade made me sleepy and I managed to doze off quickly.

It was the perfect place to lie low for a while; the horses could be hidden, and the men gather their strength for the next leg of the journey. If we had reached Cloud territory, we must've come quite close to the coast, but we hadn't been able to travel fast. We might not have come that far at all. They'd probably left some of their group before, maybe even killed the people who'd lived there in order to wait for us to reach them.

I dreamt of pigs, unsurprisingly—pigs who kept snuffling at me, trying to find the best angle to break my body open and start eating my guts. When I scared myself awake it was still very dark. They'd left us alone, probably bored with two prisoners who didn't move at all.

"Sloe?" Tjal pushed his boot into my side.

"Thank the gods," I breathed. "You're still alive."

"Where are we?"

"Probably some way south of the lake. I'm trying to figure it out, but we are far away from my home and I'm as much a stranger as you are around here. How do you feel?"

"Horrible."

"Do you remember anything that happened back at the house? Do you remember what they did to Qes?"

"Qati knocked him out with an iron cooking-pot, but I don't know what they did to him after that, I'm sorry."

"Would they have gone out of their way to kill him?"

"I don't know, Sloe. Is there water?"

"No, I don't think so. We have to wait until the guard comes back."

"It feels like something died in my mouth. Tastes like it, too."

"At least they've kept us together."

"Can you please not."

"Do what?"

"Look on the bright side. They will kill us both, it's just a question of when."

"No, I think they have something else in mind. We would've been so much less work if they'd finished us off in Goldenlake."

"You don't understand. They will put me on trial."

"Whatever for?"

"To make an example of me. To make my family pay for the dishonour I brought upon them, to make them try and get back into favour with additional contributions. They caught me with my trousers around my ankles, Sloe. No one will forgive this."

"Shut up. Shut up now."

We sat next to each other in silence until dawn, when we could look around us for the first time. The walls and dividers were covered with a mixture of clay and chopped up straw to make them smooth. The rafters had been carefully constructed, and the first layer of the roof consisted of compacted bracken lashed to a frame of sturdy hazel rods. Someone had taken great care to build a house that would serve for many years.

The floor had been scraped clean as best as possible. We were sitting on dead leaves and more scratchy bracken. It was not the worst situation to be in, even if there was no door as such. I could see that it was still snowing heavily. While that meant that all the traces we'd left would be wiped out, it also made it much more likely that we'd stay put for some time: a chance for Tjal to get better, if they didn't forget to feed and water us altogether.

When the guard finally came back, it was another man who brought a bucket and a bowl of water. I was so close to bursting that I didn't even object to relieving myself next to Tjal, although he declined to do the same.

"You're not having a shit in the corner," I warned him. "Use the damn bucket."

He shook his head.

The guard scoffed, waited until we'd drunk some water, then one of Cathil Cloud's cousins came with breakfast and the two guards chatted amicably while we were chewing our rations of more dried meat and lumps of sour cheese. None of them seemed worried to be overheard.

The plan had been in place for quite a while, even if they hadn't expected to bring prisoners along. The Clouds at the longhouse had waited for their cousins to return. The people they'd killed had been Magpies.

During the day, a steady stream of people came to the pigsty, the guards changing all the time—even some of our former housemates took on the duty and Tjal averted his face from them, set on wallowing in his disgrace. He'd been caught bare-arsed, but I'd been the one about to make the next move on him. I couldn't help but be annoyed with his attitude. Because they never left us alone, I had no opportunity to talk to him and found myself getting more and more frustrated as the day progressed. At least he could be persuaded to finally use the bucket in the evening. We had some more dried meat and water, afterwards the guards changed once again.

It fell to the one who liked to whittle to watch over us for another night by the faint light of his oil lamp. Tjal turned his back to me and fell asleep soon after. I grumbled for a little while longer before being lulled into sleep myself by the sounds of wood shavings scattering to the floor. Later, I shuddered awake from disturbing dreams when I heard laughter, quite close to me.

A single oil light was propped up on one of the dividing walls, but there were two guards—two of the Clouds I'd seen at the Roundhouse in Goldenlake, and they smelled like honey beer and fire smoke, clapping each other on the back and laughing again, then one of them started to undo his trousers. The other one came over and tried to do the same to me. It took me a moment to grasp what was about to happen and when I drew breath to scream, the other one knelt on my throat while I felt his hands on me.

Tjal started to shift—his voice was surprisingly loud when he managed to call for help before a kick in the face silenced him.

I heard more laughter and Tjal groan in pain, his nose surely broken, but he gave it another try, spitting blood and curses I'd never heard before.

"We'll do him next," said the Cloud with the open trousers, stroking himself.

"What the fuck do you think you're doing?" They both turned around, the pressure on my throat lightened ever so slightly. Olas stood next to the oil light, his face distorted, and in front of him, the Prince of Crooked Hill.

The man who was about to rape me shrugged. "Cathil said it's fine."

"Cathil Cloud does not get to decide if it is fine to assault a hostage," Ileon said, his voice controlled and low. "I will not allow this kind of atrocity within my camp."

The man who still held me down snorted in disgust. "There's not a lot else to do around here. How are we meant to pass the time?"

"Have a wank, like normal people," Olas snarled. "Get out— now." He waited until Cathil Cloud's cousins had left before he pushed past the prince and knelt next to me, to help me sit up and pull my clothes back on.

Ileon stared down at me as I felt myself start to shake.

"Thank you," Tjal sputtered.

Olas drew a flask made from boiled bark from his cloak and wet a cloth to clean him up. "We'll talk to Cathil Cloud," he promised.

Ileon came closer, his eyes glued to my face.

I wiped my cheeks on the inside of my forearm, desperate not to let him see me break down, while a whole host of emotions were visible on his face.

"You will stay with them for now, Olas. We cannot risk them getting hurt again. I am going to sort out the Clouds once and for all." He wheeled around and left the pigsty, while Olas cut the ropes around our hands.

He was visibly affected by what had happened, shocked and angry. "We should never have trusted them to keep you safe."

Tjal rubbed his chafed wrists. He was deathly pale, and still bleeding from his mouth. Olas gave him the cloth to wipe himself again.

"Can you tell us anything?"

Olas shook his head. "Better not. But you know that he will keep his word and ensure that something like this won't be tolerated."

"As long as he's around," Tjal snapped. "The moment his back is turned they will try it again. What makes you believe that they won't sell you out, as soon as they can?"

"They haven't been paid yet."

From then on, we were watched over by men of the Cities, two of them at a time, who did resent their new task immensely but didn't try to take their frustration out on us. They didn't lash us to the wall again, though Ileon had been kept bound for much longer in Goldenlake.

"Thank you for trying to help," I said to Tjal as we ate that evening. "They must've heard you in the house."

"But it wasn't enough. If Nivael and Olas hadn't come ..."

"It was enough. It's not your fault that Cathil Cloud's cousins are horrible people." I cleared my throat, but it was still painful to speak in more than a hoarse whisper.

"How can you even try to excuse any of this?" he asked.

"You're upset with *me*?"

"No, of course not. I wish I could do anything, *anything* to make you feel safe with me—but I can't."

"You heard them. They would've done the same to you and I wouldn't have been in any state to fight them. They would've raped us both."

He still looked sceptical, as if there would've been any reason for the Clouds to spare him. That night we didn't sleep, lying next to each other in hurt silence. My throat throbbed for hours, as if the Cloud was still kneeling on my neck. Every other moment the face of his cousin flashed before my eyes.

MAKE IT WORSE

We stayed in hiding for a total of twelve days. By the end, the soup became even thinner, as if supplies were running low. I knew my aunt must've felt the first sense of hopelessness and was thinking of returning to Tall Trees without me, to face the wrath of my mother.

Qati Badger had managed to provide another layer of bracken for Tjal and me. Since we were free to stand up whenever we needed to, the whole bucket arrangement worked much better for both of us. After the experience with the Cloud cousins, neither of us felt much enthusiasm to do more than seek warmth in the night and so we went back to sleeping in each other's arms with nothing else happening besides. We stayed in the pigsty the whole time, barely able to smell it anymore, even if the guards winced when they came in to start their shifts.

No one gave us a heads-up before we left one morning—they came in and pulled us apart. The horses were ready, one for each of us, which was a relief. We weren't with the pack horses, but behind the prince's entourage. The men were tense around us, hungry and already exhausted before starting off. Every group kept very much to itself: a couple of Cloud guides at the front, the rest after us, and a lot of exasperated muttering.

Although they didn't bind our hands again, Qati kept hold of our reins to avoid any ill-advised escape attempts. I had to admit to myself that I wasn't prepared to try. The snow lay in deep drifts around us. I was on territory I didn't know, had no way of procuring food, and would have starved quite quickly.

A thin layer of ice had formed overnight, and the horses crunched their way through the trees. I wasn't sure we were following a path anymore, just a general direction—further south—until we came to a broad frozen river in the early afternoon. We had to dismount and lead the horses across; the ice was thick enough to hold but so slippery in places that more than one animal fell and had to be helped up.

As soon as everyone was on the other side, we witnessed a spat between the leaders of the party. Cathil Cloud stood unmoved in the trampled snow, bulging arms crossed in front of him, snowflakes caught in his stubble, while Olas hissed at him, the prince standing by as if he wasn't a part of the altercation. We were too far away to understand what was wrong but after that it didn't take long for us to make camp for the day, in a far more shambolic way than usual. Tjal and I were allowed to share the entourage's fire.

Olas made a point of sitting down next to me. "You look better than the last time I saw you," he remarked with a cautious little grin.

"Please tell me what happened to Qes."

"I asked to leave him behind but I'm not sure how it worked out."

"He was trying to help, and he took care of all of you."

"Sloe, I know. But things go further than we want them to sometimes."

"Where are we going?"

He shrugged. "Can't you tell?"

"No, of course I can't tell. I only know that if you're planning to return to the Stoneharp, we're not heading in the right direction."

"Maybe that's enough."

"My aunt will try to find you. You might already have all the wizards of Goldenlake on your heels—apart from Cirvi Cloud."

"No one here is particularly scared of wizards."

"You experienced them at the council. Do you think it's wise to underestimate them?"

"They serve gods we don't believe in. We have no need to fear them."

"But you know Sjunil Moon."

For the first time, he squirmed. "Your aunt is indeed a formidable woman, but in the end her power is limited by her faith."

"You're lying to yourself," I realized. "I think you're the only one of them who understands what she is and how ruthless she can be when it comes to her family."

He glanced over his shoulder to the closest fire of the Clouds, where their wizard sat close to the flames, his hood pulled into his face. He looked like a man thoroughly acquainted with his own darker side, as if he'd lived a life full of moral compromises.

"You know by now that the Clouds are dangerous people. *He* knows as well." I pointed my scraped chin towards the prince. "If you're following them into one of their main settlements on the coast, you might as well cut your own throat."

"Don't," he pleaded. "Don't make it worse."

I folded my fingers into each other and held my breath. Whatever the original plan had been, the men from the Cities had started to have second thoughts. They were already deeply uneasy, and it wouldn't take much to drive Olas over the edge, to refuse cooperation. I glanced over to Tjal, who tried to shrink into the stinking blankets he still wore, to become as unnoticeable as possible to the men he'd shared so many experiences with.

At least we were relatively warm, an unexpected luxury after twelve days in the pigsty, and not quite as hungry as before. We were allowed to sleep next to the fire and I dreamt of Qes, lying in his own blood in the doorway leading into the House of Men. When I woke in the light as the guards changed, I started to pray for him again.

The forest around us transformed. Soon we rode through an area where deer had eaten all the young saplings and left only the eldest trees that stood as imposing solitaires with wide-spreading branches on rolling hills. In the summer it must've been the most beautiful landscape, but it didn't offer us much shelter from the bitter winds. Sometimes the snowdrifts were so deep that the first horses of the group would sink down up to their bellies.

We rode in single file, the snow often reaching our heels. If someone had the idea of risking an attack in such conditions, we could well have found ourselves trapped and helpless. The Cloud guides guaranteed our safety, even if I hated them for it, and I tried to remember everything Silid had once told me about them, when there'd been the possibility of me marrying a Cloud and leaving Tall Trees to build a new life in the south. They had a couple of larger villages close to the coast, the site of their assemblies being the one with a natural harbour. It was reasonable to assume that was where we were heading.

Despite all my misgivings, I felt an excited twinge at the thought of seeing the sea. Like everyone, I'd hoped to travel to the Stoneharp one day and to see the famous west coast, but at least there'd be proper waves and ships. I remembered trying to squeeze information out of Sjunil some time ago about what the sea was really like, but she hadn't been in the mood to oblige me.

"You will see it for yourself one day," she'd said, and her prediction was likely to finally come true. Maybe the sea would provide me with a means to escape or an opportunity to get a message to Tall Trees … I flinched in the saddle as the prince's bony grey gelding turned up next to me.

"What do you have to smile about?" he asked quietly.

"My mind was just wandering."

"I would appreciate it if you would not try to influence my negotiator against me."

"He's the only one who understands."

"He is skittish enough as it is. I made my decision a long time ago and I am not going to change my mind." He crossed his gloved wrists on the pommel of his saddle. "Why did you pick Tjal na Tialin? Because you knew that he was the weakest of us?"

I looked at him in surprise. "I didn't pick him. It just happened."

"Excuse me for finding that hard to believe. Tjal hails from one of our oldest families and his brother served me with valour, right to his end. Tjal was taught the same principles and his father is one of the most honourable men I ever knew."

"He said he was falling in love with me."

The Prince of Crooked Hill looked sad. "And you could not let him be? You must have known the risks he took upon himself to please you." He wiggled his left hand where the bandage still made it appear bigger in the glove than the other. "I understand that he was tempted but you should have been stronger. I expected more from you, Sloe Moon of Tall Trees." He spurred his horse on and overtook me again.

For the rest of the day I entertained myself by trying to think about the best way to murder him.

We reached an abandoned group of stone huts in the late afternoon and the men tried to fashion them into habitable shelters. They built fires within the half-collapsed walls and stretched tarpaulins over corners to create niches where warmth could be held and the horses protected from the snow. Again, the groups kept themselves apart. The tension was palpable. The Clouds were out of patience with their allies and since they'd reached their own territory, the men from the Cities moved on thin ice. I was in the wrong group, in the same awkward situation as Qati Badger.

At least the men from the Cities hadn't tried to abuse me to pass the time. Who knew what would happen when we reached our destination? It wasn't inconceivable that all my former housemates would soon enough find themselves in shackles. Anyone who trusted Cathil Cloud further than they could throw him needed their head adjusted. The entourage didn't pick up on that, apart from Olas, and munched on their dried strips of meat as usual, while I had to force myself to swallow even a morsel, my mouth tasting like bitter herbs.

Olas insisted that they posted their own guards, and I very much hoped that the prince understood why the precautions were taken and that it would've been foolish to think himself safe for a single moment.

That night, Tjal crept close to me, but I kept my back to him, not wanting to engage in any way that might cause him further trouble and could've been misconstrued as tenderness between us. It pained me that the days in the pigsty hadn't brought us together but instead made us resent each other. I pulled the cloak up as far as I could and folded my fingers around my silver amulet, the only item bar the grimy clothes on my back that I'd been allowed to keep from the life I'd lived before. It was the only thing that still tethered me to my family—even the sky-blue cloak had been left behind and Werid's pearl taken from me. My prayers were angry and probably unjust, but then Brother Brook was known for his quick temper. If there was one of the gods who knew how I felt, it was probably him. I prayed to be delivered and I prayed for vengeance and that one day I'd be allowed to see Cathil Cloud choke on his arrogance.

UNBOUND BUT STILL UNABLE

The air started to smell weird, like salt and ice and rotten vegetables. No one remarked upon it, so maybe that was how the sea was supposed to smell. We followed a narrow strip of trees that had been planted to mark a road, broader than any we'd used since leaving Goldenlake. We reached a small cluster of shingle-thatched houses where the Clouds had stationed a group of guards, all with the clipped hair that I associated with less than wholesome proceedings.

The guides signalled at them and they let us pass. Behind us, I could hear Cathil Cloud exchange a few jokes with them. The snow on the road had been sprinkled with sand and crushed pebbles and fell off steeply towards the shore. I gasped as the expanse of the sea laid itself out before me, though to the left of us another coastline rose from the half-frozen waters, bleached and craggy.

"What's over there?" Tjal asked next to me.

"Fuck if I know," I snapped back. "Pester your new friends, why don't you."

He looked as if I'd slapped him but before I could relent, Qati saved me.

"Westlight. It's an island," he added patronizingly.

I knew about Westlight. We could see the tip of its westernmost coast; that meant we were most likely about to enter Greycliffs, at the edge of the Cloud territory. Just a few leagues to the west we would've met another family. It was one of the reasons my mother had been so desperate to keep them happy: we'd always relied on them to keep our western side protected and the Owls at bay. Suddenly I felt better. I knew where I was likely to be, even if the sound of ice crashing against the pebble beach was strange and violent.

The road snaked down amidst three rings of houses to meet the shore. Greycliffs was larger than Tall Trees, almost imposing, the houses built from the same stone as the cliff so they seemed to melt into it. Some of the roofs had been covered in thin split plates of rock, others with wooden shingles that had warped in the salty air. We saw no large ships on the beach, only middle-sized vessels that the Clouds used to fish with. There wasn't a lot of space to pull boats up to protect them from the winter storms, and I assumed the larger ships had all been stored somewhere else.

We were brought to the lowest ring of houses, where the buildings looked patched, in constant repair to counteract the occasional freak floods that happened along this coast. Even if the prince didn't pick up on the slight, it was almost laughably direct. At least we were closer to any boats that were still kept in the water.

There were few people about on the lowest level; the whole set-up reminded me of the Golden Lake shoreline, with drying nets and various equipment draped everywhere, and a long line of empty racks to process the fish as soon as it was brought in. Everyone slunk back into their houses when they saw Cathil Cloud; no one wanted to greet him in the ring, and I noticed that their wizard was glancing around as if he was waiting for someone to appear.

The house the men from the Cities were given had no special designation, seeming like more of a spare warehouse that could be used for guests in emergencies. Sleeping platforms lined the walls but hadn't been used for some time. Someone had forgotten to take their broom with them, and it leant drunkenly on the wall next to the door. Two braziers had been brought in, firewood was piled on one of the platforms; everything was cold and dusty and smelled decidedly fishy.

"You will wait here," one of the guides said as the men were ushered in.

They left three of Cathil Cloud's cousins with us, one of them the man whose face I'd never be able to forget. The other ones took the horses away. I watched the men starting to unpack their bedrolls. Qati stacked the braziers and tried to coax the fires to life, while Olas and the prince took their place at the central table. Olas pulled a parchment from his cloak. I couldn't help but step closer when I saw the map he unfolded.

It must have been old; it looked faded, almost rubbed away in the folds and drawn in various shades of ink. I could spot Westlight at the bottom of it, and someone had used a charred stick to mark Greycliffs. There were other such signs—one of them was surely Goldenlake, the other the Stoneharp in the west. It was the first time I'd seen one of the maps from the Cities. Compared to it, our own maps were rather crude affairs and focused on descriptions of landmarks to guide us through the forest.

The prince noticed me staring open-mouthed. "You can look at it if you want," he invited me quietly and I sat down next to his negotiator. I tried to identify other marks they'd made in territories of different families, but that kind of information was missing, probably because the person who'd drawn the map hadn't really known about them. From the shape of the coastline on the parchment, I saw that they'd calculated some of the distances wrong. Greycliffs couldn't be so far east if in reality you could only see the tip of Westlight. Perhaps the mapmaker hadn't been there in the first place, and who knew how many mistakes they'd added. The marks were little more than guesswork. Olas noticed the disappointment on my face.

"What's wrong, Sloe?"

"It seems impressive from far away, but as soon as you take a closer look it's very unreliable." I worried at the scabby, itching skin on my wrists where the ropes had bitten into me.

Ileon turned away and beckoned Tjal over, who'd been waiting close to the door, looking helpless and unsure if it was still expected of him to pitch in setting up the house.

Tjal obeyed with relief. "My prince?"

"Take them over there and start putting the firewood aside, so you can use the bed tonight," he commanded. "They have given us a house that is too small."

"It's bigger than the house in Goldenlake," I said, but Ileon had never set foot in that festering pit. He'd been treated to the amenities of the Moons' guesthouse as soon as he'd lost his fetters.

Tjal pulled me from the bench, and we set to work.

The wood had been damp when stored, so the bed smelled and was full of little splinters and mossy bits that had to be swept out. It had curtains made from roughly woven hemp, nailed to the frames around the platform and the dividers were built high to allow for some privacy. In the summer, the house might've even been a nice place to stay, but it felt like a punishment in winter. Neither Tjal nor I had any blankets; it looked as if we would have to make do with the rough split planks the platform was built out of. I thought about asking someone to spare a few saddle rags for us.

I flinched as the door creaked open. The cousins let in two women who carried baskets filled with bread, beer skins, and cheese wrapped in cloth. They wore the same silver-grey wool as the men and had bound their hair on top of their head into a tight knot. The rest was clipped off to resemble the style of the Cloud men. They watched the men of the Cities with curiosity, but no malice came off them. When Olas thanked them and tried to start a conversation, they fled the house.

The men gave out the first of our rations in Greycliffs. The cheese tasted different, was slightly saltier than I was used to, and they'd mixed the bread flour with dried seaweed, probably to bulk it out, which resulted in a minerally flavour that bothered me at first. I could see some of our housemates grimacing as they chewed, but no one complained. At least the bread was fresh. Afterwards, we tried to make ourselves comfortable and sleep. The planks we laid on were quite bouncy, not as hard as I'd feared them to be.

"I wish you didn't hate me now," Tjal said, lying down close to the wall.

"I don't hate you. Though I think we've had enough of each other. Maybe that's inevitable if you live so close together as we've done, with one bucket to share and the stench of the pigs around us. You must find me hard to bear."

"Yes, because you've been treating me like shit since … that night."

"Do you still wonder why?"

I saw him cross his arms in front of him and shudder into his clothes. "Yes," he whispered.

"Because you didn't even consider being treated the same as me. It seemed natural to you that they'd assault me, but you still thought that they'd spare you, just because you are a man of the Cities."

"That's not what happened," he said.

"That's how it felt to me."

"You're being unfair, Sloe. I tried to help you and if I hadn't called out, who knows what could have been."

"You really doubt what they would've done?"

"No," he admitted and started to cry—the one thing I couldn't ignore and that was dangerous to do in present company. I wrapped my arms around him, and we huddled into a smelly heap against the wall, desperate to survive another night.

I couldn't bring myself to kiss him, but allowed him to keep close until the light of a new day woke us.

The Clouds were assembled in the Roundhouse on the highest level, though their version was a square building and lavishly decorated with wall hangings and painted carvings. A half-circle of high-backed chairs stood around the largest brazier I'd ever seen, low and crouching on dragon feet, making the house almost uncomfortably hot. The town's inhabitants sat on benches, all wrapped in their grey cloaks and looking like one great mass.

The leader of their family, the woman who'd once decided against me, sat in the centre. She didn't seem to have many teeth left and was much older than Mother. Three of her daughters, her closest advisors, stood grouped around her, and in the next closest chair was Cirvi and then another wizard. Like Cirvi, she didn't wear any ornaments, only a silver pin in the shape of a sun that fastened the cloak underneath her throat. She carried a staff like Qerla Badger in Goldenlake, so long that it might also be a weapon, sanded smooth and with one iron-topped end. Cathil and Cirvi were the only men in places of honour.

They'd made the Prince of Crooked Hill sit on one of the hard benches with the other family members, and I was part of his entourage, unbound but still unable to run. Olas had found blankets for me and Tjal to wear; his was green and mine was chequered in bright colours. I'd been reminded of my aunt as I wrapped it around me, and it made me stand out so much that there was absolutely no chance of moving about undetected. A strong smell came off me, but my face was washed, my hair combed and braided. I assumed that Olas wanted me present in case he needed to ask questions about proceedings later, even if it looked like one of the formal morning prayer ceremonies to thank Brother Rain for the return of their family members.

Cirvi Cloud led the ritual while the other wizard stared at his back with badly hidden disgust. The longer the prayers went on, the more uneasy the men of the Cities became around me: apparently none of them had understood yet how much the political was tied up with the religious for the families.

Even I heaved a sigh of relief when Cirvi finally finished and sat down again, but the second wizard jumped up and pointed her staff into the crowd. It took me a while to realize that the iron band around the rod was directed at me.

"Sloe Moon of Tall Trees," the wizard said. "You speak for these men?"

❧

SUCH TROUBLE

"Your name is known to us." The wizard's voice carried into all the corners of the house. "We gather that you have accused us at the council in Goldenlake, resulting in the payment of fines we can ill afford. Now you come with the men who seek to use our power to fight the families of the east?" She sounded disapproving.

"This is a misunderstanding." I tried to glare at Cathil Cloud as menacingly as possible. "It's not what it looks like."

The wizard was angry. "It looks like all the rumours we have heard about your disreputable parentage are true."

"What?" I barked before pressing my mouth shut. I needed to be clever. All eyes were on me and I felt a dribble of sweat run down my back. "I don't speak for these men. I am but a hostage, snuck out of Goldenlake to avoid honouring an arrangement with our own wizard. I never asked for any of this."

"Yet, you find yourself in the middle of it all, and they even brought you with them today. They ensured your good treatment and allowed you to walk without restraint. You must have done something to endear yourself to them."

I wanted to turn around and stare pleadingly at Olas, but the men of the Cities had all gone deathly quiet around me. "I am a helpful person," I protested lamely, "and have experienced enough discomfort and ill-use to refute these accusations."

Suddenly the wizard smiled at me. Her teeth were very white and pointed. "You are lucky that you find yourself among people who understand that there cannot always be a single explanation, and that alliances can be complex. We will afford you the opportunity to prove yourself helpful once more. I ask you again. Sloe Moon of Tall Trees, do you speak for these men?"

My head was throbbing. "Do I have a choice?"

She shrugged. "Probably not."

"Fine. I speak for these men."

The men in question started to mumble in protest, and Olas stood up behind me. The prince caught his sleeve and pulled him down again. "Not yet," I could hear him hiss and when I looked over to Cathil, he seemed unsure for the first time since I'd known him.

"Is this why I'm here?" I asked Ileon as the assembly was dismissed. "Because you knew that you needed someone from the families to be your voice?"

"Why would I have taken such trouble over you if I had not planned on you being useful to me?"

"Such *trouble*?"

"I have made sure that you remain unharmed. I have even left you Tjal, though you know how much I disagreed with this particular choice of yours. You believe your aunt trained you to be the perfect hostage, but I think you already know that I did the very same thing. I can profit from your questionable position among your own kind."

"My own *kind*?"

His yellow eyes narrowed. "Someone must have told you how annoying this habit of yours is, Sloe. I do not need my words repeated back to me. I gather your father once made a name for himself and as a result, no one considers you trustworthy. In certain situations, this can be an advantage."

I wanted to scream in frustration. "But this means that you must trust me enough now to share your intentions with me."

"Have I ever truly hidden my intentions? I have come to Birkland to conquer. Perhaps I chose a different approach than other men would have—I believe that arrangements can be made that suit all of us, the Cities and the families. The Clouds have agreed to profit from this venture, as have the Elks and Bears. We will work on the Owls next, but I gather that the Owls still have trouble trusting the Clouds. They will be much happier with a Moon negotiating the terms." He smiled again. "This should give you an idea of where we are. Olas will fill you in on the rest."

"If you don't do it, they'll kill you." Tjal's voice sounded hoarse in the darkness.

"I see we came to the same conclusion," I muttered. "But don't you understand what this means?"

He sniffed. "It means that you play into their prejudices, that you destroy all your attempts to redeem yourself to the people who only see the blood of a traitor when they meet you." It hurt to hear it spoken aloud. Tjal touched my face, and I was too tired not to let him. "Don't you think your father might've been in a similar situation?" he asked.

"How so?"

"You know how easy it is to find yourself in a position you never wanted to be in. Maybe they called him a traitor and took away his powers because of things that happened to him. Things he never intended to do."

I pulled the chequered blanket around me. "That is an interesting thought," I had to admit.

"Perhaps all he ever intended was to be helpful."

The inside of my nose started to burn, and I kissed him before he could say anything that brought me even closer to tears.

"They have sent for you." Olas stood in front of our platform, more dishevelled than I'd ever seen him.

I started to crawl towards him, my limbs aching from shivering in the night. "Just for me?"

"Just for you. There is an escort to bring you to the upper level."

"Did anyone say why?"

The prince's negotiator grimaced. "Why would they tell me anything?"

"You realize that I never wanted this, right? That I would give this position to you as soon as they let me?"

He rubbed his unshaven face. "I still don't care for being replaced."

I tried to arrange my clothes but could do nothing about my hair at such short notice. Two Cloud guards waited for me, and I thanked Brother Brook that I knew neither of them. They marched me up the road; a cruel wind blew from the sea and whipped my braid around my neck, but patches of fog were still trapped between Greycliffs and Westlight. This was how I'd always thought of the land of the dead: ice-encrusted and wreathed in mists, though before long the wet walls of houses wafted into visibility. The smell was still new to me, still disconcerting.

The guards didn't attempt to speak to me, and I was out of breath for most of the ascent anyway. They brought me to the benches that had been placed under the roof in front of the House of Women, in a similar arrangement to the one my mother favoured in Tall Trees. The second wizard was waiting for me, sitting and leaning on her staff. She gestured towards her apprentice, a girl with huge sad eyes, who poured me a bowl of steaming tea—a courtesy I'd dearly missed since leaving Goldenlake.

"Thank you for joining me this morning," the wizard said, absent-mindedly scratching at the silver sun on her chest. "I figured it would be more efficient if we talk among ourselves first. My name is Cjanis, and I am one of Cathil's sisters."

"That can't have been easy," I said, and she laughed.

"It wasn't. I had to become a wizard to make my word count against him. I'm already thinking of the next mission to give him to get him out of our hair." She took a sip of tea and put her bowl down on a low table between us. "I know that it must be difficult for you too, Sloe, and I'm sorry for all you have suffered in order to get you here to Greycliffs. But you can see that we do need your help."

"I should be brave enough to refuse."

She shrugged. "You're far too bright to believe that. You want to survive, same as me. You know that the gods will understand this choice. The men of the Cities are a threat we need to handle in our own way. We have enough warriors to fight them off for now, but they will come back with more and they will be hungry for revenge. We need to run rings around them, Sloe, and we need to do this together."

I stared at her, horrified. "Just to make sure that I understand you correctly …"

"Cathil has always been Mother's favourite and she would've made him her heir if it would've been in any way permitted. She bends to his word and chooses not to heed any council against him. The problem is that my brother is easily bought, with promises that my sisters and I see in a very different light—so we need to go about it another way." She pursed her lips. "I wanted you to understand this before we proceed. All of our sisters voted to keep faith with the Moons, but Cathil wanted to marry someone else. Good luck to him—his husband is a spoiled little brat. I can't wait for him to join the Mice in the west. Until then, I need to keep my head low. The prince from the Cities obviously thinks himself learned in the ways of the families, but you must've noticed that none of them understands where our decisions are truly made."

"I noticed," I confirmed.

"I intend to make the most of this."

"With a double-cross."

Her apprentice looked up sharply at that, but Cjanis grinned at me. "It will be a difficult line to plough, but I hope that your aunt has taught you well." She drank some more tea. "I've always admired Sjunil Moon," she said. "She strikes me as a crafty old bitch."

"That's not the first time I've heard her described as such."

"It's something we can all aspire to."

I felt a bit sick when the guards were fetched to bring me back. The apprentice had kept an eye on our surroundings, to make sure we hadn't been overheard. It was the sort of thing Silid excelled at and maybe even Siw, but it made my heart hurt. I tried to breathe in deeply, to suck the cold air as far into my body as possible. I longed for the life I'd lived in Tall Trees. The tasks on the work rota seemed so uncomplicated: keep an eye on the goats, assist with the shearing, sort the fleece for the spinners and dyers, weed the herb gardens, pull the roots, find the mushrooms, gather the nuts, clean the cheese-making kit, wash the clothes, grind the flour, find the honey, talk to Qes.

Talk to Qes.

I had to pause. How could Brother Brook have allowed him to be taken from me? If there had ever been a situation I needed my best friend for, I was in it. I couldn't possibly confide in Tjal; I would have to sacrifice the closeness we'd gained back since arriving in Greycliffs for another betrayal, another dangerous scheme.

I couldn't help but follow my father's footsteps.

LOST TO US

The next time, both the prince and I were called to the upper levels. Olas insisted on coming too, though it was unlikely that he would be allowed to join the meeting. It was later in the day and the fog had cleared to reveal the eastern side of Westlight. The guards walked behind us; I could hear them getting impatient with my constant stops. I'd soon be used to the steep climb, but I struggled and was relieved to hear that the prince was breathing almost as heavily as me when we reached the Roundhouse.

Two small braziers had been put in the corner furthest away from the door, and the large one remained unlit. It must've used up an awful lot of fuel and so it made sense for them to keep it reserved for assemblies and other official business. Cirvi and Cjanis sat close to the flames, already arguing, and Cathil and one of his cousins stood by, both idly fondling the hilts of their longknives as if they couldn't wait for the row to get out of control.

I expected the bodily reaction Cathil Cloud's presence provoked in me: I was feeling nauseated and sweaty, though the latter might've been caused by the ascent. When the wizards realized that we were waiting, Cirvi made an abrupt gesture for Cjanis to shut up and turned towards us.

"We have sent a messenger to the Owls," he said, without any sort of greeting, "and have been received with coldness and threats of violence."

Cjanis sighed. "What did you expect? This is a new thing for them. For generations we have squabbled over the border territories, why should they trust us now? I said we should wait, but you ignored me again. Rushing over there waving longknives around will not result in any useful developments." She glared at her brother.

"Perhaps we should send a smaller delegation under my protection," the Prince of Crooked Hill suggested. "That might intrigue them enough to grant us an audience with their government."

"That sounds reasonable," Cjanis said, but the older wizard frowned at Ileon.

"This is not about you," Cirvi objected.

"It most certainly is," the prince replied in a strained voice. "I will be the one offering the advantages that await them from such an alliance."

"They have no reason to take you seriously," Cirvi said so bluntly that I found myself gasping. "They have met your kind before and no reason to trust you more than the Clouds."

Cjanis cleared her throat. "The Owls have traded with the Cities for many years, and as much as I would like to think that they are more inclined to negotiate with another of the families, in reality they may have found their relationship with the Cities much more beneficial. It will be worth a go."

Cathil took a step towards her. "I won't be pushed aside." He didn't even seem to try to make it sound threatening. It just did.

I could feel the prince straightening his narrow shoulders next to me. He'd have never stood a chance against him in any sort of fight, but he was obviously trying hard not to let him know that he felt intimidated by him. "I am not saying that I will not take any of you with me, but maybe it should not be you, Cathil. That would send the wrong message."

"It would send the message I would want to send," the warrior scoffed. "Who else would be in the position to speak for us as I would?"

His sister raised her hand. "I am prepared to give it a try," she said and I had problems swallowing. "We could take some men from the Cities and some of ours and make it look less … like a war party."

Cathil scratched at the iron pommel of his longknife. "Wizards make everything more complicated than it needs to be. It should be an easy yes or no from the Owls, and our response immediate."

"You really want to bully them into joining us?" Cjanis said softly. "The Owls are traditionalists. They will respect a couple of wizards much more than a big man poking his knife about. Cirvi? They would know that it is important if we can overlook our usual differences, and both go."

The older wizard still seemed doubtful, though he must have been able to follow his colleague's logic well enough. "That might work," he said eventually.

Cathil flushed with irritation. "I can't see why."

"It would show them that we actually gave this matter some thought," his sister replied. "That we know your presence would hurt our plans more than it would further them. You have a reputation, dear brother of mine, a reputation that can be very useful at times, but also stifles the more sensitive conversations—if you know what I mean."

"What?"

The prince shrugged. "She means that if they are afraid that you will brain them after the slightest provocation, they will not be prepared to talk openly. One of my men is an excellent negotiator. You should ask him for advice sometime."

The longknife flew out of its sheath and vibrated against Ileon's neck. He smiled up at the taller man and pushed the blade aside with his middle finger.

"My point precisely."

"It will probably take a few days before everyone has agreed to it," Cjanis warned me later, when she gave me a basket of fresh provisions to take down to the house and we had a few moments to ourselves. "But I'd say Mother will allow it in the end. Think about who should come with us, Sloe. Who could be useful for such a delicate diplomatic undertaking?"

I nodded. "Thank you. It will feel better if you're coming with us." I turned around and joined Ileon and Olas, who were waiting next to the guards. The basket was quite heavy but neither of them offered to help me lug it to the lower level. A distinct odour of salted fish crept from the cloth that covered it against the tiny snowflakes that started to drift towards us from the sea. Ileon informed his negotiator of the next journey while we returned to our housemates, and Olas made his thoughtful face.

"*Two* wizards," he said. "This is bound to end in a catfight."

"Preferable to giving Cathil Cloud a slap on the fingers every other moment. I do not want to be responsible for keeping him under control. Cirvi is a much more reasonable man and will take care of the other wizard for us."

Olas glanced over to me. "What do you think, Sloe?"

I moved the basket over to my left hip to rest the right one for a while. "That's a fair expectation to have. They'll keep themselves occupied and it will impress the Owls that both of the Cloud wizards support the scheme. There's a much better chance that they react well to a petition brought forth by a wizard than a warrior, who's been an absolute pain in their arses for the best of ten years."

Olas frowned. "Can we trust them enough, my prince? Cirvi seems an easy enough man to keep an eye on, but the other one ..." As always, Olas asked the important questions.

Ileon grimaced. "I do not think we have much of a choice. The territory of the Owls reaches almost up to the Stoneharp. We need them to join in, not work against us."

Olas nodded slowly. "But please let us be careful, my prince. We have lost enough men as it is."

Though the final word hadn't yet been spoken, preparations were made. It kept my housemates busy, and they enjoyed arguing about who'd ride with us, although there were very few places to go around.

"I don't want to see you leave," Tjal said one evening, when the fire had almost burned down. "They might take advantage of the situation."

I arranged the new blankets around me to ward off the cold air whistling through the gap between the walls and the roof. "Are you afraid for me or for yourself?"

"For both of us." He shivered against me. "We might not see each other again, Sloe."

"I don't think we should expect the worst outcome from the very beginning."

"Do you *want* to go?" he asked accusingly.

"Is that so wrong? Wouldn't you want to get out of here if you could?"

"Out into the snow again? You might freeze to death before you even come close to the Owls!"

"Sounds preferable to spending the rest of the winter as a prisoner in another smelly house."

"A smelly house that could keep you safe."

"It's not my choice, Tjal."

"That's not what I'm talking about." He sounded sulky and I knew full well what he meant. It wasn't my choice, but I would've chosen to leave even so. The chances of getting away would be much higher on the road; maybe Cjanis Cloud would be prepared to help me … I bit the inside of my cheek. He was right. Even unbound, another journey to the west would be uncomfortable to say the least. We all would be better off hunkering down in Greycliffs until the spring, but the prince was in a hurry. It appeared he was working towards an ultimatum, perhaps a timeframe his own family had set him.

I downed a bowlful of beer and stared into the brazier's last flames. My position was changing with every day: no one tried to push me away from the fire into the coldest, dirtiest corner. Instead, I was speaking for all of the men and the second snorer refilled my bowl. I turned around to thank him, but he grunted and left me to it.

Tjal sat across from me, his hands clamped under his armpits to keep them warm. He didn't look at me, studying the salt-encrusted tips of his shabby boots instead. He knew that I couldn't wait to get away from him, and that whatever had drawn me to him in Goldenlake had lost its hold. Technically, I was still their hostage, technically all that was needed was a command and my throat would be cut, but Greycliffs was a world I understood better than all of them. They finally recognized that they needed me.

I reached over to the table and broke off a piece of hard cheese. It still tasted too salty to me, but the herbs that flavoured it were nice, minty and sharp on the tongue.

"I'm sorry, Tjal."

He stood up abruptly. "No you're not."

I buried my cold nose in the chequered blanket.

I didn't sleep next to him that night. I kept the fire going and snoozed as best as possible on the bench until dawn crept over the coast. When I stuck my head out of the door there were no guards posted. At the water's edge, men winched boats up to the shore, pushing them on larded planks lined up in front of the shallow bit of pebbly beach they used for easier access. They probably expected the sea between Westlight and the mainland to freeze over completely in the next few days, which didn't bode well for travel plans of any sort.

I watched them a while, thinking of the winter tasks that would've preoccupied me in Tall Trees: checking over the goats and keeping them as clean as possible, melting snow for us and the animals to drink, picking over the stored fruit and vegetables to make sure that nothing spoiled, and the endless spinning and weaving to prepare next year's clothes. On all the levels of Greycliffs, similar activities would be put on the work rotas. Whatever the prince had in mind for us, there were aspects of our lives that would surely be lost to us before long.

TELL ME

The horses were well rested when we made them ready. We were an even smaller fellowship than expected: the two wizards on large shaggy piebalds, Olas, the prince, and me, as well as two Clouds of smaller statures and with rather nondescript faces, to ensure that the Clouds still outnumbered us. They were brothers from the lowest level and experienced guides.

Cathil Cloud was visibly unhappy as he said farewell to his sister; it was not the way he wished his family to be represented. We must've looked like beggars to him, even in our new winter gear. We'd donned another layer in the silver-grey colour of the Clouds, which made us all look the same. The cloak was surprisingly soft and an expensive present.

Olas had a similar colouring to us of the families anyway, but the prince stood out like a sore thumb, as he always would. We arranged ourselves around him and the horses started to move.

I turned around in the saddle, looked back at the house where the others had taken their positions to see us off. Only Tjal had chosen to remain inside, and I was glad not to have to see his face. All the problems a journey in the depth of winter could throw at me were better than the prospect of lying to him every single day.

After all that had happened between myself and the prince, I felt much better about withholding certain truths from him and even Olas. At the very least, Olas should have expected a betrayal.

The guides knew the landscape we moved through; they found a group of boulders for us, strewn across the plain and marked by tree clumps, where a rudimentary roof had been constructed some time ago and one of the last travellers had built a wall from compacted snow to form a serviceable shelter. Cjanis pulled me to her side as we waited for the soup to be ready.

"I have missed this," she said. "Sometimes Greycliffs is too small for me. How are you feeling, Sloe?"

"Weird," I admitted. "Guilty to leave so many of them behind."

"I am sure they will find ways to pass the time."

I hugged my right knee. "But I still feel bad."

"Is there someone you will particularly miss?" she asked.

"No. Not as much as …" My throat made a strangled noise.

"Tell me," she said, her dark eyes kind.

"A friend of mine was left in Goldenlake, probably injured, maybe dead. Nobody knows what happened to him and I can't shake the thought that he might've died because of me. It's stupid."

"No, it's not. You must love him very much."

"Qes is my best friend, though we've only known each other for a while. I miss him every moment. He made everything bearable and never laughed at me. Well, almost never, but he was never cruel to me."

"Is he related to you?"

"He's a cousin. My father's niece's son. He is … just the best person I've ever known."

"I had a friend like that once," the wizard said quietly. "But she has been dead for a long time."

"I'm sorry. What happened?"

"Her wife killed her." I waited for her to continue, but she left me wondering. "It was like something out of the stories. Jealousy, rage, a sign from the gods. After her wife was sentenced to die, I decided to become a wizard. Cirvi did not appreciate an apprentice who had been part of the government for years and so I had to learn with someone else. I was able to pass the trials quickly and when I came back to Greycliffs, Mother allowed me to stay.

Cirvi is still not happy about it, as you may have already noticed. Without my friend, I would never have started out on this path, and I am still grateful to her every day. If the worst should come to pass, you will keep him close to you in other ways."

I thought of Qes' dimpled smile and the way his eyes shone when I said something funny and sniffled desperately. "I'll swear it."

"Nobody expects any oaths from you, Sloe. Just continue to be a good friend to him."

"Maybe I should become a wizard, too."

She looked taken aback. "Why?"

"Because sometimes I think it's what I should've been—to find a direction and get closer to the gods."

"Just because your father took this position once?"

"Maybe. It could be a more straightforward path to right the wrongs he did. Whatever that was, no one is particularly forthcoming with the details."

Cjanis' chin pointed over to the prince and his negotiator. "Did you see the map they studied a few moments ago?"

I nodded.

"Your father was the one who provided most of the information to them. Perhaps he was naïve, or he did it to piss off the Badgers. The important thing is that he prepared everything that is happening now, in a way. This can be your personal reason to help me, if you really want to right the wrongs."

I thought back to the time they'd let me look at the map and the way I'd judged it. A shiver flooded down my back. "It probably could be."

"Being a wizard is a hard path to follow," she warned. "You should have a proper think about it before you make any further decisions."

"Could you use a second apprentice?" I asked.

She slowly shook her head. "Your mother would never accept that."

"You're right. She wouldn't."

"You can try to find a master after you have returned home," she said, but there was something regretful in her tone. "After you have found out what happened to your friend."

"He doesn't like you talking to her," Olas said.

"I don't think there's any way around me talking to the leader of the mission," I replied tetchily.

"She isn't our leader. You should defer to our prince or, if necessary, to the older wizard." He pointed his thumb at Cirvi, who was mumbling prayers into his shawl.

"The older wizard? The *male* wizard, you mean? This was her idea and that makes her responsible."

He cocked his head. He hadn't shaved for a few days and seemed different. "You have a weird sort of glow around you. A glow I've seen before."

"What do you mean?" I hissed at him.

"Do you always fall in love so easily?"

"I'm not in love with her!"

He smiled. "Maybe not quite yet. But you would be happy to become involved with her, right?"

"That is none of your business."

He rubbed his gloved fingers together. "Everything that happens in this group is my business. I need to know where everyone's loyalties lie, and you make a very interesting case, Sloe Moon. Whenever I believe to have understood your motives, you turn around and run in a different direction. Like a dog who desperately tries to be owned."

I glared at him. "I'm not a dog!"

"You should keep in mind why you're here. I'm still not quite sure why exactly, but I dare say he would take your betrayal very badly."

"If he would start treating me better …"

Olas suddenly looked alarmed. "He shouldn't have to, Sloe. You owe him your life."

"No. We are now even, that is all. I'd prefer to talk to him directly."

"That's not what he wants."

I made a gesture towards the snow-covered land around us. "He's no longer in a position to tell me what he wants. We are far away from Greycliffs and still very far off from the Stoneharp. I may have agreed under duress to help further his interests but essentially, we are of the same status. It may change again as we reach the Owls, but I think this is something he needs to understand."

"What do I need to understand?" The prince had stepped closer without us noticing him. Olas gave a surprised little yelp.

The moonlight reflected off the snow around us, setting silver points in Ileon's eyes.

"That my respect needs to be earned. My love as well." I crossed my arms to hold myself still.

He studied my face. "We have known each other for quite some time now, Sloe Moon of Tall Trees. You still think I do not respect you?"

"You don't *act* like it. You might admire me for volunteering as your hostage in Goldenlake, but you still scold and belittle me."

The prince made a slow movement with his right hand. Olas sighed and left us alone.

"Let us walk a while," Ileon said. "Perhaps over to the second clump of trees where the horses have cleared the path."

"Why?"

"Because Olas has extremely sharp ears." He glanced over his shoulder. "I do not want him to know everything." His gloved hand reached out to me, and I allowed him to touch my elbow for a heartbeat. We took a few steps away from the camp before he said, "I assume my son has often wanted to give me a similar speech. I do not think that I have been a good father to him, though I have wanted to protect him and always had his best interests at heart. I should never have taken his love for granted, but I did. I love my own father, though he is unjust and has a temper on him that made me afraid of him when I was a boy. I did not comprehend why my own son pulled away from me or why he has always tried to work against the fate he was born into. I was telling the truth when I said that you remind me of him sometimes. Perhaps you could meet one day, and I dare say you would become friends."

"Well, I'm not your son, even if you find us both to be useless."

"You remember that, hm?"

"I tend to remember when I'm made to feel as bad as you made me feel. Once I was all too happy to lay down my heart at your feet, but things change. Sometimes they change quickly. You could've left me in Goldenlake, and we both would've been better off." I shook with anger and suddenly thought of Cjanis' friend. Jealousy, rage, and a sign from the gods. Would I really have been able to kill him? I'd fantasized about it a lot recently, and there we both were, our feet ankle-deep in snow and me with a knife at my belt. Just a small eating knife, but it didn't take much to make a man bleed out. I'd slaughtered pigs and goats before when it had been my turn, and though he was wrapped up warmly, I still had a chance to get at his neck ... but that was not who I was, and probably never would be able to be, even if he made me angry enough to scream.

"I am sorry, Sloe. My position comes with an awful lot of privilege, but also with a need for ruthlessness and a certain pragmatic mindset. We will find a way to get along, surely?"

He smiled and I unclenched my fists.

SLIGHTLY MORE COMPLICATED

It took us three days to reach the first settlements of the Owls, but after speaking to the prince I felt calmer. To know that he actually wanted my respect made the weather and the slow hours in the endless white of the western plains more bearable.

Though this was still the land of my people, I didn't feel at home. I'd enjoyed the novelty of the sea and the scenery around me was boring in comparison: a flat horizon where my eyes latched onto every single structure that was still visible, some lonely trees, and a few rocks. Apart from that, I was largely preoccupied with the wind, the cold biting into my face, and my breath filling my scarf with ice, making it sharp-edged and brittle over my nose and mouth.

After Ileon's remarks, I kept more of a distance from the wizards who used every break to bicker about past perceived slights. I still wanted Cjanis Cloud to like me but knew that I must be more careful about my feelings. She had flat-out refused to become my master and that worried me.

We approached the houses protected by a broad ditch and a fence of sharpened poles. The settlement was situated on a slightly higher part of the plains and had probably been there for a long time. It was one of the very few places that guaranteed some sort of view.

The gate was guarded by two women, who lowered their spears and glowered at us. We wore the colours of the Clouds; there was absolutely no reason for them to give us the benefit of the doubt. They had fawn-coloured cloaks and woolly hats with two tufts that mimicked the head feathers of a great owl. Their spears were tipped with serrated blades that made me shrink back instinctively.

"We sent your messenger away," growled the smaller of them. "We will not speak to you now."

Cirvi straightened his back and nudged his piebald mare forwards. "We come with a new proposition."

"You received your answer and there will not be another warning." The guard stared up at him, her hand tightening around the spear shaft.

"I doubt that you have the authority to decide over these matters," he said pompously and urged his horse on again.

The spear hit him in the chest, its blade cutting through the layers of clothing. The mare shied as her rider gurgled in shock, then collapsed in the saddle, while we looked on in horror. The only one who hadn't stiffened in shock was Cjanis.

"He had been warned," she said with a shrug.

I jumped from the saddle and tried to catch the hanging reins of the piebald mare—blood rushed over her coat, and she was too spooked to stand still. When I finally managed to hook my fingers around her bridle and pull her to me, it was already too late. Cirvi Cloud was undeniably dead, his eyes wide open and his mouth gaping and filled with blood. My stomach lurched but I was able to hold on to my morning rations—just.

I turned the horse back towards the gate, where the two guards had started to argue. The taller one was visibly shaken; I understood that he hadn't looked like a wizard to them, that they'd realized what they'd done, even with the necessary warnings.

Cjanis stood next to her own horse, making some abrupt gestures at Olas and the prince to signal that any words from either of them were likely to have even worse consequences. Olas was quite green around the gills and his knuckles clenched white around his own reins, while Ileon's face was kept carefully blank. He was waiting for Cjanis to save the situation. She loosened her cloak to show the silver amulet of Brother Rain around her neck and the sun brooch. If the guards hadn't noticed the staff strapped to the saddle, that was the last clarification they needed. I held the mare's bloody reins and studied the faces of my fellow travellers.

The two guides had backed off, and for the first time I wondered whether they hadn't known that Cirvi was likely to be sacrificed in some way.

The wizard held her palms up to emphasize her not being armed. "I am open to coming to some arrangement here," she said, "and I hope that this unfortunate … accident will not stand in the way of us getting the chance to talk things through."

That morning, she had squabbled with Cirvi over the crispiest piece of bacon. He was dangerously listing to the left and I had to prop him up to keep his body in the saddle. She smirked as the taller guard bowed before her.

"We ask that any weapons are left at the gate," she said. "Including your own staff."

"A very sensible request." Cjanis smiled back at us. "We will do as they demand," she ordered and then winked at me.

They took the horses from us, and the smaller guard asked me to hand over the reins of the mare. She said she'd bring the body to their healer, where it could be washed and examined. She was pale—she'd soon face the consequences of her eagerness to protect the settlement. Killing a wizard could easily cost her own life. More guards appeared to escort her and the man she had killed across the centre square, while the taller guard of the gate handed our collected weapons over.

The news that something awful had happened spread fast; I could see people nudging each other, every single one looking terrified before rushing on. They were trying to get the assembly together as quickly as possible in what was shaping up to be an emergency crisis meeting. We were brought into the largest of the central houses.

Seeing the Owls around us, it became apparent that it was not a typical family village: there were no children about, no old people. It was more like a garrison, an outpost to keep other villages safe. The Roundhouse was unheated, the benches shoved together in an untidy heap, and as they left us alone for a few moments, Olas turned on the wizard.

"What the fuck …"

Her hand was around his throat before he could blink. "In case you hadn't noticed, things have changed. I can kill you too, if you prefer, but I would seriously recommend keeping your trap shut and trying to be as inconspicuous as possible. My brother is too far away to hear you scream." She looked at the prince. "Do I have to explain?"

"No," he said flatly.

"Yes!" Olas cried and she tightened her grip until all he could get out was an undignified little squeak.

"The tables have turned again." The prince sounded weary. "I have almost given up on counting how many times they have flipped. I expect Cathil Cloud will not be happy to hear of this?"

"My brother portrays himself as much more powerful than he truly is. My sisters have given me their support and their word remains the one that matters." She signalled to the guides, who suddenly produced lengths of rope to secure the men of the Cities. Olas shook with rage, the prince was eerily still.

"Did you know about this?" he asked me.

"Sort of," I had to admit, but a withering look from the wizard made me bite my tongue. I hadn't known about her plans for Cirvi, but it made sense that she'd carefully picked the guides to come with us. It was no coincidence that she'd argued against a more befitting entourage for the prince.

Ileon smiled at me sadly. "I should not be surprised," he said. "But I am."

The commander of the garrison was an older Other, with a scarred face and half an ear missing—a veteran of many border fights, who greeted Cjanis with a tired nod. Surviving the winter was hard enough, no one needed complications of that scale on top of it.

"I have seen the dead wizard," they confirmed. "I am prepared to offer my assistance to compensate you for his loss."

Cjanis shook her head. "We require assistance, but in a slightly more complicated matter."

"*More* complicated?" Their eyes under the brim of the woolly hat went wide. "What could be more complicated than the death of a wizard?"

"We won't miss this particular wizard much," Cjanis said. "His death was the means to an end."

"How so?"

"I have come to negotiate an alliance between our families against common enemies in the west."

A scandalized murmur arose around us. The commander took a deep breath. "We have already declined your brother's offer."

"This is no longer my brother making an offer—the terms have changed. As well as the enemies in question. We have brought the Prince of Crooked Hill to you to do with him as you wish." One of the guides gave Ileon a shove. "I hope this is a prize tempting enough for you to join the families against the Cities?"

"You will forgive me if I find those new developments difficult to believe," they said quietly.

Cjanis nodded. "Which is why I have Sloe Moon of Tall Trees with me. The Moons have been allies for generations, and my brother's endeavours to destroy the trust between us did not meet with approval from the majority of our government. The Clouds will continue to stand with the Moons, Badgers, and the Ravens against any threat of invasion from the Cities. We will try to win the others over, but we need the help of the Owls to do so. Having the prince in your control should provide sufficient leverage."

"That is not for me to decide," the commander warned. "All I can do is to bring you to Featherdig, to the leader of our family."

"That is all I ask of you at this point," she said.

The commander took off their hat and shook the melted snow off it. Their hair was bound into two slate-grey knots, one above each temple. "I can admit that such a plan would have my personal favour, but I cannot promise that my voice will be the one that secures your success." They came closer and studied the face of the prince. "I think we have met once before," they said. "In the camp around the Stoneharp."

Ileon smiled. "Rawil Owl, if I remember correctly."

"You have learned to speak our words," they said approvingly. "I must admit I did not think much of you back then. You did not strike me as much of a threat, just a spoiled greedy merchant. You look different now. I will see to it that you and your man are well-treated, but you should not expect the Owls in Featherdig to be as respectful. They have had bad experiences with the men from the Cities."

"I understand, and I am grateful that you afford me this honesty. This is not the first time I have been a prisoner recently and I appreciate the openness."

Rawil Owl shrugged. "We always give fair warning."

ONE OF THOSE MOONS

We left the garrison the next morning. The guides stayed behind with Cirvi Cloud's body and had orders to take him back to Greycliffs, which left me and the two men of the Cities under Cjanis' command. Ileon and Olas kept their distance from the wizard, as did I. She didn't try to seek me out again and must have realized the calculated way in which she'd allowed for the older wizard to be killed had made me aware she served her gods without regrets.

I longed to talk about all of it; things tended to go rapidly downhill if I was left too long to ponder developments, but the prince and his negotiator were no longer able to trust me. I'd shown them time and time again that my heart was able to spin around faster than a dog chasing its own tail, and I knew that I didn't deserve to seek solace with them anymore. I didn't know any of the Owls who were sent with us and the commander was far out of my league. It was a dangerous situation I'd willingly helped to create; I was responsible for the fact that I was feeling very alone and not a little stupid.

I didn't sleep for most of the night and heard Olas and his prince talk under their breath for hours. They were trying to find a new angle, a way to solve the ever-evolving riddle. The prince might possess skills with a longknife but he wasn't even left with his eating knife and was no match for the Owls around us, all trained fighters and well-experienced in border conflicts. Every one of them had at least one facial scar to their name.

When they brought the horses out in the morning, they gave me Cirvi's piebald mare; the horse I'd ridden before was laden with supplies. I accepted the reins with hesitation. Cjanis glanced over at me, but joined the queue of riders after Rawil Owl, who towered over everyone on a magnificent blue roan. At first glance, the tufts on the hats of the Owls had struck me as faintly comical but there were no smiles this morning.

Cirvi's mare was a much more comfortable ride than my previous one, a horse that had been specifically selected to serve a person of high status. They'd cleaned the blood off the saddle but there still was a pinkish stain on the grey blanket beneath it. I couldn't help but remember the slack mouth of the wizard, drooling blood, and the way his body had crumpled. He'd made the mistake of not taking the guard seriously enough, and of not dressing in the flashy way that was expected of wizards, but it bothered me that he was left behind in the garrison—a fatality in a power struggle he might not have been fully aware of. It was dumb to assume that Cjanis wouldn't have been happy to use me in the same way; I desperately needed someone to watch my back.

I turned around in the saddle and looked to the men of the Cities, who pretended to ignore me. Ileon was the man I'd known the longest, even if I still hadn't learned how to read him. It felt strange to realize that, in a way, he was all I had left. He'd been with me almost from the very beginning.

"What's wrong?" One of the Owls trotted up to me, her face with wind-bitten bright spots on the cheeks, her brows growing into an uninterrupted line. I gawped at her, and she added, "I'm Raz. You're Slow, right?"

"Sloe, like the bitter fruit."

"Ah, that makes more sense. You won't mind me saying that you look a bit like a Badger with those eyes."

"Half-Badger."

"Hah!" Raz waved at one of the other Owls. "Half-Badger— I win!"

The other Owl grimaced.

"You win what?" I asked curiously.

"Their new pair of weasel pelt gloves. They always go in way too high." She grinned at me. Her eyes were chestnut brown and very round. "Why did you look so sad a moment ago?"

"All my friends are far away."

"Why?"

"Because I was taken from them a few weeks ago."

"Taken?" She blinked.

"Things have changed a lot since then."

"Then you must've done something right, Sloe Moon. I wish I'd been granted the use of such a good horse. Are you her apprentice?" Raz's chin pointed towards Cjanis.

"No. One day I hope to be an apprentice though, to someone. Not to her anymore."

"Why? Wizards are never the easiest people to get along with. And never quite as honest as they would like you to believe."

"It might be in my blood. The Badgers like to choose people with eyes like mine to apprentice them. It could be that. Maybe I'd be happy if I'd never known about it. I could pray a bit and let it be enough."

Raz's eyes narrowed. "Pray to whom?"

"Brother Brook."

"That wouldn't be enough for him," she said flatly. "He always takes the whole arm if you offer him a finger."

"What does that mean?"

"It means that, at least in my experience, Brother Brook is one of the greedier gods. I wanted to be his when I was younger, but I couldn't handle his constant cries for attention. I chose Brother Moon instead, much more laid-back." She grinned again. "And he wanted me to ask you. I assume he couldn't bear to see another Moon this gloomy. To be honest, I must thank you—I'd wondered how I could manage to go back to Featherdig this winter, at least for a few days. My little brother has just moved there, and I haven't seen him in ages. Rawil didn't want to risk me going on my own."

"Where did you and your brother grow up?" I asked her.

"You won't have heard of it—little more than a ditch in the grass with a stable behind it. But we were only a day's ride from the Stoneharp, and we took our horses to market there."

"I always wanted to go to the Stoneharp."

"It looks very impressive," she confirmed. "I've never been inside, though. They don't let just anyone in. At least you can see it before returning back east?"

"At least that. Then I will have seen the Golden Lake, the sea, and the Stoneharp on my travels. That's something to be pleased about, I guess."

"The Golden Lake," Raz gasped. "Lucky you! Is it true? Are the waters so still that all the yellow leaves mirror themselves on its surface?"

"We came a bit late," I admitted. "When I was taken, it was frozen solid enough to walk on. It was still a magnificent sight and one day I hope to get back there and see it in its golden state."

"You could take me with you," Raz suggested.

"I could, if we still know each other."

"I will make it my business to know you," she said. "Rawil always moans about me having a relentless streak."

"Are you related to them?"

"I'm their niece. That's why they get so ridiculously overprotective sometimes. They didn't even want to bring me this far east in the first place, before we heard that Cathil Cloud had left the area."

"He's back in Greycliffs now—or, he was when I left."

"A good time to run, then. I doubt I will miss it much. Most of the time it was mind-numbingly boring. Trust me to be on kitchen duty when something exciting happens at the gate!" She noticed my frown. "Aww, sorry. Was he a friend of yours?"

"No, he most definitely wasn't. He didn't deserve to die like that, though."

"Few people do, I guess."

Raz liked to talk, and I soon noticed that she could be very indiscrete. I hadn't asked her about Rawil Owl's love life and still got the full account of their painful divorce five years before. I told her about Qes but didn't think it wise to mention Tjal just yet.

"He sounds exactly like the kind of man I should try to marry," she said. "But then, I never found these particular men that inspiring. I have the worst taste in people, I'm afraid."

"Me too," I said, before explaining the Saon situation to her.

"Huh," she said afterwards. "Can't blame you. I would've jumped him even quicker. I like the artistic types, especially the ones who can barely hide their selfishness. I was engaged for a while but that went spectacularly wrong, and Mother asked for me to be moved somewhere safer. I doubt she had the borderlands in mind, though. At least there's more choice here. I've had my heart broken more times than I can count, all in the last few months, can you believe that?"

"I really can, though my experiences are more of the 'unrequited love' kind."

"Your mother never wanted you to marry someone incredibly suitable?"

"Well, she wanted me to marry Cathil Cloud but I'm rather relieved that that never happened."

Raz's mouth fell open. "Oh—you're one of *those* Moons."

"I'm afraid I am."

She laughed. "That's perfect. Trust me to find a princeling to gossip with."

"I'm not a ... princeling."

"I know a lot of people who'd disagree with you there."

I poked my thumb over my shoulder. "*He* is a prince. Someone who never dug over the herb garden or brushed dingleberries from the goat's arses, someone who has someone to talk for him."

"Right, so you're *not* a princeling. You're just someone who's name was mentioned in connection with one of the most powerful people in the grasslands." She shrugged. "Why didn't you marry him then?"

"He refused to. Thankfully, though it hurt at the time to be dismissed like that."

"I would marry you," she said. "If you weren't so nice. You're just not my type, I'm afraid."

That made me laugh—finally.

The unforeseen development of getting to know one of my fellow travellers in such a heads-over-heels way kept me from glancing balefully back at Ileon and Olas all the time. I was distracted enough not to notice how quickly time passed on the first day on the road with the Owls. Darkness came so sudden after our midday rest that I stared at the flame-coloured clouds in wonder. The whole plain looked like it was on fire, the snow glittering in a myriad of different colours. Perhaps the Golden Lake was able to keep up with its spectacle in a few short weeks of the year, but the view before me was overwhelming. My eyes brimmed with tears.

"What now?" Raz asked, slightly exasperated.

"I don't think I've ever seen anything this beautiful."

"Really?" She grimaced. "You're easy to impress." She put the left hand behind her saddle and twisted around. "They are all crying," she said.

Olas frantically wiped his face, but the prince stared at the sky, transfixed, his face reflecting the colours, until he noticed us watching him and his expression changed from one moment to the next, turning from rapture to a sneer.

"Hmhm," Raz said. "He looks like a complicated one."

IN HARM'S WAY

Featherdig was laid out similarly to the garrison. It had a palisade and an elevated centre. It must've taken hundreds of Owls weeks and weeks to move the soil gained from digging the ditches into the middle to form a plateau, ringed by houses built from wattle and roofs made from bundles of compacted grass, covered in a thin layer of ice. The angles were so steep that the snow could only build up so far before sliding down between them; it was then carted around the village to be fashioned into windbreaks and insulation for other buildings. The family sigil was painted on everything that came to hand. Every single house was marked with it.

Rawil Owl was obviously well-known—we were let through the Eastgate without any interaction attempts from the guards, or maybe they merely recognized the horse.

Raz leant from the saddle and gave one of the guards an affectionate pat on the head. "See you later!"

"Meet you in the Nest!" he added in a booming voice.

"That's your little brother?" I asked.

"Yes, Rian is the youngest of us and lately had a bit of a growth spurt."

"Is he married?"

"Not quite yet. But he's engaged to someone very much on the jealous side. She'd rip your head off."

"Ah. I don't want to get anyone in trouble."

"Such a noble heart," she mocked. "I'll find you someone," she added. "Featherdig is full of desperate people."

"Thanks a bunch." We grinned at each other.

I'd enjoyed the journey into the west a lot more than expected. Raz and I shared the same sense of humour and had spent a lot of time teasing each other, though I still hadn't told her about Tjal. She had more than enough awful stories to share, and she told them so loudly that everyone around her was entertained as well. At one point, I'd caught Olas staring at her absolutely rapt, waiting for the anecdote to continue.

Raz was an excellent companion, someone who liked to draw the attention without letting it get to her head. She seemed to be well-liked among the Owls and there were definitely worse people to explore Featherdig with.

"What's the Nest?" I asked her.

"One of the grottier taverns, but we like that."

"A tavern? I've never been in one, I don't think."

"You're in for an absolute treat. But I advise you to wipe the bowls before we use them."

The commander brought us to the Roundhouse of Featherdig, the highest building in town, the shape of its roof even more exaggerated. A lot of Owls had congregated in the centre square. Many called out to Rawil, and they held up their gloved right hand in greeting. A fawn-coloured flag hung in front of the entrance, stiffened by frost.

We dismounted and Cjanis came over to us, took the prince by the elbow, and dragged him with her before he had a chance to protest. A gust of hot air singed our faces as she threw the flag aside to follow the commander inside. I kept close to Raz, so close that I could smell the sheepy whiff coming off her woolly hat.

A roar of many voices greeted us, as if we interrupted an assembly in full swing. Olas was pressed against me as we were swept into the house. Around the central brazier stood a large group of people that made way for the wizard and the prince—it took me a few breaths to realize that they were screaming at him in anger.

Olas started to squeeze past me, and I tried to hold him back, but wasn't fast enough to catch his sleeve. Everyone rushed at us, all the Owls in the house. The blade of a longknife was drawn with a flourish. Olas cried out and pulled me along, flinging himself in harm's way with such force that I stumbled in front of him. I saw the blade chop into my arm, the warrior not quick enough to stop himself, his dark eyes wide, his face blanching under the beard. I stared at the red scar on his cheek, then at the longknife stuck in me. I was granted a few heartbeats before the pain came.

"Julas?"

"What the fuck were you thinking?" My sister, in her full apprentice regalia, came sailing at me.

"It wasn't my fault!" I pressed my hand on my arm, but more blood welled up.

"I'm not talking to you, Sloe." Siw kicked Julas hard in the shin.

"What … what are you both doing here?" It was astonishing how quickly the sight of a blade sticking out of me had managed to disperse the Owls into the back area of the Roundhouse. Cjanis still held on to the prince and Olas gawped at me as if the realization that I'd probably just saved his life was still filtering through.

"Did you really think Sjunil would give up on you so easily? She took an educated guess, and we made our way west to intercept you." She pulled my hand off and I sobbed with the pain. "You have to let me see. You're lucky, the cloak took most of the force." She peeled back the sodden layers. "Shit. I need better light and my supplies." She turned to Raz. "Will you help me take them somewhere safe?"

Raz put her arm under my right shoulder and started to pull me up.

"No!" I protested. "I can't leave them here alone with her!"

Siw glanced at the Cloud wizard. "Julas will keep an eye on her."

He looked shaken. I suddenly understood that he'd tried to keep the Owls *away* from the prince, and hadn't actually wanted to hurt any of them. "Sloe," he said. "I'm so sorry. I didn't … you were wearing Cloud colours and …" He gestured towards my blood-spattered grey cloak.

"They need stitches—now!" Siw yelled at him. "You're responsible for keeping the prince and his negotiator alive until I come back. Understood?"

He nodded and I was dragged outside.

"What happened to Qes, Siw?"

Raz held my right shoulder down while Siw cleaned the cut, poked about to see how deep the blade had bitten. "He's with Sjunil."

"He lives?"

"Of course he does. Don't be stupid. Hold still, dammit. You're as twitchy as a squirrel!"

"It fucking hurts!"

"Be grateful that you're still able to complain. Julas isn't known to hold back but he must've tried to stop the blow just in time." The tip of her tongue appeared under her front teeth as she threaded the two bent wire needles. "Prepare," she advised Raz. "They aren't going to like this."

"Wait, wait, wait—I have questions!"

"You can ask them later."

"Where is he, Siw?"

"Further west. We split up to cover more ground. We can send for him and Sjunil after this is over."

I started to sob again, and she huffed in annoyance.

"I can't do it when you're shaking about, Sloe." She turned to Raz. "Help me here."

"I don't really know what's going on," the Owl said defensively.

Siw bent over me, took my face in her hands and wiped my tears away with her thumbs. "You will be back with him soon, I promise. It's so very good to see you, Sloe."

"I love you," I blubbed.

"I love you, too." She kissed the top of my sweaty head. "But now you need to hold it together."

At some point, I'd lost consciousness. When I came to, my left arm was wrapped in bandages and smelled strongly of Siw's favourite salve. She'd cut off my sleeve and used it to bind my wrist to my chest so I was barely able to move the arm at all—probably so I couldn't rip the stitches while asleep. My mouth tasted awful; it was no wonder Ileon had asked not to be drugged again as soon as he was able to stand the pain. Compared to what he'd gone through, my wound was a walk in the meadows, but it was still the deepest injury I'd ever received, while Raz would probably have been able to shrug it off with ease. She sat next to the table they'd stretched me out on, using Siw's waxed thread to repair one of her gloves.

"There you are," she said, relieved. "Your sister went back to the Roundhouse to help." She bit off the thread, wiggled the thumb of the glove back and forth to check the seam and smiled at me. "Why did you do that?"

"It was an accident."

"No, it wasn't. I saw your face. You wanted to protect them. You feared for their life, though they held you hostage."

"I didn't want to see anyone else hurt, after what happened with Cirvi."

"Siw promised to come back and check on you as soon as possible. I'll run down to the Nest and let Rian know that I'm needed here."

"You don't have to stay."

"I want to. At the very least, I want to see your sister do some more magic. There are always cuts and bruises to be nursed at the garrison. I could use the opportunity and learn from her." She softly touched my good arm and stood up.

The door swung open, and the men from the Cities stumbled into the building, the prince with a bloody nose. Julas made way for Raz to pass, still a bit wild-eyed, then closed the door again to stand guard over us. Olas knelt next to me with a flourish—both the prince and I stared at him in confusion.

"Thank you," he said. "Whatever possessed you to do that?"

"It was an accident," I repeated, hesitantly. Maybe Raz had been right?

The negotiator wiped at his face with the back of his hand. "We could all have died."

"Well, we did not." The prince grimaced with bloody teeth. He pulled Olas back to his feet. "This does not change anything. It only serves to show us that the noose around our neck is tightening. What do you think will happen if Sjunil Moon finds us here?"

Olas sniffed. "She'll eat us alive."

"She won't," I protested. "I can speak for you."

The prince looked at me. "Do not take it the wrong way, but I do not want you to speak for me ever again. Bad things happen to both of us when you do." He tried to clean his face with his shawl. "How are you feeling?" he asked with an unexpected tenderness in his voice.

"Not great. I don't understand what happened in there."

Olas closed his eyes as if he needed to gather his strength. "Neither do I. Perhaps they just wanted to see some blood."

"It was a group of Owls reacting to a group of people dressed in Cloud colours," the prince said. "At least you have your sister at hand to patch you up. She will make sure you heal quickly." He looked at his left hand, as if to remind himself of the ordeal he'd gone through not that long ago.

"She said that Qes is alive."

The two men exchanged a glance. "That is great news," Olas said carefully. "At least for you. I can't imagine he will be very happy to see us again."

I gave my bandage a little squeeze. "He's not a vengeful person."

"Do not touch that!" The prince slapped my hand away and groaned in frustration. "We could have saved ourselves so many days on the road, Olas. Now I am back to where we started."

The negotiator patted the dirt from his knees. "But a lot closer to the Stoneharp," he said.

HOW THE STORY GOES ON

"I'm so sorry."

"Shut the fuck up, Julas. I don't need to hear that again. Siw said it's going to be fine, and she should know." I tried to cut my apple one-handed and it jumped out of the bowl. He caught it just before it rolled to the ground and put it back.

"Do you want some help?"

"Not from you."

We were sitting in the house Raz had described as a tavern, though it was hardly more than a communal kitchen with tables scattered about and a strong smell of fermentation. There were a few other places like it in Featherdig, to make sure that all the inhabitants had access to food and drink, and no one tried to cook anything inside the living quarters to limit the dangers of fire spreading through the grass-thatched settlement. The Nest was arranged around a yard with a deep fire pit and quite open to the elements; pots bubbled away on the embers and a goat was roasting on a spit, with a few pieces already removed. Raz had ordered some of the leg for us, as well as dumplings filled with pickled seeds and a kind of root vegetable dish that I wasn't familiar with but had a deep nut-like flavour. I tried to spear the apple again.

"I can't bear to watch this." Julas snatched the apple away from me, chopped it into rough pieces and deposited them rather unceremoniously into my bowl. "I know I didn't handle things well in Goldenlake," he said. "But everything has changed."

I munched on a piece of apple, mealy and cloyingly sweet. "Why?"

"I'm with your sister now."

"You really get around, don't you?"

"I was confused back then."

"It was only a few weeks ago, Julas!"

"But a few weeks ago we were in Goldenlake and everything around us was shifting and things with Qes had come to a halt. I was scared and angry. We do stupid things when we're afraid."

"Yes, we really do," I admitted. "If you hurt Siw I'm going to chop off your pebbles and feed them to the pigs."

"I won't hurt her. She is an extraordinary woman."

I rubbed at the bandage. "You could've had her love much sooner."

"But I kissed Qes first. I didn't want to push him away, in case …"

"In case what?"

"In case he actually would be able to love me."

"You think he didn't love you?"

"He said he didn't. I still miss him sometimes, but he was right. We didn't suit each other. Siw is much more …"

"… ambitious?" I finished for him.

"That too."

"I can't believe that I would've almost given in to you." That I still dream about that fucking kiss from time to time, I added silently. That your face comes to me in the most inconvenient of circumstances.

The door behind us opened and Raz and her little brother joined us. Rian Owl looked a lot like a bear, all beard and straggly hair. He had the same single eyebrow as his sister but one of his front teeth was chipped.

"Glad to see you up on your feet," he said. "More or less."

Raz slipped onto the bench next to me. "I managed to catch up with him eventually." She pulled her bowl back to her to finish her abandoned breakfast. "I think it's warmer today."

Rian's brow vanished into his hairline. "Wishful thinking. We have at least another month of snow."

"It smells a bit like spring to me. I can't wait for the grass to grow again." She licked grease off her thumb. "They said they will bring the prince further west."

"Who said that?" Julas jumped in.

"Apparently, the Cloud wizard wants to get rid of him as quickly as possible. Rawil has offered to arrange for transport to the coast. They want to put him somewhere really safe."

"But I probably shouldn't travel yet!" I squealed.

Everyone stared at me. "What makes you think that you're going with them?" Julas asked quietly. "Sjunil had very precise instructions for us. We're going home, Sloe."

"The fuck we will. I'm not leaving them behind."

"Is the prince your boyfriend or something?" Rian asked.

I felt the blood rush to my head. "Of course not!"

"Have they made you swear anything? The wizards will take care of it, don't worry."

"No, but …"

"But what?" Rian asked, still chewing.

Raz sighed. "You feel responsible somehow."

"He's a valuable person, important to all the men of the Cities. I don't know if Rawil realizes how much they can get for him if they find the right angle." I worried at the bandage on my upper arm, wincing as I irritated the stitches by mistake. "It sounds daft but … I feel … not just responsible. It's as if the gods had planned for us to meet."

Julas groaned and slammed the point of his eating knife into the table. "Horseshit, Sloe."

"Siw would say that nothing is impossible—nothing the gods have set their minds to."

"I'm sure your dear aunt would find dozens of arguments against it," Julas said. "You should be grateful that you're still alive. There were days on the road when it was difficult to remain hopeful. Sjunil said she just knew you weren't already dead, but Siw was in quite a bad state."

"I bet you loved cheering her up."

"Stop it. You owe it to her to get your arse out of danger. If you won't do it for yourself, do it for your sister."

"Siw would want me to follow the path the gods have given to me."

"Yes—the path back home, the path back to Tall Trees."

"Nah. Sounds boring."

He looked as if he wanted nothing more in the world than to slap me so hard that my teeth rattled. "Sometimes you're just like Qes, you know that? It must be the Badger in you."

"I need to know how the story goes on, can't you understand? When will I ever have the chance to travel this far into the west again? It would be stupid to turn around now."

He threw up his hands. "I'm done arguing with you. And I won't protect you, either."

Cjanis waited for me under the sloping roof of the House of Women in Featherdig, her beautiful face pale and immobile. "I think we should talk," she said. "I know that you feel disappointed in me, but I hope that this serves as a lesson to you."

I tried to cross my arms, but the stitches wouldn't let me. "Why did I need to learn a lesson?"

"Because you need to leave some things to the wizards. You're not a wizard, Sloe. You never will be, even if you find someone irresponsible enough to take you on as their apprentice. Your mother made the right choice for you—I don't think that you have what it takes to withstand the power of the gods."

"What are they going to do with him?"

"They will keep him until someone offers an adequate price, what else? It's all in the hands of the Owls now and I must say that

I am glad to be rid of him. He has bought me what I wanted, and I am more than happy to release him. I cannot understand for the life of me why you have such a soft spot for him, Sloe. He is not a good man."

"Are you a good woman?"

"What do you think?" She stared at me, her dark eyes glittering.

"I think you're an opportunist, Cjanis Cloud. And a sweet-talker, who is able to hide an iron core long enough for people to fall for your words. I think you enjoy causing pain as much as your brother does, though you despise him so much. You're dangerous, and that probably makes you a good wizard, of much value to the gods who treasure this sort of ruthlessness. But I think *you* think that behind all of this you're a good person, because you sweet-talk yourself just as much. I might be weak and poor wizard material, but at least I don't have any illusion left about myself. You can't break me down enough for your purpose, I'm afraid. What will you do now?"

"Negotiate with the Owls, forge an historic alliance—a pact that will be talked about for generations to come. You don't get to make this sort of impact if you aren't prepared to take some risks in life. I see you have found new friends among the Owls. They will tell you as much."

"No, they won't. They're the people caught up in the alliance. They'll be the ones who truly take the risks—the warriors and guards who'll never have the chance to govern their families."

"They, too, will disappoint you. You are the type of person who always ends up cursing themself for placing their trust in the wrong people."

"You don't really know me," I said, my voice wobblier than I would've liked. "I'm so relieved that you didn't allow me to become your apprentice, to make myself beholden to a wizard who embodies all the worst aspects of the job."

She folded her long fingers around the staff. "What makes you so angry with me, Sloe?"

"The way you pushed Cirvi on to die."

"I did not kill him."

"You knew that his arrogance would doom him soon enough."

She shrugged. "But that is hardly my fault. You need to learn, Sloe. So much."

"No more lessons from you." I turned away from her. "I wish you luck with your negotiations. Give my best to your brother when you stab him in the back next time."

The silver felt warm, soaked in the heat of my skin as I pulled the amulet from my tunic. Snow blew over the centre square of Featherdig and when I closed my eyes and breathed in until my chest hurt, I could almost persuade myself to taste the salt of the sea again, though we were still at least two days away from the coast.

It was a short prayer, to forget Cjanis' words and to not let them sting, lacerate, destroy me. In all the weeks I'd spent away from Tall Trees, I'd started to suspect that I'd been cheated out of the right direction, just because Qarim Badger had proven himself to be unworthy so many years ago. I didn't want to be the kind of wizard she was—even my aunt wouldn't have suited me as a master, but somewhere someone would be brave enough to take me on, to risk their reputation for Sloe Moon of Tall Trees, to help me come closer to the gods—closer to touching their hands and pulling them down to meet my eye. If Brother Brook was a greedy god, as Raz had said, that might make him suit me best after all, even if I didn't crave the kind of power that Cjanis hungered for with such impatience. I wanted to know what happened next; I wanted to know how I could stay in the story, as a witness, or as more than a witness.

"You shouldn't be out here." My sister, her herb bag slung over one shoulder, stepped closer. "You should stay warm and keep your strength up."

"Siw, do you think I would make a good wizard?"

She winced. "Maybe once. It's too late to catch up now. There is so much to study that I feel like I'm falling behind all the time, but apart from that, maybe there is a certain sensibility. Sjunil must have wanted to train you for a reason."

"Do you ever feel as if you've not come far enough?"

She smiled and took my wrist. "All the fucking time."

SOMEONE NICE

The commander considered Raz and me with an air of resignation. "I suppose I can't forbid you to come?"

They studied their niece, twiddling an inky reed between their fingers. A message lay half-written in front of them. The room was small and stuffy; it smelled of work and boredom and was little more than a shed attached to the back of the Roundhouse. It served as a storage area for benches and a rusty pile of smaller braziers, but also had a table and a rickety folding chair, a row of oil lights, and a binder filled with paper cut to different sizes—paper made from pressed grasses, sanded smooth enough to write on.

Raz gave me a little shove and I cleared my throat. "I need to go," I said.

"And I *want* to go," Raz added.

"Cjanis Cloud warned me that I would find it hard to shake you off, Sloe. But she also said that you might indeed be useful. As long as you explain the situation to your aunt. I don't want to get on the wrong side of Sjunil Moon."

"I will," I promised, a little too eagerly. "Can I see them?"

Rawil Owl scratched at their neck and accidentally smeared some ink on themself. "Just for a moment."

"A moment will be enough."

Olas looked as if he'd had a sleepless night. "I suppose you're here to say goodbye?" he asked wearily.

The two men from the Cities were huddled together in a corner of the small guesthouse. The fire in the brazier had burned down in the night and no one had come to bring more fuel.

"No. I'm here to let you know you won't get rid of me that easily. I'll be coming with you."

The prince, his face still a bit swollen around the mouth, scoffed. "You are unbelievable. This was your chance to get out of the whole mess."

"I quite like being in this particular mess. You might need someone else to translate at some point."

Olas seemed relieved. "Thank you, Sloe. In a weird way, you have been the most loyal man of all."

"Not a man."

"Apologies. The most loyal person of all. I'm not sure why you're doing this, but I have no doubt that we'll profit from your commitment in one way or another." He poked his elbow at the prince. "You should thank them, not mock them."

"I didn't expect him to thank me. I just wanted to inform you that we will leave Featherdig shortly."

"To meet up with your aunt?" Ileon asked.

"I very much hope so. I don't know where she is right now, but it won't take her long to find us, I'm sure."

"Will you stand by us when she tries to rip me a new one?" the prince asked.

"A new what?" Olas asked, but then thought his way through the words. "Oh."

"I will try," I promised.

"And hopefully explain that we were not responsible for your injuries?" He pointed at the bandaged arm strapped to my chest. "Before she sees us, preferably."

"Why are you so afraid of her?" I asked.

"Because Sjunil Moon could give Cathil Cloud a run for his money," Olas answered for him. "She just uses words instead of blades."

"I thought you didn't believe in wizards?"

"This has nothing to do with wizards or your horribly pedantic gods," the prince snapped. "This has to do with the fact that your aunt is the most dangerous person I know."

"Pedantic?" I asked. "Why do you call our gods pedantic?"

"Because they seem to demand full control over the smallest things."

"I would call that 'detail-oriented'."

Olas laughed at that. "I've missed this," he chuckled.

"Thanks to my gods I'm back with the families now—and with the *right* kind of family. I don't have any reason to complain." I nodded at them and pulled the door closed behind me. Julas stepped aside to let me pass. He'd joined the rota of guards keeping watch over them.

"How did you find them?" he asked.

"Argumentative, as always."

"How's the arm?"

"Still a nuisance, thank you so very much."

He came closer. "Do you really still love him? After all that happened to you?"

I wanted to throw another snarky remark at him but instead I swallowed my words. "I don't know," I confessed. "Would that be so strange?"

"It's strange that you let him do these things to you but have such a hard time forgiving me for kissing you."

"I kissed you," I clarified, turning to walk away from him. "And I can't forgive *myself.*"

I met Raz and Rian in the Nest to celebrate our last evening in Featherdig with beer brewed from grass seeds, more roasted goat, and cake made from ground nuts and honeyed berries. I didn't look forward to living off dried rations again, even if we had a chance of eating fresh fish at the coast. The beer was strong and had a bitter taste I wasn't used to; it took only one bowl for me to feel woozy and a bit too warm.

I ripped my grey shawl off. "I can't wait to see Qes again. He must've had such adventures of his own."

"And I can't wait to meet him after so many glowing endorsements from you. Are you sure you don't want him?"

"We're just friends. I would still welcome your expertise in those matters."

Rian coughed into his beer. "Expertise? Have you told them about …"

"Yes," his sister said. "I've never pretended to know all the answers. But I know lots of eligible young warriors, some of them tried and tested by yours truly. Wait until you get your heart broken—your luck can't hold forever."

"Luck?" He tried to smooth down his beard. "Just because I don't fling myself at everyone who lifts their hand to greet me?"

"Not all of us are blessed with such self-restraint," Raz bit back.

"Or confidence," I added gloomily, feeling the effects of the beer all too keenly.

"What exactly are you looking for?" Rian asked me, cutting a piece of goat into steaming slivers.

"Just someone nice."

He snorted. "*Just*?"

"Someone who doesn't make me feel bad about myself. Loyal. Funny. Kind."

"… and handsome?" he finished my list.

"Maybe."

"I doubt Raz knows many people who fit that description. With us Owl warriors there's always a certain kind of … unhelpful arrogance involved."

I thought of Julas and shuddered. "Which can probably be quite attractive."

"It depends," he said. "Do you need someone to marry or someone to bed?"

I felt myself blush. "To bed. For now."

Raz laughed. "Thank the gods—that makes it so much easier!"

Quite a few people came together to watch us leave. I could see Cjanis Cloud standing with a large group of important-looking Owls; it seemed as if the talks around the alliance were progressing well. Rawil pulled their blue roan close to me and their shawl tighter around them.

"I hope you don't regret your decision already," they rumbled. "Horrible weather to set out across the plains."

A strong northerly wind whipped the snow about the streets and would be a lot worse once we were out in the open. "Not quite yet," I said. The one thing I regretted was to leave my sister again. Siw and Julas stood next to the Roundhouse. They were set on following my aunt's instructions and turning back east as soon as possible. Siw was obliged to follow her master's will, and perhaps she secretly longed to get back to Tall Trees and start preparations for wedding celebrations. I saw her holding on tight to Julas' hand, then pulling him across the square to me.

"Promise that you'll come back home as soon as the prince has been exchanged."

I'd decided to call the piebald mare after her late owner, though I hadn't liked him half as much as his horse. I arranged the reins over Cirvi's stripey mane. "I can't, Siw."

"Mother won't like it that I found you and let you go again."

"She doesn't have to like it. It's my decision."

"A stupid decision." She touched my knee, pleadingly. "Don't forget to take care of the wound. The stitches need to come out soon—you will have to find a wizard in the west. Don't let Sjunil do it, she's not good with fiddly stuff."

"Noted."

Her fingers squeezed and I yelped. "Not funny," she said, and I could see that she was close to crying. "I need you in Tall Trees when the baby comes."

I stared at her. "What?"

"You heard me." She released my knee and stepped back from the mare.

I was too stunned to concentrate much on my surroundings after that. The thought of Siw being a mother was nothing less than terrifying, and it was more than likely that her master wouldn't be too happy about the development. But Sjunil had sent her off with Julas ... she must've known that something like that could happen. But then, a pregnant apprentice was bound to only be around for a limited time ...

"What's wrong?" Raz asked eventually, the same question that had started off our friendship.

"My sister is going to have a baby."

"With the guy who almost cut your arm off?" Raz pulled her tufted hat over her ears to protect them from the wind. She had to scream at me to make herself heard.

I managed to nod. "The guy who fell in love with Qes, and then wanted to get off with me."

She shrugged. "Unhelpful arrogance, like Rian said."

"I'm not sure what it is with him. Maybe it's not confidence as such. I wonder whether he'll be a good husband to her. He'll have to, to keep the favour of the gods."

She grinned. "That sounds painful enough."

I stared out into the snow, at the big haunches of Rawil Owl's gelding powering through the drifts in front of us. "I don't want it to be painful, for either of them."

The wind pressed into my bandages. I'd tried to patch up my cloak as best as possible, but nothing really helped against the force of it; Cirvi was carrying her shaggy head low, and I could feel her labouring breath. It was questionable whether we'd get very far. Maybe it had been foolish not to wait for a few more days, but every step brought me closer to seeing Qes again, to having him hug me after I'd imagined him dead for weeks.

With my left hand bound to me beneath the cloak, I had to drop the reins and push them under my knee to touch the amulet.

Brother Brook, please make my sister happy.

TO FIND MYSELF SO DRAWN

The wind relented on the second day and it seemed to be a bit warmer than before, the snow clumping together so that from time to time we had to clear the horses' hooves out to avoid the snow building up inside them. The provisions we carried with us were much tastier than the fare in the garrison, and so we ate well. The men from the Cities kept away from me. Whenever there was a problem, Olas sorted it directly with the Owls. It looked as if the prince meant what he'd said to me before: I was no longer required to speak for them.

Rawil Owl was also more of the quiet type, though their orders were clear and plenty enough. The warriors around us had been stationed in Featherdig for a while and obviously enjoyed the opportunity to get out of town. One of them had a good singing voice and could often be heard humming away at the end of the group when the wind left off. We were transporting hostages, but the mood was different with no wizard among us. Raz helped me with the bandages and the small pot of salve Siw had bestowed upon me to tide me over until I was able to find another healer at the coast.

On our last evening on the road she was tucking in the ends of the cloth strips when she said, "Sloe, I have been thinking."

I took another drink from the skin filled with strong honey wine. It always helped with the pain when Raz prodded the stitches. "Hmhm?"

She cleaned her hands on the seat of her trousers. "If you want someone to bed, you could just have me."

I barely managed to swallow the mouthful of wine before I started to cough. "What?"

"I can't promise you that it won't be awkward or just plain weird, but I really like you and maybe it's time for me to make some better decisions. We both will marry other people one day, but it would be nice to have some company." Suddenly I noticed how close she was to me, arranging the sleeve of my tunic over the bandages to hold off the wind. She sat back on her heels. "What do you think about that?" She smiled at me with no hint of unease about her, nothing that made me worry that she wouldn't take a rejection with a quick laugh.

"You really mean it?"

"It seems as if we're both searching for similar things. Rian said I should ask you."

"You know for sure that this is going to be awkward. I'm … I'm not that experienced—I've only ever been with two people. Two men."

She shrugged. "I can show you what I like. And if it doesn't work, you'll be on your way east before long anyway, and I bet Rawil will have their plans for me as well. It's a suggestion, Sloe—no need to get your smallclothes in a twist." She rocked back to stand up.

"Wait—Raz, please wait." My hand shook as I took her wrist and pulled her closer. "Promise me that you won't be mad at me if it turns out that I'm not what you want after all? I really like you, too and it would be horrible to lose you just because we are both so desperate for something else."

"I'm not sure I can promise, but I can certainly do my best." She grinned. "I assume this is a yes?"

I swallowed nervously. "Let me try something." I let go of her wrist and reached around the back of her neck. She leant over me and our mouths met. She tasted of the spices and herbs the dried meat strips had been marinated in, her nose pressed into my cheek, and her tongue—I felt a deep shudder running through me as her hands cradled me.

"Did it work?" she asked, still so close that our lips touched when she spoke.

"Oh gods, yes."

"Well, they say that practice makes perfect." She got to her feet and began to clear the dirty bandages away.

I looked up and saw Olas and the prince staring at me with hanging jaws, while Rawil hid a smile in their soup bowl.

"What was that?" It'd been days since the prince had spoken to me.

I pulled up my good shoulder. "We wanted to test something."

"You are with her now?"

I stabilized the next bowl against the ground before I scrubbed it clean with my right hand. "Probably."

No one expected the two hostages to do work in the camp, but he pushed the pile of dirty bowls over to me with the tip of his boot. "I thought you liked men."

"I like them. Doesn't mean I can't be interested in something else, too."

"Whenever I believe that I am starting to understand you ..." he said sourly.

"Why do you need to understand me?"

"Because you are in my life, Sloe Moon, and I like to have a handle on my life. Admittedly, at the moment I do not feel in control of it most of the time. Perhaps that is why I am taking this news with less grace than I should." There was a strange vulnerability in his face. "Maybe it is just loneliness." He turned around and left me to the rest of the dishes.

Rawil came to me next. "What did he want?"

"To voice his displeasure. He likes everything in clear categories, as all of them do."

The commander squatted next to me and started to dry off the bowls. "I've noticed that," they said quietly. "I suppose that is what makes them so ill-suited to work with the families instead of against us. Let me know if they are bothering you, will you? They might need a reminder of their new status, though they will find themselves without a doubt as soon as we reach our next destination. Featherdig is a well-equipped settlement, but the arrangements in Beakdig aren't that comfortable." They put the damp cloth over their shoulder and took up the pile of clean clay bowls. "I probably won't have to warn you about my niece, right? You're both sensible and reasonable enough to know what you're doing?"

I thought about the kiss we'd shared so publicly and felt the blood rush to the top of my ears. In just a few heartbeats everything had changed, and it felt as if I'd suddenly found myself hanging over a cliff, longing to plunge down and experience the fall.

"That's a very generous assessment," I murmured.

"Maybe more aspirational than accurate," they said, with another of their enigmatic smiles. "But we all live in hope."

"Did one of them try to talk you out of it?" Raz asked as we found ourselves alone before I started the first watch of the night.

"Not really. But I think they both had their concerns."

She dug out another handful of split wood from the pack we'd brought with us and moved it closer to the fire to dry off some more. "Are you worried?"

"A bit. What if I don't do it right?"

She laughed, rubbing her forehead with the back of her glove and left some dust from the firewood behind. "You will try again. It's not magic, Sloe. But we should probably wait until we have reached Beakdig to give it our first go. I don't fancy all of them holding their breath while we fuck."

I exhaled, relieved. I'd done that too many times already. "Sounds good."

"I'd hoped that you'd agree." She glanced over her shoulder. "Do you want me to stay?"

"No, get some rest while you can."

"Who has second watch?"

I jerked my thumb into the direction of the warrior who was already snoring in his bedroll. "See you tomorrow."

She stepped over the new log pile and took my face into her gloved hands. Our second kiss didn't shake me quite as much, but I felt myself pushing into her nonetheless and was glad to find myself so drawn to her. "See you tomorrow."

Temperatures dropped overnight and the snow was covered with a thin layer of ice that was sharp enough to cut into the horses' fetlocks. The commander's gelding had the largest hooves and thickly feathered legs, so he trampled the path clear for the rest of us. We followed in single file, drawn out over the plain. I was becoming more familiar with Cirvi and started to feel safe with her. Raz rode a few places further back and I was glad not to talk through the morning, but to focus on my expectations for Beakdig.

I was impatient to see the sea again, to be at the west coast for the very first time in my life, and was getting nervous about the plans Raz had for me. When she spoke about it, it all made sense, but we hadn't known each other long at all and though she'd seen me partly unclothed when cleaning my arm, I was still apprehensive about disappointing her. Having had her way with almost all of the garrison, she probably expected me to measure up, even if I pleaded ignorance. At least in that respect, things with Tjal had been easier. It still hurt to think of him, of the way I'd pulled away from him in the end. Who was to say I wouldn't feel the urge to do the same thing to Raz?

I didn't notice that the commander had reined in their horse. Cirvi's nose bumped against the chestnut mare in front of her and she started to nibble at the top of her tail before I had my wits about me again. The chestnut mare screeched and stomped one of her hindlegs; I had to turn Cirvi's head aside to avoid an altercation, my attention on getting her away from the other mare—but the smell was back, the smell of the sea.

We'd reached a slight ridge in the landscape. Before the commander's blue roan, the ground fell gently into a dip and after another expanse of snow, rose again to the coast where a rectangular settlement had been built along the highest stretch. Behind that was the ice, pushed up in ragged-edged plates and refrozen, though undoubtedly in the process of thawing. Beakdig had three crude watchtowers positioned at the corners and in the middle of the village, on the tallest, a fawn-coloured banner was being raised: they had spotted us on the ridge.

I turned around in the saddle, but the prince was too far behind me in the line of horses to make out his face. We were only a day's ride away from the Stoneharp and that probably meant several things to him. He'd sailed from the Cities to the west coast because the Stoneharp was unmissable and its coast easily accessible to seamen not familiar with our waters. No captain from the Cities would've been stupid enough to try their luck at Greycliffs without a native navigator on board, but the west coast had better landing sites, used by the families for generations.

For the prince, it must've felt like coming full circle.

For me, it was proof that I'd actually done it; I'd reached the sea again. Soon I'd see the Stoneharp and really have something to tell back home.

Raz gave Cirvi a pat on the arse as she overtook me. "It's quite a sight, isn't it?"

"I hadn't expected the sea to be frozen. It wasn't at Greycliffs. Will you visit your family while you're here?"

She scrunched her face up. "Nah, I don't think so. I left under quite a dark cloud. I can't even think about the last words I yelled at my mother without wanting to punch myself in the nose. I hope you'll be able to see it when spring has properly started. This is one of the most beautiful places in the world." She had a light in her eyes I'd never seen before, and I couldn't help but wonder if she would still want me to stay in the west after our first night together.

❧

START PRAYING

The commander of Beakdig was a youngish man with a braided beard and a hat with the biggest wool tufts I'd ever seen. I wasn't sure if it meant his rank surpassed Rawil's, or if it was merely an affectation. For a man stationed at the furthest edge of the Owl territory, he was suspiciously well-groomed.

"This is the prince?" He fiddled with the glass bead at the end of his beard. "I hadn't imagined him this … scrawny."

Rawil seemed mildly annoyed. "Careful, Rovan. He can hear you perfectly well."

"No gold, no sealskin cloak? Are you sure you have the right man?"

"I'm sure." He couldn't have missed the edge in Rawil's gravelly voice.

"We'll find a shed for him somewhere. Why don't you keep him fettered?"

"Because it would have been impractical for travel in the snow."

"I didn't realize you could be so reckless, Rawil."

I could see the older commander's right fist clench in their glove, but they didn't say anything else. They just turned around, made a face at me, and pushed past the door on the ground floor of the middle tower. We were all exhausted and dirty, from the guards to the hostages. I followed them outside, though the last thing I wanted to do was to leave Olas and the prince with the young commander.

"Is he always such a …"

"Dick?" Rawil Owl growled. "Sometimes I'm not sure he even knows that he has that effect on people."

"Do I need to be concerned? Will he do something stupid as soon as you go back east?"

"Probably." Rawil's hand took my good arm. "But if I'm not very much mistaken, I'd say you can handle him, Sloe Moon. You're under no obligation to obey him, or even respect him."

"And you are?"

"He used to be my husband and rose to his position with my help. It's no one's fault but my own." Their smile was slow and sad. "I'm going to find myself some honey wine and drink until morning. Please don't try to find me."

I waited in front of the tower, and it only took a few moments for the young commander to appear with two muscular Owls behind him, each of them bundling a hostage along. I joined them, though the guards gave me an irritated glance, and I saw the relief on Olas' stubbly face. They were brought to a building that reminded me of the pigsty Tjal and I had spent so much time in. It was crammed in between the common kitchen and the stables for the garrison's horses.

When Rovan Owl kicked the door open, an unhappy yellow dog growled at him, reluctant to be banished from his lair. He took it by the scruff of the neck and hauled it out into the cold. The shed smelled of dog blankets and mould; broken tack had been flung into a corner some time ago and apparently been forgotten, a tangled mass of straps and leather covered in spots of mildew. A couple of benches were put on top of each other and could be turned into a narrow sleeping platform. The heat from the horses next door seeped into the shed. No wonder the dog had sought shelter there.

"That will do for now."

The men from the Cities were pushed into the dark as the commander's eyes found me. "Get them something from the kitchens and more blankets. You will make sure that the guards are changed every two hours and if there is a scratch on them, I'm holding you responsible." His brows drew together. "Who are you again?"

"Sloe Moon of Tall Trees."

"Slow Moon?"

"Sloe, like the bitter fruit."

"Whatever." He made a dismissive gesture. "You're Rawil's new …"

"Their new what?"

His eyes were hard. "I never knew they liked them this fat."

"No! No, I'm not involved with them at all!"

That surprised him even more. "Why are you here?"

"I'm here for them." I gestured towards the men of the Cities.

"You're their servant?"

"No."

He chuckled joylessly. "The Moons have truly lost their bite. See to them, then." He left me standing with his guards, staring after him.

"Is he always this …"

"… yeah," mumbled one of the guards. "That's him all right."

Raz helped me organize the watches.

"You didn't tell me that I would be insulted by their former husband!"

"He always was the jealous type," she said with a shrug. "Don't let him get to you—he's throwing his weight around to get back at Rawil."

"Why would they ever get married to someone like him?"

"The usual—family politics. In the end, it lasted longer than all of us thought it would." She narrowed her brown eyes at me. "Would you care for some distraction, Sloe?"

"Now?"

"Later there'll be too much to do. Come with me." She grabbed my good wrist and pulled me with her into the stable, where a girl watched over the horses, ordering the tattered bridles we'd pulled out from the shed earlier. Raz made an impatient gesture at her.

"Off you fuck, little cousin."

She looked up, noticed Raz's hand on me, and grinned far too knowingly before scuttering away.

Cirvi had been stabled in one of the last stalls and turned around with hay between her teeth when we joined her. Raz carefully leant me against the dividing wall and kissed me. I'd never known such a good kisser; she did something to me that made my legs shake. The sweet smell of the hay was around us and I was almost able to forget that Olas and the prince were just a few wooden boards away, probably scared and almost hungry again. Raz's fingers dug into my arse as she pulled me to her, and I wasn't able to stifle a moan. She turned me around by my good shoulder.

"Undo the laces," she said, and my right hand fumbled with my trousers. "I'm going to touch you now," she whispered. "If you still want to go ahead with this?" I tried to turn around to kiss her again, but she stopped me. "Say it, Sloe."

"Yes, of course I still want it!"

"Just making sure." She buried her mouth in my hair, her left hand sliding between my legs while she ground into me, her thighs hard with muscle, her breasts riding up against my back. My forehead was pressed against the wall, my breath coming in deep, desperate gulps.

"Slow down," I croaked. "Otherwise it's going to be over too fast."

She allowed me to turn around. She'd already unlaced herself and wiggled her trousers down a bit more when I tried to reach into them. My head was in the crook of her elbow as she held me, the left hand covering my fingers, directing me.

"More to the left. That's too far the wrong way. Here. Just here."

She felt unexpectedly soft and sticky; the tip of her middle finger was on mine as she pushed me down and in. I could feel her breath getting erratic, her eyes were half closed.

"Try a second finger," she said, and I had little difficulty following her command. "Brother Moon," she gasped into my sweaty temple.

"Good?"

"Excellent—keep going. Don't you dare to slow down."

I flinched as her own hand found me again and we stared at each other, before giggling helplessly.

"Try again," she said then. "You almost had me there."

Afterwards, we sat for a while against the wall, her head on my shoulder. "What's the verdict?" I asked.

"Promising beginnings." She kissed the side of my neck. "Believe me, I've had worse experiences. Much worse, in fact." She sat up straight.

"What do you mean?"

Her face clouded over. "We'll talk about it later. Now I'm hungry. Aren't you hungry?"

"I'm always hungry. But if you start kissing me again, I might be up for another round."

"Then you liked it." She smiled. "I wasn't sure at first."

"It did feel a bit weird, but that's just me."

"We'll find some time," she promised. "I should talk to Rawil." She got to her feet. Cirvi snuffled at her and Raz stroked her long bony nose. "She's such a sweetie," she said. "You're lucky, Sloe." She fixed her laces and left me in the stables.

"Do we really need the small one?" the young commander asked sceptically. "He'll be another mouth to feed, and our provisions are starting to run low."

Rawil sniffed. "He's his negotiator and an important man in his own right—Sloe?"

Both commanders turned around to face me; my thoughts had been with Raz's hand wedged in my smallclothes and the moment I'd felt her shudder against me and stammer Brother Moon's name a second time.

"Huh?"

"I'd say Olas da Ozanil is worth keeping alive," Rawil said quietly.

"What?" It felt as if someone had pushed me in the river after the snowmelt.

"Rovan here is of the opinion that resources are limited and that it would be easier to dispatch him forthwith."

"You can't be serious!" I barked at Rawil's ex-husband.

He smiled at me. His canines were sharp and white; he reminded me unfavourably of a ferret. "For the good of the garrison. Early spring is always a very lean time around here."

"What about fish?"

"The closest landing site is at the Stoneharp, and everything up there is expensive. This is not the time to get sentimental—there are plenty more men of the Cities."

"But we need this one!"

"Do we really, though?" Rovan asked.

"Yes, we do! If the Owls are supposed to find any arrangement with them, he needs to be kept alive and well. Otherwise, the prince will take his revenge as soon as he feels himself able to do so—you'll see. Your head will be on a spike before anyone can say 'totally dumb idea'."

"Why is a Moon this invested in the fate of two men of the Cities?" He propped his elbows on the table. "Which one of them have you fucked? Both of them?"

"Neither of them. It's against all the rules to treat hostages this way, if you actually want to achieve something, isn't it?" I glanced at Rawil, pleadingly.

They pulled up their right shoulder in a half-hearted shrug. "He knows that, Sloe."

"So he's just trying to be a …"

Rovan's brow furrowed expectantly. Chances were that he just wanted me to insult him so that he could kick me out of Beakdig.

I tried to breathe in deeply. "I've spent a lot of time in the company of both men, and we indeed need both alive. We will find rations for them until they are moved on."

"Then pray for a quick thaw." Rovan sneered. "Before we start roasting *all* the rats. Last year, conditions were so bad that no one was able to come through for weeks. In the end, we had to sacrifice ten horses for the pots. You could volunteer your horse."

"It won't come to that."

"Just start praying, Sloe Moon."

THINGS THAT SHOULDN'T BE RUSHED

Brother Brook listened to me, at least for a while. It got noticeably warmer over the next few days, and everyone in Beakdig seemed to heave a sigh of relief. One night, I woke up because rain came down hard on the roof of the small Other House. They'd given me my own platform. There were only a few Others in the garrison, but they'd kept their distance, probably aware that I wasn't their commander's favourite person.

I'd watched the warriors train in the square, all of them going through the same form sequences before breaking up into smaller groups to beat the living daylights out of each other. No wonder Raz knew how to deal with cuts; even the wooden training swords had edges thin enough to slice.

All the Owls in the garrison had lived such a life for many years—had been chosen from early childhood and the training had formed their bodies as it had formed Raz's, the one I was becoming more and more familiar with. I'd enjoyed watching her train and besting quite a few of her comrades, before she received a blow to the side of the neck that made her tap out.

They were the Owls Cjanis Cloud needed to fight her brother and though the Clouds had a fearsome reputation, I didn't envy them the prospect of getting up close and personal with the force stationed in Beakdig. Rawil Owl, they of the deep sighs and hanging shoulders, underwent the most astonishing transformation as soon as they drew a longknife. The weapon they favoured was rather crudely made but changed with them, becoming sleek and ever so deadly, the tip filed to the finest of points. Rawil's air of resignation gave way to precise movements, measured and eerily calm as their opponent huffed and sweated through the exercise.

Raz stood next to me, pressing a scarf filled with snow against her neck. "What did I say?"

"They are amazing. Do you think I could've learned how to fight like this?"

She shrugged and winced as she repositioned the scarf against her skin. "If you'd started a long time ago maybe, but not like them. I've always wanted to be as good as them but probably never will be—which is fine, though it makes watching them bittersweet. Are you up for a meeting in the stables later?"

"With that crick in your neck? It's going to be a massive bruise—it's already getting purple."

"You just need to talk me out of being on top again." She gave me a little shove. "How are your ducklings today?"

"Grumpy and fed up with the horrible food. I took them out for a walk this morning, but the weather doesn't agree with them."

As I listened to the rain battering down, I knew that it would make things worse. When I poked my nose out of the door the next day, everything was coated in ice—beautiful, but more than impractical for the running of Beakdig.

There was no training that day and the warriors were busy trying to keep parts of the settlement walkable, spreading crushed pebbles and sand around, digging blocks of snow from the streets to melt down for drinking water. Raz and I were surely not the only ones trying to make the best of the time, though I couldn't persuade her not to straddle me; she liked it that way. It was easier with my arm as well, though I'd stopped strapping it down. The stitches would have to come out very soon, even if they had no wizard in the garrison.

My head was propped up at an uncomfortable angle against the wall and I tried to stuff more hay under my neck. We were used to rushing through our encounters, but she lowered herself slowly downwards and started to peel off the layers that covered the lacing of her breastband. It took her a while to get the knot out of the greasy linen tape, then she pulled herself free. It was the first time I'd seen her so naked. The cold air puckered and hardened her, but her skin still flamed against my mouth.

She cradled my head as I caressed her; she tasted like salt and her breasts folded around my face. I'd felt them before, but only ever underneath all those winter clothes; she shivered and moaned, gently guided me over to the other side, while she moved on me, languidly, her right hand snaking down, cupping my arse. She'd asked me early on if I liked to be touched in that way and I waited for her fingers to slip into me while she lifted me deeper into herself. It usually didn't take me long to finish after that, but she made me beg for it, distracted me with her breasts again until I'd made her come for the first time. When I managed to get her off early, she could usually squeeze in a second time if we kept going, and for once, there were no chores waiting for her. She surprised me as she let herself glide off me and rolled around. I'd barely caught up with her as someone cleared their throat behind my horse.

"I thought I'd probably find you both here." Rawil had turned their broad back to us. "This arrived from the north for you, Sloe." They brandished a squashed tube of grass paper. "Looks urgent, I'm afraid."

Raz sprawled in the hay next to me while I was trying to make out the glyphs. "What's wrong?" she asked.

"My aunt is angry. She writes that I should've stayed with Siw and Julas."

"You knew that and you decided to ignore her instructions."

"She's easier to ignore when she's not here. Can you make out this word?"

She leant over and squinted at the crumpled paper. "Incensed?" she guessed. "Gods, her handwriting is bad. They drilled it into me from the beginning that legibility saves lives in the right circumstances, but I suppose that doesn't usually trouble a wizard. What will you do?"

"I'll wait for her to come and get me."

For the first time, she looked worried. "You're sure about that?"

"You've heard Rovan. As soon as my back is turned, he'll give the order to clomp Olas over the head. I'm not going back now. I need to see the Stoneharp before I let anyone do that to me."

She laid her wrists on her naked knees. "What are you hoping to find there?"

"Answers. Not … actual spoken answers, but … maybe I'll be able to understand my father a bit better if I'm actually there. With him, in a way. Do you know what I mean?"

"No." She slowly shook her head. "Are we going to go on? It's getting a bit chilly, even for me, and I'd rather wrap up again before my nipples drop off."

"I don't think so, sorry—I'm not in the mood anymore."

She started to dress. "I got what I came for," she said.

"Thank you," I mumbled, before hitching up my trousers. If something could take the joy out of being with Raz, it was Sjunil Moon's voice in my head.

Raz closed the pin on her cloak, pricked herself in the finger and cursed softly. "Why do you need to understand your father? He's dead, isn't he? I'd rather focus on your living family."

"Everything in my life has happened because of him, of his mistakes, his bad reputation. I have some memories of him, but I don't know if I haven't honey-coated them in hindsight. He was here in the west, met the men from the Cities all that time ago, and learned words from them he taught me back in Tall Trees. I don't know why, perhaps he just needed to find something to do with a child who wants to learn about the world. Those words let me speak to the prince and things developed from there. Ileon didn't have many of our words before we started teaching each other. You see, it's all been snowballing up to this moment. I'd never have met you, Raz. I'd have missed out on quite a lot of other, more specific learning experiences."

She sucked on her thumb. "Do I need to be flattered that this doesn't count towards your regrets?" she smirked. "I can vouch for your willingness to learn. Maybe he really threw the words at you to give you something to do." She jumped up and held out a hand to pull me up with my good arm. "Will you write back to her?"

"No. I could pretend never to have received the message."

"She won't believe that."

"No, but it will buy me some time, until Rawil knows how to proceed from here. I need a few more days, that's all." I stuffed the paper into my tunic and laced up my trousers properly.

She sighed. "I'd say you're playing quite a dangerous game. If life has taught me anything so far, it's that the main thing to avoid is to thoroughly piss off a wizard."

"She's *my* wizard, I can handle her." But, of course, that was a lie.

The healer of the Beakdig garrison was a stressed looking man, bald under his woolly hat, with the same style of beard sported by the commander. He sniffed at the remnants of Siw's salve in the pot.

"Interesting. You wouldn't have the recipe to hand by any chance?"

I shook my head as I gritted my teeth. His hands were trembling, and I wasn't looking forward to him pulling my stitches.

Rawil stood next to me, their lined face exuding deep exhaustion. They'd accompanied us to Beakdig because they'd hoped to talk things through with Rovan, I realized. There was no other reason for them to have taken an interest in me and my decisions, but they were up to their neck in it, stuck with me.

"Could we please get on with it?" they asked.

"There are some things that shouldn't be rushed," the healer grumbled and poked my arm so hard it made me hiss in pain. I should've taken one look at that beard and refused the help. He obviously didn't like Rawil Owl one tiny bit and them coming with me was turning out to be a mistake.

"Is there something you can give them to lessen the discomfort?" Rawil asked.

The healer shrugged. "My stores have almost run out. I'd rather keep the rest back for serious cases."

"Just do it," I pleaded, sweat running over my face.

The commander and the healer exchanged a slow glance, then the healer picked up a pair of small iron scissors from his table. The blades were so cold against my skin that it already hurt. He started to try and wiggle the stitches free. I cried out.

Rawil took my face in their hands and turned it to them. "You might have waited a bit too long and I'm sorry, but you know that you need to get this done. Look at me, Sloe." Their fingers dug into my cheeks. "It's going to be over in a moment."

I tried not to cry, but the tears came with the pain. Every single stitch was agony and I whimpered and groaned and wished to fall down dead, while I tried to count the scars in the commander's face, to think about what they must've gone through and why they still wanted to be close to a man they had divorced and who was as unlikable as Rovan Owl.

"… and finished." The healer doused my arm with vinegar and I howled for the last time. Rawil released me.

I stared at the angry red line with the dots surrounding it, where fresh blood welled up from the procedure.

"I'm sorry," I spluttered.

Rawil's brow furrowed. "Why?"

"Because I'm so weak that a little cut can bring me to tears."

They laughed, bent down, and kissed my sweaty forehead. "If you knew how much I cried when he treated my ingrown toenail, you would never worry about that again."

YOU HAVE A LIFE

"He's not doing too well." Olas had ushered me into a corner of the shed. "He's losing hope."

"Because he expected a rescue mission, as in Goldenlake?" I scratched at the smaller bandage that covered my upper left arm. "You knew that was extremely unlikely. We're too far west, and no one in their right mind will travel further in this weather than they absolutely have to. Even so, Cathil Cloud will assume that his sister's betrayal was done with the prince's blessing."

The negotiator, already a slight man when we'd met, looked gaunt and desperate. None of the tidy fussiness was left; he was as dirty as the rest of us, with dark circles under every fingernail. "He wouldn't," he disagreed, in a tone that let me know that he needed to persuade himself.

"You'll have noticed that Cathil Cloud isn't the sharpest knife on the rack. He will assume that his sister has made her decisions out of greed, not because she wants to hold on to the old ways. And in order for her to profit, the prince needs to be on board. She has the backing of the Cloud government and by now Cathil will have been set free, if he hasn't cut his losses and decided to fall in line again. Knowing him, he'll probably have taken his entourage and gone into exile to sulk for a few years. He's not in a position to rescue anyone."

"What about the others?" Olas asked. "You think they have been killed?"

"If Cathil was still in charge, I wouldn't have put it past him to make such a stupid mistake. I'm expecting more from his sisters. They'll keep them as hostages in Greycliffs, for when the time comes."

Olas had wrapped strips of cloth around his gloves to provide more warmth. He pulled at the ends, not wanting to meet my eyes. "One of the guards said that you've pleaded for my life," he said.

"Do you resent me for it?"

He glanced up at that. "No, of course not. I know that it must have brought danger to your door, Sloe Moon, and I wonder why you do such things if you hurt yourself over and over again."

"I've promised to stay at your side, and I'll be there if I can, as long as they let me. You won't be surprised to hear that my aunt is less enthused about my principles."

"Your aunt …" A weird smile crept on his face. "I must admit, I miss her from time to time. She was a good adversary to have. Has she ever … been married?"

"No. And I doubt she would marry a man."

"Ah."

"She might sleep with you, though, if you ask her nicely."

He blushed violently. "Goldenlake was such a happy time in comparison. I didn't expect that this adventure would bring us so low. When we were still in Seagard, it all sounded like an invite to a garden party. Go over there, throw a bit of coin around to impress the natives, set up trading posts, and spend the rest of the year haggling for the treasures of Birkland. We didn't expect to be so unwelcome."

"Seagard? Is that one of the Cities?"

"Yes, founded a few decades ago, but already set to achieve great fame across the known world." He looked at the sleeping prince. "He has invested quite a lot of his own capital there and owns a house where we met to discuss the details of the voyage. His family in Crooked Hill sponsored the endeavour, but it is to be expected that they won't throw him a feast anytime soon. Not after all the things that have gone wrong so far. It was a horrible crossing—I never puked so much in my life. Coming into the landing bay at the Stoneharp, we had to admit that the reports we'd heard in the Cities had somewhat … embellished the nature of the set-up over here. We'd expected large numbers of our countrymen in a good-sized town. Instead, we found shacks and tents on a stony beach and men who couldn't wait for the opportunity to get away. But he still kept his hope, even after these disappointments. He found people to help, he worked out routes, and divided us up to travel with a greater chance to slip into the east undetected. He even kept his head when we came upon him in Goldenlake, battered and bereft of his most loyal of friends. But now … what little food there is, he doesn't eat. He sleeps most of the time and he doesn't talk to me. Whatever happened, he has always talked. Is there something you can do?"

"I'm trying my best to get him to the Stoneharp as quickly as possible. The Owls will ransom him and make sure that he is sent back to the Cities, to … Seagard. He will have to accept that the families in the west don't like you, either."

"What about the Bears and the Elks?"

"If the Clouds are back with the Moons and we are now bringing the Owls with us, they don't have the numbers anymore. No one will fight against such heavy odds. Silver is not food. I'm not sure what Cathil Cloud dreams of buying with the riches he was promised. A better horse, a bigger boat, stone shingles for his houses? He still needs to feed his family and they'll eat the same things they've always eaten."

Olas sniffed. "Which is a good reason to want more from life, isn't it?"

"I don't know. Cathil and I do not see eye to eye on most things. Just thinking that I was ready to get married to him at some point …"

He smiled. "I married my wife without ever having met her, but she is a quiet, intelligent, bookish woman and we suit each other well. Sometimes it can work out, I suppose."

"But you're still interested in my aunt."

"I'm alive, aren't I?" He laughed drily. "Don't tell her that, by the way."

"Of course I'll tell her. It's too good to keep to myself."

We had another spell of icy rain and I hoped Sjunil wouldn't expect me to send someone back with a reply. I read the message a dozen times, tempted to ask Rovan for paper, ink, and a reed pen, but then tried to distract myself with discussions about the improvement of the rations and more visits to Cirvi's part of the stable—until the morning when I woke up in the Other House and could hear rain again, the noise it made as it splashed into the sleety puddles that had collected in the yard. I pulled my grey cloak around me and left the house to visit the tower closest to the house I slept in. Rawil Owl still snored in their own corner. It was barely light out and probably wouldn't get much brighter over the day.

I climbed the steps to the first platform that looked out to sea. Most of the ice had gone translucent and moved with the swell of the waves. It wouldn't take long for the beach at the Stoneharp to be accessible again, because the climate in the west was milder overall. The snow would probably remain longer in the forests and the eastern steppes. Things would start moving quicker: the rains would turn the plains into a sea of mud before long, the meltwaters would make the rivers overflow and find their way to the coasts, and we still had a good while to wait until the first fresh food became available again.

My heart hammered away at the thought of all the difficult decisions that lay in my future—Raz being one of them. Whatever we had between us was something I'd rather not lose; each time we rolled through the hay was another opportunity to get closer to her, to discover more—and not just about her.

I rubbed my grumbling stomach and made my way across the sodden yard to the kitchens, where the first shift of garrison cooks had the grass seed porridge pot on the fire and tried to scrape together anything to make it taste of more than watery paste. Saltfish was soaking in large wooden tubs for the unavoidable stew around noon and everyone had the same stressed expression as the healer. These people knew exactly how much food was left in the stores and even my wide, sad eyes could only get me a small bowl of porridge sprinkled with bits of seaweed and ground-up brown shrimp. The roasted goat we'd had in Featherdig was an eternity away in Beakdig, where such luxuries were unthinkable. The few spoonfuls barely stopped the growling in my guts.

"How's the porridge this morning?" Raz slipped onto the bench in front of me.

I pulled a face. "Meh."

"I'll take 'meh' over 'burned' anytime."

"Ask them to skip the shrimp," I advised. "I think a few of them must have gone mouldy."

She secured her breakfast and came back to me. "Rovan wants to see you. It looks like someone made it through from the north last night."

"You mean from the Stoneharp?"

She nodded. "Or a settlement very close to it."

"I thought that things might start to move now, and that I'm not prepared to leave you behind."

She lowered her spoon. "You won't have a choice, Sloe. Even if your dream finally comes true and they let you ride along, Rawil won't want me away from them that long."

"Even on such an important diplomatic mission?"

"Unless they are prepared to go north themself."

"Can you talk to them?"

"Sloe, we both knew that this was going to be a short-lived arrangement. I loved every moment of it, but that doesn't mean that we can keep it up for months to come." She patted my hand.

"You don't want me, after all that?"

"You have a life in Tall Trees and I have a life here. Don't make it more complicated than it has to be. Your aunt will catch up with you and drag you back by the ear. Maybe you're not marrying Cathil Cloud, but you're still an important asset. I'm no one anyone marries to forge an alliance, not after everything that happened."

"Can you at least tell me what that was? Why won't Rawil let you out of their sight?"

She pushed her half-eaten portion of porridge away from her. "Because I'm generally treated as bad news."

"What—why?"

"I've mentioned the engagement, right?"

"Yes …"

"It wasn't just one engagement, it was five. And they all died fighting the Clouds. I tried to find someone to stay with me, but stories spread." She rubbed her right cheek. "So they would fuck me but … but that's it. And they don't want me to come out with them on patrol. Rawil took me with them because they'll have to answer to my mother if one of their warriors sticks a knife in my neck."

"Oh, Raz …" I tried to take her hand but she pulled away.

She smiled and then her eyes went wide.

I turned around and saw warriors running through the puddles, their heads pulled between the shoulders to dodge the heavy rain. The feeble squeak of a horn announced that something was happening at the gate; we heard shouts echoing all around us.

"Should we go and see?" Raz suggested. "Here, eat the rest of it—it's horrible today."

I gulped down her cold porridge and we pushed out into the yard to join the others. The gate was opening with a slow, unearthly creak.

"Who is it?" Raz bellowed at one of her colleagues, who gave a shrug. No one seemed to know why they were gathering at the gate.

A rider trotted through, on a dark wet horse, a sky-blue cloak wrapped around his broad shoulders. He threw back his hood and glanced around. On the left side of his head, the black curls had been clipped short and a fresh red scar curved over his scalp. Another scar ran from his lower lip down to his chin. Some of the softness had gone from his face, but the smile he gave me when his eyes found mine was as warm as ever.

"Qes!"

POT OF MAGGOTS

"I hope you don't mind that I took your cloak." Qes released me from the longest hug of my life.

"It's your colour much more than mine—keep it. You look so different." I stroked the stubble on his left temple, careful not to touch the scar.

"Qati is stronger than he seems." He leant into the touch and kissed my palm with his cold mouth. "He has quite a way with a pot lid. Thank the gods Siw was there to sew me back together."

I pulled up my own cloak. "She did mine, too."

He stared at the puckered skin. "Oh, Sloe."

"I thought you were dead for the longest time. None of them wanted to tell me what happened to you in Goldenlake."

"For a while, it could have gone either way, I suppose." He rubbed the back of his neck. "I've never seen Sjunil in such distress. She called the council so early in the morning that Werid's hair was still in curling-rags. They really weren't amused—when politics get involved with their beauty regime, things get personal. The prince wasted a good chance to resolve all of this gracefully. Sjunil won't be able to trust him again."

"Tell me what happened to you, Qes."

"I got whacked on the head and spent the next few days puking and bleeding. Knocking me out must've been the very first thing they did. When I came to, the house was a battlefield—they took everything they could carry and destroyed the rest. The Bears weren't happy. Siw stitched me up and proceeded to comfort Julas."

"I hope you don't hate her for it."

"She's welcome to him."

"She thinks she's pregnant."

He laughed. "Of course she is. Trust her to get the last word in. Sjunil hatched a plan to hunt the prince down, but Werid persuaded her to try something clever. And it worked. The Owls have taken him off our hands and will be the ones made responsible for the punishment. I'd feared to find you bound and broken. But here you are. I've always told you that you are one of the most resilient people I know."

"Where have you been in the last weeks?"

His face fell. "At the Stoneharp."

"Really? Sjunil is at the Stoneharp?"

"No, Sjunil is in Clawdig. She didn't want to risk getting into Mouse territory just yet."

"But she sent you."

"I volunteered. I thought if you find yourself with the opportunity at all, the Stoneharp would be the likeliest place for you to resurface."

"You can take me there!"

"No. Sloe, Sjunil wants you to come to Clawdig, as soon as possible. She figured you would probably try to ignore her letter but that you'd have more difficulties ignoring me."

"Crafty old bitch."

"Have you sworn an oath? Have they forced you to make a promise to the gods?"

I shook my head. "It's all of my own making. It's hard to explain but it almost feels as if it was …"

"… meant to be?" he finished the sentence for me. "You think Brother Brook has an interest in keeping a man from the Cities alive?"

"I see it more as a test for myself," I admitted. "Whatever he throws at me, I will attempt to master it. I need you to meet my new friends, Qes. Rawil Owl and Raz, their niece. They have both saved my arse."

He nodded slowly. "Valuable allies," he said.

"… and there's Cathil Cloud's sister. She might be an ally but she is … I was very impressed with her at first, but then … Would you ever have thought that we'd find ourselves so far in the west one day?"

"I remember sitting at our fire in Tall Trees and dreaming of exploring the coast," he said quietly, "but I don't think I've ever factored in the pain of seeing you cut and sewn up. All of this certainly came at a price."

I went in for a second hug. "Will you come with me, Qes? Please. We can send a note to Clawdig to explain. It will only be a few days until we're ready to ride north, until the invitation comes through."

He slipped his gloved hand into the sky-blue cloak, pulled out a folded paper sealed with grey tallow. "This is the invitation, but you're not on the list."

I gasped. "Why not?"

"Because you're not welcome at the Harp, Sloe. We will need to go to Clawdig and let your aunt yell at us for a bit."

"I can't, Qes."

"You don't understand. The Stoneharp is not open to everyone."

"It was open to you!"

"Not exactly. I've not been *in* it as such. I looked at it from the outside and was sent away, time and time again."

"Is this about my father? Why were they so eager to deny me?"

"I don't know. I've stayed with a Badger in the winter camp close to the landing beach and he wasn't forthcoming, either." He pulled me to him and for a heartbeat our foreheads touched. "I'm sorry," he said. "I wish I could bring better news."

"I need to get the invitation to Rawil Owl, and negotiate again."

Qes looked worried. "Negotiate what?"

"I'm going to find a way into the Harp, if it kills me."

He let me go. "It *will* kill you."

The old commander pressed their eyes closed. "Holy fuck."

Raz pushed against them, trying to get a glimpse of the message. "What?"

"The council of the west will assemble in a few days and they have summoned the prince. I gather he has some experience with these kinds of gatherings?"

I nodded, dry-mouthed. "He spoke to the council in Goldenlake."

"The council of the west is going to be a more … flammable affair."

"*Flammable?*"

"Let's just say that your friend Cathil Cloud will move mountains to get his foot in the door, and I gather he has recently married into the Mouse family? Well, that gives him yet another claim to complicate things further. You need to stay well away from this, Sloe."

"I won't. I will ensure that the hostages are exchanged fair and square."

"You're half Moon and half Badger. Half the wrong Badger, at that. You have no right at all to be present. Neither of your families has been called." Rawil smoothed the paper down on the table.

Their former husband played with the glass bead in his beard, his eyes fixed on the words. "You are entitled to a personal guard, Rawil."

"Are you actually suggesting smuggling Sloe in? You can clearly see that they're a Badger."

"Appearances can be changed." I stared at Rovan Owl, astonished that help might come from him.

The young commander smiled at me, his sharp teeth glinting. "We could try an eyepatch?"

"This is madness." Rawil's voice had gone growly. A hank of grey hair had come loose from the bunches of their traditional hair style and fell over their cheek, making them look more dangerous than usual. "I know how much you enjoy these kinds of games, Rovan, but this is not the time to indulge your wish to distract yourself with amusing schemes."

I saw a flicker of pain on Rovan's face; some of the words must have hit home.

"I could do an eyepatch," I said softly and Rawil turned on me.

"For the gods' sake, shut the fuck up, Sloe. This has gone far beyond your misguided notions of honour and loyalty. If you are specifically forbidden to attend the council, any attempt to disobey this directive will end in you getting strung up from the highest tower of the Harp—by the ankles, so you can bleed out for all to see."

I thought of Tjal's brother in the forest, the blackish yawn of his cut throat, the congealed blood in the leaves. "It might still work."

"It's not just your own life you'll lay down. They will kill everyone who is involved—Raz, Rovan, me, your friend Qes, maybe even your aunt and your sister. Are you really willing to risk this for an arrogant twat from overseas?"

"Two arrogant twats," Raz corrected.

The disappointment washed through me. "No, of course not."

Their broad shoulders relaxed. "You're a sensible person at heart." The commander leant forward and kissed me on the head.

Rovan coughed at the display of affection. "But maybe there's another way …"

Rawil's hand was around his throat before either of us had the chance to even blink. "You will keep *quiet*."

Rovan's eyes were wide, his fingers clawing at Rawil's hand, but there was something in his face, a longing that made me cringe.

"In case you can pull your head far enough out of your arse to actually think it through, you will realize that the council will not resolve anything. They will scream at each other and throw some curses around but in the end, we will be expected to ready our warriors for some sort of conflict. You will have a part to play in things to come and we will need every single person who can hold a longknife the right way up."

Rovan went slack in Rawil's grip. "Why can't you love me?"

Raz grabbed me and bundled me out of the door.

"Ouch, what—"

"This is not a conversation any of us should be a part of," she said.

"But we were still discussing how to get into the Harp!"

"The discussion was well and truly over. Why don't you take me over to the kitchen and introduce me properly to your friend. After all you told me about him, I hadn't pictured him this … hot."

"What do you mean by hot?"

She grinned at me. "I like my people scarred, in case you couldn't tell." She boxed me in the good arm. "Don't worry, I know he's off limits. But I would like to get to know him even so." She pulled me across the yard where Qes sat on one of the benches, staring miserably at his bowl of watery soup.

"Qes, this is my friend Raz."

He looked up, the scar on his lip distorting his careful smile. "So nice to meet you. I hear you have kept an eye on Sloe."

"A little bit more than an eye." She patted my cheek and I saw Qes blink in confusion.

"What about Tjal?" he asked.

Raz's face went blank. "Who's Tjal?"

"Thank you oh so very much," I spat at Qes, "for opening this pot of maggots."

THE PATH

After my revelation, Raz pulled even further away from me. I hadn't expected Raz to take the story about Tjal so badly, given all the people she'd slept with, and I wanted to talk with her, to assure her again that I hadn't planned to keep my last relationship a secret from her but had feared that she might despise me for getting involved with one of *them*.

The fact that she would have the opportunity that I was denied made it difficult to listen to her describe the preparations Rawil Owl's entourage were making in order to follow the invitation. I led Qes to the shed and saw him recoil from the smell of unwashed men and bad food.

"I'm glad to see you alive," Olas said as we'd put down their bowls and they'd wolfed down the small portions they'd been offered.

I was relieved to see the prince eat. The news that he'd have to make his way north seemed to have woken a new will in him to pull through.

The negotiator pushed the empty bowls away. "Sloe almost drove us up the walls with their constant yammering. What happened to your hair?"

"Qati Badger took all his anger and fear out on me. Siw had to cut it in order to keep the wound clean."

"It suits you, somehow," Olas said. "I'm sorry about that. And I'm sorry to part ways so soon. I understand that we are to be taken to the Stoneharp under the sole protection of the Owls and that the involvement of all others has been strongly discouraged."

The prince played with his wooden spoon. "I understand, Sloe. No need to do something stupid."

"But I promised—"

"Sometimes circumstances go against us." His yellow gaze lifted to meet mine. "You will serve to honour your pledge in different ways."

We sat together without anyone wanting to speak: four people around a wonky table in an evil-smelling room mere paces away from the thawing sea. Every single one of us exhausted, disappointed, and hurt in various ways.

Olas and the prince had been starved for days, as had we all, with a more than uncertain future in front of them. They'd remain prisoners, but they wouldn't have me to watch out for them, and Qes … I hardly knew him anymore. We'd have to take some time to get into the details of what happened to both of us. There was so much I needed him to understand.

The prince flicked the spoon and it jumped across the table, bumping into my left hand.

"I hope that one day we will have the opportunity to speak again." His dirty face, covered in silvery and coppery stubble, glowed in the darkness of the shed. He looked at Qes. "Take them away."

"I'm failing them," I howled.

Qes looked sorely tempted to roll his eyes. "He said that he understands."

"I owe him."

"What?" he snapped. "What can you possibly owe the man who abducted you, who broke his solemn promise to the council of wizards in Goldenlake? You can't imagine the waves that caused, Sloe. He doesn't deserve this. It reminds me far too much of what you went through with Saon. Someone who kept you close and away from him at the same time, who is out of bounds and available, who feeds you with little tokens of affection to keep you at his side."

"He says I remind him of his son."

Qes stared at me in disbelief. "Can all of this still be about my cursed uncle? The man who had the chance to be one of the greatest wizards of our time and blew it? Who had to flee into the forests and drink himself to death because he wasn't able to stand the boredom of Tall Trees? I would love to see him come back from the dead just to punch his teeth into his throat." Qes' eyes looked hard as flint. "And I want to shake you until your head adjusts itself. I had such hopes when you said that you'd made new friends here but Raz ... she seems flaky. I understand what you find so attractive about Rawil Owl, but they won't be able to help you, either. You're moving in circles again and I can't bear to watch you anymore." He stood up. "We will leave tomorrow for Clawdig. I will drag you by the ear if I have to."

I went to bed early but was so hungry that I turned over for hours, the platform making a tortured noise with every movement. I tried once again to settle in a comfortable position when a heavy hand pressed into my good shoulder.

Rawil Owl sat down on the edge of the platform. "Sht, Sloe. I want to talk to you before you leave us." They crossed their arms. "I will take on your burden," they whispered, their face hidden in the shadows of the Other House.

I struggled up to come closer. "Really?"

"I have conditions, though."

"What conditions?"

"You will find a wizard and talk them into taking you on. You will not listen to your aunt if she opposes you. I have never met anyone who is so desperately in search of the path."

I hugged them and for a moment they held me close. They smelled of damp wool and woodsmoke as I pressed my face into them, shuddering as their left hand cradled the back of my neck.

"I wish I had met you a long time ago," Rawil said into my hair. "When things hadn't been decided for you, when you needed someone to help you find the things you wanted to have in your life. I won't have children of my own, but …" They kissed my head again. "Whatever happens, I will always help you if you want me to."

Qes waited for me in the yard. He stood between the horses, tall and unmovable as a boulder, the hood drawn over his hair, curls spilling down the right side of his neck. Cirvi had put one of her hind legs up and rested it on the rim of the hoof, her bottom lip loose and her eyes half closed in the watery sunshine. I'd hoped that the weather would fulfil Rovan's prophecies and prevent us from leaving, but Brother Rain had other plans.

I turned around and saw both commanders standing on the first level of the tower above the gate of Beakdig, both with furrowed brows, but Rovan's right hand clasped around Rawil's left as if he knew Rawil needed his help for the occasion.

Raz stepped to my side. "It's been fun," she said and gave me a kiss that couldn't be missed by anyone around. She managed to make my knees wobble for one last time. "I'll see you soon, right?"

"Right. Give my best to the Harp."

She sniffled and stepped back again.

It felt wrong to leave the garrison, after all the days it had taken me to reach it, in snow and ice and the cruel winds of the plains, after the things Raz had taught me and the things Rawil had said to me. I pressed my eyes closed to get myself back under control. Rawil had given me a way out and stepped into danger. Their lined face looked down on me, stony still, an angry crease on their forehead. I'd found a lot of different kinds of love in the west.

"Get a move on," Qes barked at me.

I stumbled to my mare, fumbled with her reins and made her snort in irritation as her doze was interrupted. Qes pulled himself into the saddle, the blue cloak blazing like the summer sky against the black coat of his mount—the cloak Saon had given me not so many months ago. He looked forbidding, impatient to finally leave.

I tried to gain more time by fussing with the reins and his eyes narrowed beneath his hood. "I want to get you out of here before you start blubbing," he hissed at me.

I pressed the heels into Cirvi's belly and she took the first steps forward.

The gate started to open, the stark landscape of the west flooding towards us, the grey ground in ripples, with the slightest sheen of new growth holding the mud together.

The horses walked gingerly out into the open.

Sloe's story continues in

SLOE MOON
STONEHARP

out 15 July 2024
available for preorder now

visit www.cmkuhtz.com for more information

AUTHOR NOTE & ACKNOWLEDGEMENTS

Writing Sloe's story has proven to be the most rewarding and most intimidating challenge. I started to outline the series in autumn 2021, shortly before the November 2021 lockdown in the UK when I was still planning a trilogy. I realized about halfway into Volume 3 that three books would never be enough to cover everything I wanted Sloe to experience. I don't stick closely to first outlines, but Sloe really took me on a wild ride.

Sloe is not me. I know that this is a statement I will have to continue to make, as we share quite a few crucial attributes: we are both fat and we are both nonbinary. Growing up reading fantasy novels, I never had the pleasure and assurance to join a main character who looked like me and felt like me on their journey. The fantasy stories I read as a kid and young adult treated people who look and love like me either as villains or sidekicks available to be bullies or be bullied. The original idea behind the series was to finally have a hero who learns more than they bargained for but who goes through their adventures *in a fat body* and no one asks them to change that or their personality. With Sloe I wrote the hero I desperately searched for growing up as a fat kid in the 1980s and 1990s, always feeling deeply at odds with my surroundings and made to feel wrong and called upon to transform, to fit in, to make myself smaller, less weird, less easy to hurt.

I have always spent most of my free time scribbling away in a corner, have used reading and especially writing both to escape and to ground myself, and as fantasy novels are the ideal vehicle for wish-fulfilment, it was easy to retreat into other people, who had a shitload of other problems, but being fat and queer in a fat-hating and queer-hating world was not one of them. I only started to specifically write fat main characters a few years ago, and back then it felt like one of the most vulnerable experiences possible.

There are some rules you make your own: no one can ever want me just as I am. Every social situation is a potential trap. When someone wants to get close to me romantically, it *must* be a joke. Even if Sloe is able to voice their longing, these rules still lie underneath many of their interactions. For them this isn't so much about their body but based upon their parentage and general feeling of otherness, but it's there—and they find their courage to express desire and many different kinds of love anyway. I hope that Sloe's story will help to change the perception of who is allowed to be a hero and worthy of adventures, romance, and friendship.

Many people accompanied me along the way and need to thanked:

Isa, who has lived in the Eastern Cities with me for almost three decades and is probably the only person on this planet who can read my handwriting without breaking a sweat. You're the Sloe to my Qes.

Marlen, who is never afraid to go deep. For knowing me too well to let me have the easy way out and for showing me where the best cake lives.

Dorit, graphic designer and flatmate extraordinaire. For the many late nights in our wonky Hildesheim kitchen, talking about our lives to come.

Diana, Nicole, and Bouke, who continue to go on the adventure with me. For being friends, fellow writers, and first readers, and for believing that all that bloody effort is worth it.

Elena and the Marshalls, who took me in as part of their bubble and have become my found family in the UK.

Lorna, who teaches me about art and shares my enthusiasm for extraordinary places.

Claudia and the Cabbage Club, who help me to make sense of the bewildering country we have all come to live in.

Suzanne, whose generosity planted the seed.

Jenna, fellow writer, who gave me so much encouragement when I needed it most and managed to rein in my panic when things didn't move quickly enough.

Rachel and Tanner, for their invaluable beta-reading insights and giving me so much to think about.

Britt, for an amazing and endlessly rewarding copyediting experience—I can't wait to get started on working through the next five volumes with you!

Casey, for capturing the spirit of the series in her beautiful cover illustrations.

My parents, for coming around to support the choices I make. For teaching me that life is too short to live in a cage. For being role models for adventurous cooking and travelling, for making me interested in how stuff works and all the books, art, and love— and French cheese!

My brother Henry, who shares the story-telling bug. For all the road trips into the wilderness, storm or no storm, snow or no snow.

Hamish, the one true Prince of Crooked Hill, who is missed in every single moment.

Everyone who picked up the book and found something in my flawed, passionate, yet anxious hero to relate to.